Outstanding praise for Emmeline Duncan and *Fresh Brewed Murder*!

"Coffee lovers, this book is for you. A fresh take on the cozy mystery genre. This is a great debut!"
—*Criminal Element*

"Portland's beloved food carts provide a tantalizing backdrop for a new cozy mystery by Portland author Emmeline Duncan . . . A creative way to address both the quirkiness and the more dismaying aspects of life in contemporary Portland."
—*The Sunday Oregonian*

"Lively characters help propel the intricate plot. Cozy fans will hope to see a lot more Sage and friends."
—*Publishers Weekly*

Books by Emmeline Duncan

FRESH BREWED MURDER

DOUBLE SHOT DEATH

Published by Kensington Publishing Corp.

DOUBLE SHOT DEATH

Emmeline Duncan

Kensington Publishing Corp.

www.kensingtonbooks.com

KENSINGTON BOOKS are published by

Kensington Publishing Corp.
119 West 40th Street
New York, NY 10018

ISBN: 978-1-4967-3342-9 (ebook)

ISBN: 978-1-4967-3341-2

First Kensington Trade Paperback Printing: May 2022

10 9 8 7 6 5 4 3 2 1

Printed in the United States of America

For Miriam

Chapter 1

A few years ago, if you told me I'd be humming while pulling a trailer down the freeway, I would've laughed. But that was before I'd decided to build a coffee empire. While I'm still a dedicated bike commuter and prefer to zoom around Portland, Oregon, on two wheels, some days, like today, I use the official Ground Rules Subaru to pull a coffee cart around town.

And I drive it with panache. I'd been raised to believe that, with practice and tenacity, not only could I learn to do anything, but to do it with style.

My copilot, Bax—aka my boyfriend singing along with the radio as I drove—was a side perk of starting Ground Rules, since I wouldn't have met him if I hadn't leased the warehouse space next door to his studio. The employee joining me for the weekend, Kendall, was making his own way to the festival.

Yet, here I was, co-owner of a coffee company consisting of a roastery, two food carts, and employees. The cart closest to my heart was stationed at the Rail Yard food cart pod in Portland. And I was backing the second cart into my designated spot at Portland's beloved Campathon Music Festival.

Attendees were in for three days of music under acres of trees of a farm just outside the Portland city limits during the dog days of summer. They wouldn't be caffeine free since Ground Rules was on-site. We were the first food cart to show up, and I knew by the end of the day there'd be seven others collected in the festival's makeshift food cart pod.

A few minutes later, Bax waved me back another few inches, then held his hand up for me to stop as I backed the Ground Rules cart into its home for the weekend. So I put the Subaru in park and hopped from the car to scope out the situation for myself.

Bax gave me a high five, and I turned to inspect my parking job. The converted horse trailer turned into a coffee stand was centered inside the lines of Food Cart Spot 1, aka my assigned location. Exactly where I'd aimed for.

Alexis Amari, one of the Campathon organizers, looked up from her clipboard. "Sage Caplin of Ground Rules! You're in the running to be my favorite vendor of the year. Thanks for showing up exactly when you were supposed to. I wish all of my contractors were so diligent."

I approved of Alexis, whom I'd first met when she stopped by the Ground Rules cart to try our coffee before formally handing over our festival contract. I'd talked to her a couple of times since she was in charge of scheduling the bands and food carts. Everything about her, from her straight posture to her belted sleeveless shirtwaist dress and tidy bun—which were both heat-appropriate and professional—said she had everything under control and didn't appreciate nonsense. But she also had a mischievous smile, which she flashed my way.

"Thanks again for including us. We're excited to be here," I said. Alexis nodded and started to open her mouth like she had something to say. But then her eyes widened, and she hustled by me. I turned to see two food carts, one a red boxy truck that said BREAKFAST BANDITS on the side, alongside a rectangular black cart pulled by a giant pickup, both in the middle of the parking lot.

The driver of the boxy red truck jumped out the passenger's side door. "Back up!" she yelled.

"We were here first," the driver of the pickup said through his open window.

I glanced at Bax.

He shook his head like he was disappointed in the drivers causing a scene. "The red truck just cut off the pickup for no apparent reason and blocked his way forward. If I were you, I'd avoid these carts over the weekend."

"You're in our way!" The woman stood a few inches from the pickup and glared at the driver like he'd insulted her mother. A guy from inside the red boxy truck slid into the driver's seat.

"You back up. If you hadn't cut me off, we'd be setting up our carts by now." The guy in the pickup looked forward, like the woman glaring at him wasn't worth his notice. But the set of his shoulders said he wouldn't back up, even if you paid him a million dollars.

Alexis strode up. "Bianca, what's going on?" Her voice was clipped.

"This truck is in our way."

"I thought food cart owners were cool," Bax said.

I laughed. "Most of us are. But there are a few strange apples in the bushel."

"This should keep you in the running as favorite food vendor of the festival." Bax swung his arm around my shoulders. Remnants of his citrus-and-sandalwood aftershave floated around me. He smelled like safety.

After a few hand waves by Alexis, Bianca had climbed back into her red Breakfast Bandits truck and backed up. But she inched back millimeters at a time. Part of me admired Bianca's dedication to passive-aggressive compliance, although I also told myself to either avoid her or stay on her good side.

"Fingers crossed, especially since I want them to invite us back next year." Regular gigs, especially high-profile ones like this festival, would show I'd been right to advocate for buying our second cart.

Once Bianca had finally inched far back enough for the black pickup to safely pull his cart through, he did. The side of his cart said KAUAI VIBES over the logo of a hand giving the shaka sign and a drawing of a surfboard.

Since the road rage show was over, Bax helped me unhook the Subaru from the Ground Rules cart. I carefully edged the Subaru away from the cart, taking care to avoid the Breakfast Bandits truck parked next to me in spot #2, and sedately made my way to the parking lot for vendors. After I parked, Bax snagged our tent and a giant bag holding our sleeping bags and camp pads from the backseat of the Subaru. "I'll find us a great camping spot," he promised. The smile on his face lit up his blue eyes. Bax's enthusiasm felt like a jolt of espresso as the finish after a perfect meal.

"I can't believe I almost didn't come to Campathon this year," Bax said.

"Come find me once you're done," I said and watched him head into the trees. We'd already discussed which section of the festival we wanted to set up camp in (the quiet area). One of the (many) advantages to bringing him included allowing me to focus on getting the cart up and running yet still have first dibs on a primo camping spot. Most festival attendees would pitch a tent somewhere on Campathon's forested grounds, although there was also an area for RVs and campers.

I focused on getting the cart up and running. The action felt automatic, like the hours I'd spent running Ground Rules had trained all the muscles in my body on how to get the business ready to brew multiple forms of world-class coffee.

About an hour later, a low, melodic voice interrupted my thoughts.

"Someone needs to stop me. Else I'm going to stab Nate and then throw a party before spending the rest of my life pining away in jail, only able to play the blues for the rats who inhabit my lonely, barren cell," a familiar voice said.

I looked up from calibrating the espresso machine and eyed Maya Oliveira, aka the woman standing in front of my cart. Something about her always gives me pause. I gave her a quick once-over. Glorious curly black hair loose over toned shoulders. Green eyes. Freckles over her nose. Skin the shade of driftwood foundation, with a mercurial temperament that reminded me of the sea. Even her tranquil moments have a restless undercurrent.

Maya held both hands to her forehead, then dramatically lowered them. As she leaned her elbows against the counter of my cart, Bianca of the Breakfast Bandits stared at us with wide eyes. I waved at her. She scurried back inside her van like a squirrel who'd just seen a dog and needed to flee for her life.

"Have you got anything ready yet?" Maya asked. Her voice was as addictive as espresso, and I wished she'd keep talking. "I'd kill for caffeine. I might even be desperate enough to drink instant coffee."

"There's no reason to resort to instant. If it stops you from committing homicide, you can try the next shot." After drawing and sampling, and then dumping, multiple shots to ensure the quality met our Ground Rules standards, our espresso should sing as brightly as the singer-songwriters scheduled to perform (and maybe be more on tune than some). I quickly ground a fresh sixteen grams of our espresso blend, tamped it down, and set about pulling the perfect shot into a clean white espresso cup. When it finished brewing, complete with the perfect head of crema, I handed it over to Maya.

"Sugar? Cream?" I asked.

"I take my coffee black, just like my soul." Maya grinned, then looked down at the shot. She closed her eyes as she sipped it, rolling it around in her mouth like she was savoring every molecule. She wore a vintage-looking Metallica T-shirt with the sleeves cut off. Cutoff red corduroy shorts and black cowboy boots finished off her look. As usual, she managed to effortlessly look like a rock goddess.

"Who's Nate, and what did he do?" I took a sip of bottled water, then held the ice-cold, sweating bottle to my forehead. August in Oregon can be mild and pleasant in the low eighties. But Mother Nature had decided we needed a heat wave. Hopefully we were on its final day, and the weekend would be mild versus a hot, sticky mess. Just in case, I'd borrowed a second generator to power our ice machine since I suspected we'd sell a lot of iced drinks and coffee sodas. If we hit triple digits, we might need to start handing out ice by the handful to help people cool down.

"Nate exists," Maya said, like that answered my question. Her lips pursed together like she was replaying something annoying in her mind. Then she glanced around, and she smiled when her gaze settled on my small display of merchandise.

Maya picked up one of the Ground Rules–branded travel mugs I'd stacked to the side of the front counter. We had two styles: the camp cup I'd fallen in love with, and the slick keeps-coffee-hot-for-hours tumblers from Japan that my business partner, Harley Yamazaki, preferred. "These mugs are lit."

"Thanks. I'm fond of them, too," I said. The cups were our best-selling merchandise and a symbol of what we were becoming. Ground Rules had kept me hopping all summer. Between our cart at the hip Rail Yard, this festival along with a series of farmers' markets, plus the brick-and-mortar shop in a development about to finally break ground, the business had kept me hopping for months. But being busy was good. We'd hired a couple of stellar employees. We were working on getting our beans carried by grocery stores and cafés around town. I'd framed an article from a local magazine when they called our brick-and-mortar shop one of the most anticipated coffee openings of next year.

Acquiring the smaller cart had been a stroke of luck. We'd bought the horse trailer from a coffee roaster who'd hated doing events. It was perfect for festivals, farmers' markets, and special occasions. Hopefully a strong showing at Campathon would encourage other event organizers to book us, and our promise of excellent and creative coffee, to justify the investment in the second cart.

Campathon. The name sounded like a melody to my ears. Held on a farm not too far outside the Portland city limits, a few thousand people showed up to spend four days listening to music and camping out under the trees. Attendees had their choice of three venues—the City Lights main stage and the Pine Burrow stage, plus a kids' area complete with its own stage. Campathon had declined our original bid to be part of the festival's food cart scene, but when the coffee company they'd chosen bowed out, Maya had convinced Alexis to give us a shot. We'd been lucky she'd been in the festival office at the right time. I'd only met Maya a handful of times, but she frequently worked with the video game development company my boyfriend, Bax, co-owns and runs. Her band, the Banshee Blues, was in the festival lineup.

Spending the weekend at a music festival was part work, part fun, especially since one of my newish employees, Kendall, was splitting time in the cart with me. I'd handle the morning rush, we'd pass the torch around noon, and he'd take care of the afternoon crowd. We'd made a sign that said LAST CALL FOR COFFEE AT 3:30 since we'd close at four, and anyone still desperate for coffee could get on-tap nitro cold brew coffee in the beer tent, also provided by us. And I knew the main Ground Rules cart in the Rail Yard was in good hands, since my business partner, Harley, was taking care of it.

Maya took another sip of espresso, and I followed suit with my water.

"Oh, monkey on a cupcake. The almighty Nate himself approaches," Maya muttered. She bolted down the last of her espresso.

Nate. I eyed the tall guy with longish brown hair decked out in ripped jeans and a faded black T-shirt who walked up. Like Maya, something about his swagger said he'd embraced the rocker look. Or maybe I was reading into it since the only people on site today were either bands or attendees who'd sprung for the VIP pass.

His face triggered a memory of the music section of the *Willamette Week*, the local alt-news weekly paper. He was the lead singer of a Portland-based band, the Changelings, who'd been getting national attention. They had one of the most played songs on all of the current hip music streaming apps. My memory clicked a few more times.

Nate Green. The article had called him the leading contender to be the new voice of his generation, highlighting his moody lyrics and unique chord arrangements. They'd said he wasn't reinventing rock, just turning it upside down and stamping it with his unique spin. After reading the article, I'd listened to one of his songs and thought it'd sounded like an up-tempo Nirvana rip-off with layers of pretension. But while I like music, it's not my passion. Maybe Nate's revolutionary elements were lost on me. Perhaps musically, my taste was akin to cheap pit stop coffee.

As I watched her, Maya clenched her jaw again. I debated pouring a pitcher of water in case I needed to throw it on them to break up a fight like they were cats fighting over turf. Except I had to haul water to the coffee cart, and dumping it on dueling musicians would be a waste of my labor.

"Everything okay here?" Bax popped around the side of the cart, like a genie sent to cool troubled waters.

"Bax! Buddy! I haven't seen you for a few years." Nate nodded at him, then glanced at Maya, who stared off into the woods, her back to Nate. Maya strode away, her cowboy boots kicking up puffs of dust behind her.

Bax's easygoing expression from earlier had already shifted into a wary look, like the world had resettled on his shoulders. I made a mental note to ask Bax about Nate later, since he and Maya both knew him but I hadn't met him before today. And I expected Bax to tell me if he knew the people on the front pages of our local papers; that's Relationship Logic 101.

Nate's gaze returned to me, and he smiled. Charm practically oozed out of his hazel eyes and soaked my face, and slid through my hair. Something told me Nate had spent most of his life trading on his charisma. "Can I get an iced latte?" he asked.

Behind Nate, Bax lifted his lip in an Elvis-like lip curl, then smiled at me.

"Sure. Do you have a mug?" I asked, and tried not to laugh at my boyfriend.

Nate handed over his official Campathon tumbler. The festival strove for zero waste. Part of the vendor contract included no disposable cups or packaging, and I hadn't even packed a single sleeve of cups. For the weekend, attendees needed to provide their own drinking vessel or buy a Ground Rules reusable mug. The festival sold sleek stainless steel tumblers with the Campathon logo, like the one Nate had, and attendees needed one if they wanted to order beer from the bar tent. Or attendees could bring their own cups for water and nonalcoholic beverages.

"Coming right up." I set about crafting Nate's latte.

"You know, Bax, you were in the crowd our very first show." Nate's voice sounded relaxed. Slightly lowered in charm, but more intimate.

"The first after you joined the band, you mean," Bax said.

Nate continued like Bax hadn't said anything. "Since you're here to see us this weekend, you do realize you'll be one of the few who've seen the band's full progression?"

"I'm definitely looking forward to seeing Maya's new band this weekend." It seemed like Maya's dislike of Nate had been transferred along to Bax. He was fully on Team Maya, making me wonder what game they were playing.

Another man walked up, most likely in his mid-thirties, dressed in a crisp button-down shirt rolled up over his elbows and dark jeans, followed by a girl, maybe twenty, who carried a phone in her hand and tote bag over her shoulder.

"Ian, have you met Bax?" Nate asked, nodding his head toward my boyfriend. "He runs the Grumpy Sasquatch studio in Portland. You've played some of their video games."

"Oh yeah, I've met local musicians you've worked with. They say good things." Ian's voice had an overly smooth note that told me he was used to glad-handing people.

"Ian's my band's manager," Nate said.

"Ian Rabe. Nice to meet you." Ian offered his hand, and Bax slowly shook it. Bax's professional look slid over his face, hiding the sparkle in his eyes. He glanced upward like he always does when he's annoyed.

"This is my assistant, Faith," Ian said and nodded toward the girl behind him. My eyes zeroed in on her hair since Faith's light brown mane was twisted into an elaborate side braid. I almost asked her if she could show me how she'd managed it.

"Intern," Faith said without looking up from her mobile phone. Her coral linen dress looked perfect for the weather. I noted her bag was a this-season Coach, which seemed brave given the dusty conditions. I'd brought my trusty Timbuk2 since it could handle an apocalypse with aplomb and just need a simple wipe down to look brand new at the end of the weekend.

As I handed Nate his latte, Ian was still looking at Bax. Maybe I imagined the gleam in his eye felt speculative, but then he said, "You know, I have some musicians who'd love to compose music for video games."

Bax slid his wallet out of his pocket, moving slowly like he wanted to be anywhere else. As he opened it, he said, "I'll give you my card, but I'm not thinking about work this weekend. I'm here to listen to music and help out Sage if she needs me." Bax looked at me, and out of the corner of my eye, I saw Ian glance over. Nate wandered away.

"This must be Sage," Ian said. He took the business card from Bax.

"Yep, co-owner of one of the best coffee roasters in Portland," Bax said.

"One of?" I tried to make my voice sound outraged, but the laughter peeked through.

"Sorry, the best!" Bax grinned at me, and the sparkle in his eyes came back out.

"Can I get a pour-over?" Ian asked. "An Ethiopian single-origin bean, if you have one?"

"We have a single-origin from a small farm in Harrar with us this weekend," I said. "It's sun-dried, which is normal for Harrar, and it really brings out the fruity and floral notes."

"Harrar?" Ian asked.

"It's one of the iconic coffee bean–growing regions of Ethiopia. It's the highest altitude coffee-growing area and plenty of people think they produce some of the best beans in the world," I said.

"That sounds fine."

"A pour-over will take a few minutes. Do you have a mug?"

"Oh, that's right. I left mine on the tour bus. Is there any chance you have any paper cups?"

"Sorry. We didn't even bring any cups 'cause they're against the festival's rules. I have cups for sale, or you can get your mug. I'll be here for a while." I knew several things. One, I was talking too fast. Something about the vibes of this group made flickers of nervousness flow to my hands and mouth. Two, I'd be saying my "we don't have paper cups" spiel all weekend. And I hoped we'd sell the travel mugs, since I'd brought more than normal out of a sense of optimism.

Ian glanced at Faith, like he was debating sending her to fetch his tumbler, then said, "Faith, give me your mug."

She glanced at him with a slightly annoyed look, then pulled a festival mug out of her tote bag and handed it over. Her eyes returned to her phone. But I could tell she was listening to everything her boss said.

"Here, sweetie, hold this card for me." Ian handed over Bax's business card to Faith, who looked up briefly to grasp the card and stash it in her tote without saying a word.

Sweetie? Seriously? Did he think he lived in the 1950s? I set water to boil for the pour-over, and while I waited, I rinsed out Faith's mug. Ian handed over his VIP pass, and I entered his number in the VIP log on our point-of-sale system. The festival sold special passes that included unlimited food and drink, and they'd reimburse me and all of the food cart vendors at the end for the VIP food sales.

Ian turned back to Bax. "One of my clients is obsessed with your *Dreamside Quest* game. He truly gets what you do, and he's a talented musician in addition to being a gigantic video game nerd."

I almost snorted as I set up the pour-over station, topped with a Kalita Wave filter with a glass carafe underneath, and took a moment to tare the scale. I set up a small bowl under the grinder we used for pour-over and drip coffees, all the while thinking that if you want to glad-hand a video game developer, referring to their target demographic as "nerds" isn't the route I'd take. However, "geek" can be appropriate, depending upon the context and lack of contempt.

Bax's tone was patient, but I could hear an edge underneath. "As I said, I'm taking a mini-vacation over the long weekend. Off the top of my head, I can't think of any immediate needs. But shoot me an email, and I'll let you know if we need any extra help. We're happy with our current freelance musicians, but it's always good to have more in mind."

I ground the beans, drowning out Ian's response, and weighed the bowl to make sure I had twenty-one grams of coffee grounds. The actions felt automatic, like I didn't need to think. Which is amusing, since pour-overs take several minutes, and so they give me plenty of time to get lost in my thoughts. Or, on slow days, chat with customers. But I was content to let Bax carry the conversation weight with Ian.

As I poured water from the gooseneck kettle through the grounds I'd set up, Alexis walked up, still carrying her clipboard. I waved with my other hand.

Alexis waved back, but her smile faltered when she saw Ian. But she threw her shoulders back as if she'd mentally girded her loins and was ready to take down a lion. Ian's look back was a bit smug, like Alexis was part of his territory. I resisted the urge to tell Ian that female lions are in charge of their prides.

"Hi, Sage. Can I get an iced herbal tea? And this." She picked up one of the Ground Rules tumblers and handed it over.

"We have a couple of options for tea, including some herbal tea sodas and iced teas." I motioned to the list of teas and grabbed the tumbler with one hand while I continued to pour the last ounces of water into Ian's pour-over, which reached 375 grams, telling me it was ready to drink. I discarded the water I'd used to preheat his cup, then emptied the three hundred milliliters of coffee into his baby blue tumbler. Or, rather, his assistant's. It was a sleek ceramic travel mug from a brand that claimed it was spill-proof.

"Oh, these all sound excellent! Very creative," Alexis said as she read the special Campathon Menu we'd created, full of summer drinks with a mix of coffee, tea, and naturally decaffeinated options. Her nose scrunched up slightly when she read the strawberry-sage drinking vinegar special. Her gaze kept flicking between two of the decaf options: peach and lemon iced tea or mint and lemon verbena iced tea.

"You must like lemon," Alexis said.

"Note one has lemon verbena, not actual lemons," I said. As I handed Ian's coffee over to him, I explained to Alexis how lemon verbena is a plant frequently used in herbal teas because of its naturally sweet lemon flavor. "I grew the mint and lemon verbena myself."

At least, I'd planted the herbs in a pot in my dad's backyard, and he'd kept them alive. Ian took his coffee and turned back to Bax. My boyfriend's posture tightened like he was fighting down annoyance and was gearing himself to rebuff Ian again.

"I still have a few things to do to help Sage get ready," Bax said and disappeared around the edge of the cart. I'd been debating what I could do to help his escape, but clearly, his flight-or-be-annoyed instinct didn't need any assistance from me.

"I'll have to try the lemon verbena and mint tea, but I'm coming back later for the peach iced tea," Alexis said. She handed over her VIP pass. "For me, you can log the tumbler as a VIP purchase, but please don't do that for anyone else."

"No problem. Do you avoid caffeine? I can think of a few more options for you, if you'd like," I said. I logged in her pass and handed it back, and then rinsed out Alexis's new Ground Rules tumbler.

"I quit caffeine cold turkey, and it hurts my soul," Alexis said. Ian's gaze turned to Alexis, and his look was oddly soft for a spilt second before his professional mask smoothed over his face.

I looked down to scoop ice into the tumbler and filled it with some of the herbal iced tea I'd brewed this morning back in our warehouse. The tea wasn't my favorite since its smell reminded me of my brother's favorite cleaning product, but it had taste-tested well when I experimented with summer drinks at the Rail Yard's Ground Rules cart.

"Alexis, we need to talk," Ian said.

Alexis took her new tumbler filled with tea from me, and she closed her eyes for a second like she didn't want to deal with Ian. She slowly reopened her eyes, then turned to face Ian, like she was staring down a lion. "Yes?"

Maya walked up as Ian said, "The Changelings should be in the prime spot on Saturday evening instead of relegating them to Friday and Saturday afternoons. Not having them close the biggest evening is a mistake."

"Chill out. We did the best we could with the schedules. Plus, I got your new Waffle Twaddle band in even though they're unproven. I had to vouch for them personally, so they better not let me down," Alexis said.

"You know the Changelings should close out Saturday night. It's the biggest spot, and they'll draw a crowd because of their recent buzz. They're the hottest band here."

Maya snorted. "You know the Changelings aren't the biggest band here, right?"

But Alexis's steady gaze didn't waver from Ian's face. "I need to go direct traffic in the RV area. Ian, we did our best, and you're going to have to live with it. Even if I wanted to change the schedule, it's too late now."

Alexis walked off with her tea. Ian stared at her, and there was something in his expression I couldn't interpret. An undercurrent that implied they'd been arguing about something other than the festival. I shook my head to clear it. Not my problem. And from what I'd seen, Alexis was capable of handling Ian.

Maya turned to Ian and eyed him like she was ready to stare him down. She crossed her arms over her chest. "Where's Joe?" Maya asked.

"Haven't you heard? Joe's out for a few months with a 'family emergency.' Do you remember Aaron Jacobs? He's filling in on bass for a while," Ian said. He practically put air quotes around "family emergency."

A woman, maybe in her early thirties with hair dyed a dramatic burgundy red and wearing funky purple glasses, walked up and showed me her VIP pass, and requested an iced mocha. She handed over her festival mug without me asking.

"Are you in one of the bands?" I asked her.

"Nah, I just wanted to get settled in before the crowd descends," she said. "And I love how the VIP ticket is basically an all-you-can-eat pass, too."

"The VIP pass was a stroke of brilliance," I said. I wondered how many fans had taken advantage of buying a pass, which also allowed them to set up their tents or RVs the night before the general admission opened. And like the burgundy-haired woman said, the pass also allowed the holder to buy as much food as she could eat, and as many nonalcoholic beverages as she could drink.

As I made the mocha, I could hear Maya talking with Ian. On the Maya intensity scale, I suspected she was up to about an eight.

"You've been ducking my calls." The undercurrent of anger in Maya's voice made the muscles in my back tense up again.

I handed the burgundy-haired VIP her mocha, and she nodded thank you. She turned and watched Maya and Ian like they were part of the festival entertainment.

"I told you I'm investigating. We'll get this taken care of. It's really not a big deal." Ian sounded dismissive. Bax walked back up, and he eyed Ian warily.

Maya kept her gaze on Ian's face. "You better take care of this soon or else you're going to have a major problem."

"I remember those glorious days when I thought I wouldn't have to deal with you ever again," Ian said.

Maya's mouth dropped open and she sputtered. Ian smirked before turning and walking away, with his intern Faith in his wake. Bax glanced over at Maya, and she responded by slinking up to him and bumping her shoulder against his. I could only see the side of Maya's face as she looked intently at Bax. Unlike me, she could look him in the eye since she was about an inch taller than him. And at 5 feet 10, he's slightly taller than average, at least in America, since 5 feet 9 is the standard here. He'd be short in the Netherlands, though. Unlike me, since I'm short pretty much everywhere.

"Well, that was fun. I thought for sure someone was going to get slapped." The VIP walked off with her mocha.

Bax's phone rang. From the way he let out a breath, I bet his ex was calling, and it had something to do with their son, who was supposed to join us on Saturday for the festival. Campathon billed itself as family friendly and had a play area next to the kids' stage featuring a lineup of child-friendly musicians and talks, along with games.

"Sorry, I have to take this." As he stepped away, Maya stepped up to the counter.

"Ian makes me so angry," Maya said. "He's worse than Nate."

"Why is that?"

"You know the Changelings album *Sanguine Sunrise*?" Maya asked. "I wrote five of the songs on it, including 'Mid-morning Blues.' We'd been playing them for a few years when I was still with the band. But I haven't received any royalties. And 'Mid-morning Blues' is hella successful. Ian keeps saying he'll figure it all out, but he's just blowing smoke."

"So they've made money off your song." Maya's anger made sense to me on a primal level. I'd be furious if someone had claimed ownership of my creation. I mean, I'd been partially vexed and slightly chuffed when a coffee shop started selling coffee sodas almost identical to the recipes I'd developed for Ground Rules. But a sage simple-syrup coffee soda isn't overly original, even if I hadn't heard of any other shops in town offering it.

Maya stared off in the distance. "It's not just the money. It feels like the band stole my voice."

"Just call you Ariel," I said.

She turned and locked eyes with me. It felt like we were in sync. "Exactly."

As Maya walked away, I had a mental flash of her as an armored mermaid, ready to go into battle with a trident. Would she risk her voice in a bargain with the Sea Witch? But one thing I've learned over the years is that people will battle for all sorts of things if the stakes are high enough.

Chapter 2

All of the food carts were in place by evening, although they were closed, including Ground Rules. The crew behind Campathon had fired up a couple of grills and set up hamburgers, hot dogs, and garden burgers stations, along with a selection of salads and a dessert table. The festival invited everyone with a VIP pass for dinner, and Alexis had extended the invitation to the food cart owners. Although I'd noticed a couple of the cart owners set up their carts and take off. Some of the food vendors were commuting each day instead of camping. Owners leaving made sense, especially since some of them probably needed to spend the mornings prepping food in a commissary kitchen. Most of the carts opened for lunch through dinner, versus my zero-dark-thirty caffeine preparation mission.

"Would you like a beer?" Bax asked me. The beer and wine garden was open, although it wasn't part of the free dinner.

"Nah, but you go ahead. Want me to grab a burger for you?"

"Please. You know what I like."

As Bax headed into the beer garden, I put together a couple of cheeseburgers on my speckled green camping plate. Like the carts, while the festival provided tonight's dinner, we needed to bring plates unless we wanted to carry food with our hands.

I filled my second plate with a collection of salads, all of which were carefully labeled and listed allergens, showing the festival was serious about providing quality options that catered to allergies and lifestyles, chosen or forced. They'd done the same thing with the food carts. Which is one of the many reasons Ground Rules scoring a spot at Campathon felt like an accomplishment. This festival was special, with its green focus and eclectic mix of bands. Plus top-notch food offerings.

The woman filling a plate with a large scoop of Texas caviar looked familiar. She'd been driving the Breakfast Bandits cart and had scurried away when Maya made a joke about killing Nate. Yet she'd been willing to throw down the Kauai Vibes owner over who got to park first. I smiled at her and made sure my voice was friendly.

"Hey, I think you're our food cart neighbor. I'm Sage."

She looked at me with slightly narrowed eyes. "I'm Bianca."

"This weekend should be a blast. Do you know which bands you're going to check out?"

Bianca moved to scoop pasta salad onto her plate and didn't say anything. Like I had major cooties. We weren't going to move into "braid each other's hair" status anytime soon.

I tucked a can of sparkling water under my armpit and navigated toward one of the picnic tables with my loaded plates.

Bax joined me and offered me a sip of his beer. Based on the crisp taste with notes of pine and citrus, he'd chosen an IPA, which I could've guessed without trying. Bax knows what he likes: IPAs, video games, and blondes like me.

"I'm guessing that uses Mosaic, Citrus, and maybe Nugget hops?" I asked and handed it back.

"How do you do that?" Bax asked. But I just smiled at him, not telling him I'd researched the local brewery serving the festival last week, meaning I'd scoped out their website and draft list. They'd listed the hops in each beer prominently, and I'd mentally noted the stats of their on-trend IPA. "You sound like you want a beer, too."

His words made me crave a crisp lager. "I do, but it'd make me tired tomorrow morning, which seems like a bad way to start the festival." A few months ago, I'd ceded to age and acknowledged that having a drink in the evening made early mornings impossible for me. This didn't stop me from imbibing on occasion, but I'd turned strategic. I missed my college days when sleep had felt optional and late nights were the norm.

My employee, Kendall, paused and waved to me before heading out of the beer garden, carrying a loaded plate. He'd cut his dark blond hair since I'd seen him two days before, and he looked more dapper than normal in a polo shirt and linen pants. He disappeared into the trees, like a wood nymph who was wandering around. But I knew one of his friends who lived in Colorado had sprung for a VIP pass and brought her parents' RV, so Kendall was probably hanging out with her. I knew he was sleeping in the RV instead of finding a spot to pitch a tent.

And he was dressed to impress his friend.

Maya slid into the spot next to Bax. She put her tin bento box, which held a bun-free hamburger and hot dog, along with a pile of fruit salad, down in front of her.

"Did you get settled in okay?" Bax asked Maya.

"I set up my tent in the jam area." She speared a chunk of watermelon and eyed it for a moment before biting off the corner.

Alexis dropped into the spot next to Maya. Her plate held a collection of salads.

"This day," Alexis said. She looked like she needed to curl up and sleep for a week.

"'I don't mind a reasonable amount of trouble,'" Maya said.

Alexis laughed. "*The Maltese Falcon*, right?"

"Yep." Maya turned to me. "Alexis got me totally obsessed with Dashiell Hammett last winter. I ended up reading all of his novels, and I'm still working my way through his short stories."

"'The problem with putting two and two together is that sometimes you get four, and sometimes you get twenty-two,'" Bax said. Both Maya and Alexis turned to him, like he'd said something earth shattering. Then they grinned in unison.

"*The Thin Man?*" Alexis asked.

He nodded. "I have a hazy, noir-themed video game idea that's been percolating in my brain for a while."

"Bax, you should do it. I'd love to score a noir game," Maya said. "We can do something dark and creepy, with saxophones. You know, the sort of jazz that makes you want to smoke a cigarette in the rain."

A man sat down next to Alexis. A couple of years older than her, maybe mid-thirties, like Bax. The new guy had dirty blond hair pulled back into a low ponytail, and he wore a faded shirt that advertised an earlier year of Campathon.

"Hey, Logan," Maya said. He grinned at Maya like they were old friends.

Alexis looked at me. "Sage, have you met Logan? He's my boss."

I heard the hidden explanation of her words: Logan Pembroke being her boss meant his family owned both the farm and Campathon. But if you based their work rank on their appearance, Alexis looked like CEO material in comparison to Logan's overgrown-pot-smoker vibe.

"We haven't met, but we did email once or twice." I smiled at him and didn't mention I'd emailed him three times. He'd finally replied to one of my emails when I'd cc'd Alexis.

"Logan, we can thank Sage for filling in last minute as our coffee vendor."

"We're so happy you could come. A weekend without coffee would've led to riots," Logan said.

"And this is Bax," I said and nodded toward my boyfriend.

They glanced at each other, followed by mutual nods saying they found each other acceptable enough to eat at the same table.

"Now is the calm before the storm. Ten million fires and tornados will descend on us tomorrow," Logan said. He picked up his hamburger and bit into it like it was going to fuel him for the next several days.

"And you know they'll sing their complaints in dissonant chords," Alexis said. She speared a bite of a pasta salad and looked at it like she couldn't decide if she was hungry. Her eyes tracked behind me, and I stole a glance. Ian and his assistant, Faith, sat a few tables behind us. Ian stood up.

"Maybe this weekend, all of your dreams will come true," Ian said to Faith and tapped her on the nose. She looked faintly annoyed as she watched him walk our way.

"Hi, everyone." Ian stood behind me. Alexis looked up at him with a guarded look on her face.

Maya stood up. "I'll see most of you tomorrow." She glared at the air behind me, making me glad she couldn't light Ian on fire with her eyes. Else I'm pretty sure I would've gotten caught in the cross-hairs.

"There's no need for everything to be this way, Maya," Ian said.

"'Keep on riding me, and they're going to be picking iron out of your liver,'" Maya said and turned away. Logan's eyes widened.

"*The Maltese Falcon*," Alexis said.

"Oh, it was a movie quote," Logan said. He turned back to his plate.

"It's also a book," Alexis said. "Although maybe that line is only in the movie."

"Maya is such a drama queen," Ian said. He turned to Logan. "I wanted to check in, and say thanks for keeping the festival going. My bands are all happy to be here."

"You know Campathon is my life," Logan said.

Bax nudged me, and I nodded. He headed toward the bathroom, and I took our plates to the dishwashing station.

As I was debating if I should stow my now clean but damp plates in my bag or carry them, Bianca of the Breakfast Bandits walked up.

"Did you get into the festival by kissing up to the owner? Because we got in on pure talent," Bianca said.

"You'll just have to wait and find out, right?" I said. I sauntered away.

★ ★ ★

Bax had set up our tent in a spot he hoped would be far enough away from the beer garden to be quiet but close enough that I wouldn't have to stumble too far in the dark when it was time to brew coffee for the masses. Plus, we were a short walk from the nearest porta-potties, but not in smelling distance.

In other words, he'd done good.

We'd set up our camp chairs outside the tent, and the festival grounds felt calm as the sun faded and shadows overcame the campsite. Bax wore a headlamp so he could read a graphic novel, while I'd brought a flashlight that pulled out into a small lantern and a nonfiction book about a feather heist from a natural museum that'd been on my to-read pile for a while.

Occasionally people would walk past. From my last trip to the bathroom, I'd noticed most of the activity seemed centered by the RV area, aka where most of the bands had set up. But the bustle and snatches of music had barely appealed to me. This quiet moment felt like the right way to start the long weekend.

Bax looked over at me, making me squint when his headlamp shone in my eyes.

"Sorry about that," he said and turned his head, so I wasn't in the spotlight. "You good?"

"Perfect. But I might hit the hay." I shivered, wishing I hadn't left my hoodie five feet away in the tent. "So what's the story with that Nate guy? You never mentioned you know him."

Bax was silent for a moment. "Nate isn't a friend, and he's the last guy I want to waste brain space on."

"He's not your cup of coffee?"

"Nate's way too bro for me. I met him a few times through Maya after he joined her band, but we never clicked."

"Maya isn't a fan, either."

"You can't blame her. Nate kicking her out of her own band is unforgiveable."

"I can't even imagine." Although I could. It'd be like losing

Ground Rules despite putting my soul into it. More sympathy for Maya flowed through me.

A few minutes later, we headed into the tent. Bax had set up the sleeping bags side by side in the center on top of a couple of Therm-a-Rests. We talked for a few minutes, and I felt like this moment was a good omen for the rest of the weekend.

Way too early the next morning, I quickly shut off the alarm app on my phone. Bax groaned in his sleep beside me in the tent. He promptly fell back into his "imitate a log" state. I pulled on my hoodie and grabbed the drawstring bag I'd packed the night before. After slipping out into the cool morning air, I re-zipped up the tent and headed to the locker room. The festival had brought in portable showers along with the porta-potties, but Alexis gave me the key to the employee locker room by the barn, which had several shower stalls. She'd made me promise not to tell my fellow food cart vendors since she'd only given keys to me and the Breakfast Bandits since we opened early. She said the others could fend for themselves.

The front half of the locker room building held the public bathrooms, and I followed the path along to the back of the building and unlocked the door. I flipped the lights on as I entered, and the compact fluorescent lights slowly lit up the gray lockers on one wall flanked by a bench and the three shower stalls on the other side of the room. A doorway led to a room with several sinks and toilet stalls. I locked the door of the locker room behind me.

Thankfully each shower stall had two cubes inside, with a changing area with a small bench and several hooks on the wall separated from the shower. I bolted myself into the stall on the far left, listening to how quiet the world felt, how spooky. Soon the festival would be bursting with noise. But now, it was like a ghost town with faded dreams of its glory days.

The hot water felt like a luxury as I took a quick shower, although I jumped in place when I heard a clank inside the locker room. I paused and listened but didn't hear anything more. I finished my shower in a hurry and quickly dressed in a Ground Rules T-shirt, jean shorts, and hoodie, with my hair wrapped up in my camp towel.

As I put my bag down on a bench and started to plug my hairdryer into a socket, the lock on the door flicked with a creak that made me jump. Alexis walked in at a fast clip, with a sick look on her face and one hand on her stomach. She headed straight to the room with the toilets, so I turned my hairdryer on to give her some privacy. I gave my hair a quick dry before pulling it back into a ponytail.

The food carts were in the parking lot next to the barn, which held the home stage, and I caught sight of an amazon in black cowboy boots striding away from the barn. Maybe Maya.

A glance at my phone's clock told me I was on schedule but needed to shake off my sluggishness and kick it up a gear to open at seven. Attendees weren't allowed to bring stoves or start campfires, so as the coffee vendor, I needed to open early for the safety of any caffeine addicts in attendance. And their friends, since caffeine headaches are the worst, and who wants to be grumpy during a weekend of fun?

My first order of business: fill my cart's water tank. I pulled out the handcart and loaded the water tank, even though it was light enough to carry while empty, and wheeled it over to the commercial kitchen attached to the barn, which used a different key on the ring Alexis had assigned me. Whoever had remodeled the barn to make it an event venue had done a fantastic job, and it didn't take me long to fill a couple of jugs, although it took me several trips to fill the cart's water tanks. A gallon of water weighs eight pounds, so each thirty-gallon tank weighs 240 pounds. So if you stuck my business partner, Harley, and me on the same side of a teeter-totter, and one of the thirty-gallon tanks on the other, we wouldn't be able to budge the tank. But maybe Kendall and I could budge it. I'd never asked him what he weighed, since that'd be weird.

After I delivered my last load of water to the cart, I noticed my bag with my wet towel on the cart's counter. I grabbed it and power walked my way over to the Ground Rules Subaru. My sneakers crunched loudly on the gravel lot, like little peeps in the morning quiet. After stashing my bag in the car (and hanging the pack towel), a flash of burnt orange in the green underbrush along the parking lot caught my eye. Had someone lost a jacket? My feet walked over. Even though I told myself to keep getting the cart ready.

Then I noticed dark blue jeans and a dusty pair of brown oxfords. I raised my hand to my mouth.

Ian lay in the underbrush, holding a Ground Rules coffee tumbler in his hand. His face was a little swollen, and his eyes looked bloodshot. Like he'd been crying.

I felt woozy but forced myself to kneel and feel for a pulse on his throat while pulling my phone out of my pocket. He felt cold. There was a poker chip on the ground next to him.

A scream followed by a crash made me jump, and I dropped my phone as I wheeled around. Was the murderer after me, too?

But it was Bianca, the Breakfast Bandits cart owner, with a broken bowl of something green by her feet.

I picked up my phone and dialed 911 while stepping back to Ian's body. I couldn't find a pulse no matter how hard I tried.

Chapter 3

Since the festival grounds are outside the Portland city limits, the Multnomah County Sheriff's Office showed up. A couple of uniformed officers arrived first, followed by a detective and crime scene techs. Kendall responded to my SOS text and opened Ground Rules since it was outside the police perimeter. He'd brought me an Americano, and I still clutched my dented travel mug although I'd long since drunk the contents. The caffeine on an empty stomach made me feel even more jittery.

Bianca and the guy working at Breakfast Bandits kept popping out of their cart and staring at me as I sat on a folding chair on the edge of the crime scene. From the way the man kept touching Bianca, stroking her shoulder or hugging her, I was willing to bet they were married, or at least together. Bonded together by their love of breakfast foods.

The detective, a woman wearing a charcoal suit and hair pulled back into a bun so tight it seemed to draw the top of her face upward, approached me. She pulled a folding chair over and sat down facing me.

"Hi, Sage. I'm Detective Adams. I heard you found the body. Tell me how that came about."

Up close, she looked about forty, with brown hair that was a few shades lighter than her eyes. Something about her reminded me of my dad. Maybe it was because she was going for a sympathetic approach, versus the last detective I'd met, who'd gone straight for the jugular, trying to knock me off balance. He'd failed, but not for lack of trying.

I tried not to stammer as I explained how the cart was supposed to open at seven. I walked the detective through my morning, including my fateful trip to the car. "The dark orange of his shirt stood out, so I walked over."

"Did you touch him?"

I nodded. "I tried to see if Ian had a pulse. And I dropped my phone in the dirt when Bianca of the Breakfast Bandits screamed."

Detective Adams paused. "What's this about bandits?"

"It's the name of the breakfast food cart. They specialize in breakfast sandwiches and burritos. I met Bianca last night, and she introduced herself as the owner." Bianca felt off to me, but the detective wouldn't care about that. Before bed, I'd joked with Bax that I wouldn't be exchanging espresso drinks for a breakfast burrito with Bianca. Which still rankled me, since food cart owners should always band together. Given the chance, I sensed Bianca would throw me under a bus without blinking.

"So you weren't the only person here."

I shook my head. "I saw Alexis in the locker room, which is the building on the other side of the barn. Later, I saw someone walking away, heading toward the City Lights stage. There's a public bathroom attached to the locker room, so it could've been someone who didn't want to brave a porta-potty. You can't blame anyone who prefers actual running water."

"What did the person look like?"

"Tall. Dark hair." My hands felt a bit shaky as I debated if I should tell the detective I thought the person was Maya. But I wasn't positive. "You know, I thought someone came into the bathroom while I was showering, but I didn't see them."

"Could it have been the person with dark hair?"

"It could've been Big Foot for all I know. As I said, I didn't see them." The thought of a murderer coming into the locker room while I was showering made me feel sick. Especially when an image from the movie *Psycho*, of a knife and a shower curtain, flashed through my brain. I shivered.

"How did you know the victim?" Detective Adams's gaze was intent on my face like she was taking in more than just the words coming out of my mouth. She made me feel guilty, like I'd done something wrong, instead of being at the wrong place at the wrong time.

"I don't know him, not really. I met him yesterday for the first time when he stopped by my cart to talk to one of the singers he manages. He bought an Ethiopian pour-over." And he'd felt slimy to me but maybe he would've seemed normal to most people. People who are too glad-handish always make me feel creeped out. It's like they always want something from me I don't want to give.

"Singers he manages?"

I appreciated the way Detective Adams acted like this was a friendly conversation. Part of me wanted to help her, no matter the cost. But I kept myself grounded and focused on the facts. Just because she seemed sympathetic didn't mean she wasn't weighing my potential as a murder suspect.

I chose my words carefully. "I don't know much about Ian, but he manages multiple bands that are performing at the festival, including the Changelings."

"The local band? They performed on one of the local morning shows a while ago?"

"That sounds possible. They're a Portland band. The lead singer, Nate Green, is the singer I mentioned. But I overheard someone say that Ian had multiple bands in the festival lineup. One is named Waffle-something."

"Did you see the murder victim this morning?"

I shook my head as my heart started thumping in my ears. "Not until I . . . found him. I didn't even notice anyone near where he was . . . lying." The feeling of horror that flowed through me when I'd touched Ian's cold body swept over me again, like a sneaker wave. How long had Ian been there, waiting for someone to find him? And a voice in the back of my brain chimed in, asking why it had to be me. Why couldn't someone else have found him first?

After a few more questions, Detective Adams handed me her card. Her first name was Trisha. Her name didn't feel formal enough to me. She needed something stately.

The detective studied me again. "You know, I met a detective with the Portland Police Bureau a while back with the last name Caplin."

"If his first name is Christopher, that's my dad." I wondered if she was looking for a family resemblance. I'm a carbon copy of my mother on the outside, although I like to think I inherited the important bits of myself, like my principles and desire to release good into the world, from my father.

We exchanged the look. The one that wasn't quite an insider's— since I hadn't followed my dad into law enforcement—but it recognized that I knew, at least as an observer, what it was like to be in the trenches. I'd seen the toll it took. I'd talked to my dad once about how one of the things he likes about cold cases is being able to see the big picture laid out in front of him, even if solving the cases usually came down to a small detail, like finally being able to test DNA. The families he deals with appreciate seeing justice served. Even if they haven't given up hope, the shock of the crime has settled in and become part of the landscape of their lives. Detective Adams was wading in as the tsunami hit and fighting against the force of the waves that threatened to tear Ian's family apart. They'd never be the same.

Since the detective said I could go, I walked toward my food cart. But as I made it to the world outside of the police perimeter, something about Ian, and what I saw, bothered me. Something was wrong, like if you tried to substitute a checker for a missing pawn while playing chess. But I couldn't bring it into focus.

As one of the police officers held up a piece of yellow crime scene tape for me to duck under, I passed close to Alexis and a woman in a suit. Alexis looked like she was sweating, even though she was only wearing a short-sleeve dress and the morning air was chilly. I was thankful for the hoodie wrapped around me like a hug. And her eyes were red like she was holding back tears.

"One of the musicians, Maya, threatened Ian yesterday afternoon," Alexis said. Her voice was rough. "And the man with Maya was snippy with Ian, too. They looked close."

The guy with Maya? My feet froze in place. She was talking about Bax, and Alexis knew he was dating me. Not Maya. Although from the way Alexis was throwing Maya under the bus, maybe they weren't good friends after all, even though they shared book recommendations. The detective looked my way, so I continued forward, and then it hit me. I knew what was wrong.

Ian hadn't bought a Ground Rules mug yesterday. Yet he'd been holding one when he died.

But Alexis had bought one.

Chapter 4

"Have you been busy?" I asked Kendall as I stepped into the coffee cart. He was scrubbing down the counter, which collects coffee stains like no one's business.

Kendall turned and studied me for a second, leaning one jean short–clad hip back against the counter. His hair was a bit flat on the side, like he'd sprung out of bed and rushed to the cart without brushing it. His teal Ground Rules apron clashed against his orange T-shirt, but it worked, somehow. Maybe because Kendall has a natural, low-key vibe, like perfectly balanced cappuccino with just the right amount of cinnamon and sugar sprinkled on top to keep him interesting.

"It's been slow, but better than I expected. Probably because everyone wants to know what's happening," Kendall said. "I'm sure it'll pick up when the festival fully opens."

"I'm sorry for waking you up early." I snagged a mason jar of chia-seed pudding from the cart's fridge. I'd made individual servings of puddings for breakfast since they're easy to eat while working. My stomach growled.

"It's okay. It's not like you planned to find a body." Kendall's head tilted as he looked at me, like a golden retriever I suspected he secretly was at heart. "This isn't going to become a habit, right? Harley told me about the last time."

"Finding bodies? Hopefully not." The one murder investigation I'd run into had permanently bruised part of my soul, and I couldn't imagine the cost if I kept brushing up against death. As it was, finding Ian would settle in alongside the collection of scabbed-over wounds.

"So, who was it?" Kendall asked.

But a couple holding hands walked up to the cart before I could answer, and Kendall waved me back and took their order for a couple of lattes. They handed over their VIP passes to be scanned. I ate the pudding, which was simply coconut milk mixed with chia seeds, although I added fresh banana chunks as I ate. The wolf inside me tamed slightly as the food settled inside me. If you'd told me yesterday that I'd scarf down chia seeds like they were my favorite food, I wouldn't have believed you.

The main gate formally opened at 11:00 a.m. for attendees who hadn't bought a VIP pass. A steady stream of people arrived, searching for camp spots under the shelter of the trees so they could get set up before the first bands played in the afternoon. Even though he could've left me to handle the cart on my own, Kendall and I served up a steady stream of coffee drinks. After working with Harley for months, I'd had to adjust to Kendall's rhythm. But he was an excellent barista, always able to break out a charming smile. And more important, he'd listened carefully to Harley's and my teachings and learned to pull a mean shot of espresso.

Kendall looked at me during a break in customers. "Do you think the festival is really going to happen? Or will they cancel last minute due to the death? Is it right to hold a festival when someone died here?" Kendall had gone back to school last spring to study actuarial science, and I could almost see the gears turning in his brain.

I felt shaky inside again. "Good question. I have no idea."

A few minutes after Kendall left to grab lunch for us, Alexis walked up to the cart, looking like the weight of the world had settled onto her shoulders and she was barely able to keep herself upright.

"You need some caffeine?" I asked.

She smiled and handed me one of the festival stainless steel pint glasses, even though I'd sold her a tumbler yesterday.

"Don't tempt me. I think it's time to try the decaf peach and lemon iced tea," Alexis said.

As I poured out her tea, I wanted to ask about Ian. But instead, I said, "Are the bands carping on you? It must be hard making everyone happy."

"We will never please all of the bands, although plenty are happy to be here and are lovely about it," Alexis said. She waved her hand. "But Ian's . . ."

Her voice trailed off, and tears started to form in her eyes. She rubbed her face. "Ian's gone. And his death could ruin the festival."

"The festival is still going to happen? You won't cancel?"

"That's the plan, although Logan's still waiting to hear from his lawyer. Other festivals have had fatal overdoses and kept going. But there's no way Ian overdosed, and while it doesn't look like his death was a failure on the festival's part, I'm worried."

It felt like Alexis had wanted to say something else. But a woman wearing a Timbers shirt came up and ordered a latte, and while I was steaming the milk, Alexis disappeared with her tea. But Bax showed up, which made a knot of tension inside me loosen. Like he was my emotional support animal.

I was smiling as I put the latte down on the counter. When the woman grabbed it, she yelped and pulled her hand back. "That's hot!"

"I'm sorry. I should've warned you. Metal conducts heat," I said. I added a reminder to my mental list to suggest customers use the festival's reusable cups for iced drinks only.

"Do you have any sleeves?"

I shook my head. "We couldn't bring any cardboard sleeves because of the festival's goal of zero waste, but we do have these handmade ones for sale." I pulled out a box of knitted cup sleeves Harley had made while stuck at home. She'd gotten fancy with a few, knitting hearts or owls into the sleeve. A couple had stripes, and a few had sequins. Most were simple. But they were charming in an occasionally lumpy, handcrafted sort of way.

"Oh, that's a brilliant idea!" The woman rooted around in the box and pulled out a purple cup sleeve with a knitted owl, complete with two sequins as eyes. After a moment, she also chose one in yellow-and-green Timbers stripes. "I'll take two!"

I rang her up and helped her put the purple sleeve on her cup. She tucked the second into her tote and split.

Bax leaned his elbows on the counter. "Coffee is hot, huh?"

"I should've warned her, 'cause hot coffee in the festival cups is painful. She's not going to be the first." I leaned forward and kissed him briefly.

"Coffee isn't the only hot thing around here," Bax said when I pulled away. He eyed me for a moment. "Are you okay? I stopped by earlier, but you were behind the police tape."

The words made me feel tired. The shield I'd put up to deal with finding Ian faltered, and I wanted to collapse. Take a nap in the shade of the trees.

"I'm okay, overall," I said. Bax tilted his head ever so slightly, and his expression softened like he knew I was putting up a papier-mâché façade painted to look like brick. I took a deep breath and told myself to be strong, as falling apart now wouldn't help anything. Bax reached over and took my hand. Like the contact would keep me in the here and now instead of floating off into the ether.

"You know you can shut down the cart or something, right? You don't have to power through this." Bax squeezed my hand tightly for a second, then relaxed his grip without letting go. It felt like my whole hand disappeared into his.

"I don't want to let the festival down. Can you imagine a whole weekend with no caffeine?" I said. But from the way Bax's eyebrows narrowed slightly, he knew I was trying to lighten the situation.

"I'm sure the festival won't blame you if you need time to recover from being traumatized. And if they're jerks about it, then it's not a contract you'd want anyway, right? Your well-being is more important than selling coffee." Bax's gaze on my face was thoughtful, like he was trying to get a lock on what I was genuinely feeling deep inside.

"I'm fine. It wasn't particularly gruesome, to be honest." I blinked hard as tears suddenly flooded my eyes, and Bax squeezed my hand again.

Ian's body flashed through my mind. His burnt orange shirt had been dirty. Had he rolled around in the dirt? One of the details that had been bothering me settled into the forefront of my mind. How had Ian died? There hadn't been anything obviously wrong with him.

"Any chance you can hook me up with an iced latte? I'm in serious need of caffeine." Bax motioned to his travel mug with the hand not holding onto me.

"As I have an in, I'm sure I can help you with that." I picked up his well-used travel mug with a logo of a grumpy Sasquatch on the side. He'd given them out to his whole staff as a gift a few years ago after they'd launched a new game.

"By the way, the knitted cup sleeves? I'm always impressed about how creative you are, product-wise."

I shook my head. "Thank Harley for that. Although I don't know if she'll want to make up another batch when we run out, since these were a stress knit project," I said. I set about pulling a shot of espresso for Bax. When Harley knitted the sleeves after a bad break-up, she'd used up random bits of leftover yarn from old projects in her stash, which always made me laugh since it sounded edgier than bins of yarn tucked in any available cranny of space in Harley's tiny apartment. Maybe one of our friends wanted a small side hustle. Or we could find a commercial shop to make them, although they wouldn't have the rustic handmade look of the current batch.

"You just need to add a Ground Rules patch or something to really set it apart," Bax said. "You definitely need to find a way to offer reusable coffee sleeves since they're very Portland."

"What are you looking to do? Is the research something I could use for a class project?" Kendall arrived carrying two plates of chicken teriyaki from the Kauai Vibes food cart.

As I poured milk into Bax's iced latte, he snagged a couple of the chicken chunks from my lunch. Bax grinned at me when I caught him.

I explained the knit sleeves idea to Kendall, who nodded.

"It has the sort of DIY sensibility that fits in with your corporate branding," Kendall said.

As Kendall droned on, I realized Bax was trying not to laugh. Kendall's enthusiasm reminded me of myself when I was a student, so I kept my expression serious.

"If you want to spend time researching this idea, go ahead and come up with a proposal, and track your hours. We'll figure out compensation. But talk to me first if you break the five-hour mark."

"Noted, boss."

But the smile on my face faded when Detective Adams walked up.

"Would you like a coffee, Detective?" I asked. The cheerful note in my voice sounded forced, but the detective didn't seem to notice. As I glanced at Bax, we locked eyes. *Be careful*, I thought at him, not that he'd understand. But something in my expression made his eyes turn wary, so maybe my attempt at telepathy had been successful. Or he was smart enough to know me saying hi to a detective meant to be careful.

"Are you Lukas Evan Baxter?" Detective Adams asked.

Bax nodded, and his jaw tightened. "And who are you?"

"I'm Detective Adams with the Multnomah County Sheriff's Office. I have some questions for you."

"I'm not sure how I can be helpful but go ahead." Bax took a sip of his coffee.

"Would you like to talk somewhere private?"

"This is fine." Bax eventually consented to move to the side of my cart, away from the order window, but I could still hear everything. Kendall didn't even pretend to work as he listened in.

"Tell me about your relationship with Ian Rabe?" the detective asked.

"What relationship?"

"You were seen arguing with the victim yesterday."

"*Arguing* is a strong word." Bax sounded calm, but I could hear the control under the tenor of his voice.

"So you admit you did know him."

"*Know* is also too strong of a word. Nate Green introduced me to Ian yesterday, and Ian immediately tried to glad-hand me. He wanted something my company has: potential freelance jobs for musicians. I brushed him off, although I did give him my card. I expected him to hound me next week."

"What's this about jobs?"

I made a round of iced drinks as Bax explained how he co-owned a video game development company. "One of Ian's former clients freelances for my company regularly, and the few times she hasn't been able to pencil in my job, she's referred me to someone fantastic. I found Ian to be rude, so I wasn't planning on making much time for him."

"I heard you fought with him over your girlfriend?"

"Sage made a coffee for Ian, but they didn't argue. If anything, he tried to charm Sage when he realized he wasn't making any ground with me."

I glanced outside, trying to stay in the shadow of my cart as I watched them, wondering if Bax's pun had been on purpose. Given the stiff set of his shoulders and the wary look in his eyes, it wasn't. The detective had the same intent look in her eyes as when she questioned me. Bax almost looked guilty, which made me wonder if every innocent person acted this way around the police. Maybe the people to suspect are the ones who are too relaxed. Too open. Which made me wonder if people like me, the ones who turn into high-speed chatterboxes, rank on the guilty-or-weird scale.

Or maybe my brain was making stuff up and needed to take a break.

The detective's next words broke me out of my thoughts.

"I'm talking about Maya Oliveira."

A tiny tinge of jealousy pinged me. I pushed it down. But then I remembered Maya bumping Bax's shoulder and the look they'd shared, the kind that communicates without words because you know each other so well you don't need to say anything.

The skin between Bax's eyes crinkled as his eyebrows furled. "Maya's the musician who freelances for me. She's not my girl-friend."

"You didn't leap to Maya's defense?"

"Maya doesn't need my help defending herself." Bax laughed. But there was a note in the undercurrent of his laugh that said this wasn't funny. I wondered if the detective had noted it. I wondered if she saw it as guilt.

Alexis must've laid it on thick if the police thought Maya and Bax were an item.

Or maybe there was something I didn't know. The ball of worry that found its way into my brain when I'd found Ian's body grew, taking over my throat. Until finding Ian's body, I'd thought life was going well.

But maybe it was all a lie.

Chapter 5

"Are you sure you'll be okay by yourself?" Kendall took off his apron, so I saw the graphic of a coffee cup with a heart inside on his T-shirt for the first time.

"Your shirt's adorable," I said.

"Yes, I know it's precious," he deadpanned. "My sister bought it for me. You sure you want to be solo in the cart for a while?"

"Kendall, go. I can handle it the rest of the day since you pitched in this morning."

"No, I'll be back for the last hour of the afternoon shift. Call me if you need me."

Kendall finally left, leaving me to a brief moment of quiet in the cart. I'd looked forward to today since we'd signed the festival contract, visualizing myself selling coffee in the mornings and listening to music in the evenings. If the weekend was a color, I'd seen it as sunshine yellow. But finding Ian's body had never been part of the plan. Being a murder suspect, even peripherally, also wasn't on my agenda.

My hands clenched into fists. Bax being a suspect was absolutely not okay.

And I didn't want Ground Rules associated with a murder. We had plans for the future and being known as a deadly coffee company scuppered all of them.

A woman with bright purple dyed hair that matched her handmade shirt that said I ATTENDED THE FIRST WOODSTOCK walked up. She ordered a round of iced coffees. After topping them all off with oat milk, she carried them off to a group of women with matching Woodstock shirts. A brief flare of jealousy flickered inside me, since they were a group of friends having a good time, while my festival had been derailed. I told myself to woman up. Be strong.

I leaned my elbows against the cart window. Who would've wanted to kill Ian? And what thought process could have possibly decided Campathon was the right time and place to do the deed? Had this been planned? I paused, remembering this morning. Had Ian's murder been a spur-of-the-moment decision?

I pulled out the pad of paper from under the counter and wrote down three names.

Maya.

Nate.

Alexis.

All had been here yesterday, along with other bands and VIP pass holders. All three knew Ian. Most of the festivalgoers were out of the running unless they'd snuck in.

Or bought a VIP pass. Maybe someone had bought a pass just to gain access to Ian.

Could one of the other bands have had it out for Ian? Or someone who was accompanying a band, which seemed to include girlfriends and boyfriends, friends, managers like Ian, and more? The paved section of the grounds designated for band RVs had filled up about halfway last night with more rolling in today.

I paused, my mind turning back to the big question continuing to itch at the back of my mind: How, exactly, had Ian died? It hadn't been evident to me, but I hadn't spent time examining him. But maybe he'd had a stroke, or heart attack, or something else tragic and, more important, natural? Or something that was a fluke, like a bee sting when he didn't know he was allergic?

Maybe his death was merely unfortunate. An accident. Not a

crime. A tragedy that could have been avoided with prompt medical attention.

But something inside me couldn't believe Ian's death was an accident, even though I hoped it was. Although if it had been easily preventable, it'd feel like a different sort of soul-crushing tragedy.

A couple of dudes walked up, and I made them iced coffees. Attendees continued to trickle past, like a slow funnel of water through a Kalita Wave filter, lugging their gear to their camping spots and getting ready for the festival. Everyone looked so happy. So free.

Since I was alone, I took a deep breath and forced myself to do something I'd been putting off all morning. I texted Harley. *You should know I found a body.*

My phone rang almost immediately.

"What?" Harley's smoky voice came through the airwaves.

"Someone died at the festival, and I found his body this morning when I was setting up."

"Are you okay? Is Ground Rules okay? Are you or Kendall in danger? Or was this like a fluke accident type of thing?"

As Harley's list of questions grew, a tiny meow made me look down. An orange cat hopped inside the door of the cart like he was our newest barista reporting for work. The kitty rubbed his head against my leg and chirped. His tail stuck straight up in the air in a happy-cat pose.

"I'm not sure you're allowed in here. Health codes," I told the cat. He ignored me, crawled in a gap under the counter, and curled up into a ball.

"What was that?" Harley asked.

"Nothing. To answer your questions, I think we're fine. The show is going on, by which I mean, the festival hasn't been canceled."

"We really need the new cart to do well," Harley said.

"Trust me, I'm aware." My heart beat a little faster, like it wanted to sync with the emotions flowing through Harley's voice.

"I know. I'm just panicking here," Harley said.

"We should be fine. But I thought I should tell you before you heard some weird rumor."

"You know how some people, like, dowse water? You're the body finder."

"That's really not funny. Finding him was horrible." I shivered again.

"Sorry, that's my pathetic attempt at dark humor."

We said our goodbyes. Which allowed me to watch the small kitty in peace. "Where did you come from?" I asked, but he, or maybe she, let out a little squeak and curled up tighter.

"I guess it's nap time." Did the farm have a colony of feral cats? But I couldn't see a feral kitty hopping into Ground Rules and making itself at home. The cat was small, making me wonder if it was petite or only partially grown.

Customers approaching with a focused look that told me they were on a coffee mission made me forget the cat, and they were followed by another wave. As I was handing a couple of mochas over to a group of college-aged girls, Ian's intern walked up. Faith still carried the same trendy leather tote bag, although she wore a light green sundress. I glanced at her feet, and her wedge sandals gave me immediate shoe envy, especially since, for safety's sake while working, I needed to wear closed-toe shoes. I'd packed my favorite retro-inspired sneakers for the festival. At least they were purple, even if they weren't as hip as the intern's.

"Can I get an iced oat milk mocha?" Faith handed over her festival pint glass and her VIP pass. I entered her VIP pass number into the point-of-sale system, and when I handed the card back, I noticed how her jade-and-gold earrings shone against the light brown braid pulled over one shoulder. As I pulled the shot for her mocha, I decided she must be taking her internship seriously if she'd packed a polished wardrobe. Or she was just one of those people who look like they have a personal stylist following them around. And she was probably staying in an RV versus a tent. There's no way I could look that put together if I was staying in a tent.

After putting ice in Faith's tumbler, I said, "Are you doing okay? I'm so sorry for your loss."

"I feel like someone pulled a practical joke on me," she said.

"And later today, I'll find Ian laughing at me like this was one of his stupid pranks."

"Was he a jokester?" I asked. The memory of Ian calling his intern a pet name still rankled me.

"Ian thought he was a freakin' comedian." Faith looked up at me as she took the mocha I handed her. A whiff of perfume cut through the scent of coffee on the air around us, a sweet smell. I recognized it through the perfume section of a local store. Pink Sugar. Something about the notes of vanilla and caramel reminded me of cotton candy.

Faith inspected her light pink fingernails. "I'm keeping the bands going for the festival. It's the least I can do for my brother."

Wait, what? My gaze snapped back to her face. "Brother?"

Faith looked up and tried to smile, but it wavered. "Half brother, if you want to get technical. But I just met him a year ago. Meeting him was amazing 'cause he looks like my dad's younger twin. He acts like him, too. And don't get me started about how they sound identical on the phone."

The memory of meeting my own half brother for the first time when I was thirteen flashed through my mind. My grifter mother had disappeared with me when I was two, and we'd traveled the world for years. Then she'd dumped me in Portland when I was thirteen and getting too old for her to handle. I'd moved in with my dad, who'd felt like a stranger. Jackson had just started college and, to my horror, had been hired to babysit me when my father worked, although a few other extended family members had also helped out. My brother had been sarcastic and responded to me being a pain by giving as good as he got. Jackson had been part high school tutor, part life coach, occasional lawyer, and my staunchest ally over the years. Part of my brother would always see me as the barely teenager hiding her fear behind a façade of anger and snark.

Faith's phone beeped, and she pulled it out of her bag. She frowned when she read the screen. "Wish me luck. I'm supposed to talk to some detective chick now."

"She doesn't bite." Although I'd love to see Detective Adams's face if she heard a college kid call her a "detective chick."

"This reminds me of when my soccer team played in the state championship," Faith said.

"How that'd go?"

"I didn't embarrass myself." Faith squared her shoulders as she strode away.

My heart broke for her since I couldn't imagine being in her shoes. Ian calling his assistant "sweetie" now felt less offensive, knowing he'd been asking his younger sister for a favor. And, arguably, "sweetheart" is nicer than my family nickname, "Bug."

I wondered about the story behind Faith and Ian's relationship since she hadn't known her brother growing up. Meeting as adults must have felt strange. Jackson's father and my mother had been teenagers when they'd had him, and his paternal grandparents, the Hennesseys, had raised him. A few years ago, when Jackson inherited a house from his grandparents, I moved into the attic suite, paying less in rent than I would for a dinky apartment. We'd bumped along as roommates, especially since Jackson had developed a strong bromance with Bax.

Speak of the brother. I looked up to see Jackson bearing down on the cart in full badger mode with a pissed-off look on his face.

Chapter 6

Jackson bypassed the passenger window and took up shop in the doorway to the cart. He folded his arms over his chest as he leaned against the doorjamb. He was scowling, but he always has the male equivalent of RBF, which I joking call Resting Brother Face.

"You found a body and talked to the police without me?" Jackson asked. He sounded like I'd done something boneheaded when I knew better.

I knew he had a point. But all I could say was, "Want a coffee?"

"Yes, and don't change the subject."

Jackson's eyes practically burned a hole into the back of my head as I refilled the gooseneck kettle and set it to boil. Given his usual preferences, I assumed he'd want one of our single-origin pourovers. Like me, he preferred Central and South American coffees. I opened up a box tucked under the counter to pull out a stash of extra-special beans. I caught a small flash of orange. The cat was still napping in the cart.

At least this glimpse of orange made me want to smile, versus the orange of Ian's shirt earlier.

I knew I should stay quiet and let Jackson break the silence first, but words started pouring out of my mouth, flowing too quickly, like too-coarse coffee grounds in a Kalita filter. "You know, Harley just perfected this fantastic single-origin from Guatemala, and I brought a small stash. It's from a coffee farm in the Fraijanes region, grown by the Pacaya volcano, which nourishes the soil with potassium and volcanic minerals in the ashes. It's full-bodied. I brought it for my morning tipple, but I'm happy to share it with you."

Jackson snorted. "Okay, I guess it's time for you to babble about coffee instead of answering my question."

"Are you asking as my brother or my lawyer?" I kept my eyes focused on the coffee counter.

"Both."

I set up the Kalita filter and ground the beans, and when the cart was silent again, I said, "I don't think the police suspect me this time around."

Jackson snorted again.

"Besides, it happened this morning before you got here. All I did was tell the detective what I saw when I found the body," I said. Standing here reminded me of a time years ago when Jackson grilled me about my high school classes. I'd snapped at him then, reminding him he wasn't my father.

A couple walked up, and I sold them cold brews while the gooseneck kettle came to a boil. When I started pouring water for Jackson's coffee, he spoke again.

"What happened this morning? Bax didn't tell me much."

I bowed to the inevitable and told Jackson the story, from meeting Ian yesterday while setting up to finding his body this morning. "Detective Adams seems competent."

He gave me a look like I was naive. "Don't be fooled, and more important, don't talk to the police without a lawyer. I thought you knew better."

I looked down and checked the small glass carafe. It hit three hundred milliliters, so I moved the pour-over cone into the cart's sink and let the last of the water seep through the grounds while I poured Jackson's coffee into his travel mug. "Where'd you set up your tent?"

"We're on the edge of the jam camping area." Jackson and a group of his friends had been coming to the festival since they were in college, the collection of people altering over time to include marriages and evolving friendships, but the core group mostly stayed the same.

"Bax set up our home base in the quiet area."

He shook his head at me like he was disappointed I hadn't joined him in the area of night owls who'd play guitar into the wee hours of the morning.

"I'm here to work, remember, not hang out and listen to music all night," I said. "I have a self-imposed curfew."

Jackson started to say something, but my eyes locked onto a llama in a top hat walking on the pathway. He turned and followed my gaze. The llama's handler wore a sleeveless tuxedo jacket, and they walked away, toward the Pine Burrow stage.

"It'll have to be a good festival since the No Drama Llama stopped by," I said. "Although I'm not sure what tunes llamas like to jam to. Acid rock?"

"You said that llama isn't into drama, right? So maybe reggae. It feels laid back even if the lyrics are politically charged."

I hummed a few notes of "Three Little Birds."

"Don't quit your day job." My brother snorted.

As Jackson took his first sip of the pour-over, the woman with the hip purple glasses walked up. She flashed her VIP pass and set her stainless steel pint glass down on the ledge. "I'd like an iced mocha."

"I could've sworn you came by just an hour ago," I said as I picked up her glass.

"I have a VIP pass. I can order as much coffee as I want," she said. To the side, Jackson looked like he wanted to laugh as he stirred cream into his coffee.

I held up my hands in a calming gesture. "I'm sorry if that came off as critical. Are you a fan of cinnamon? Because our cinnamon mochas are the bomb."

"That sounds lovely."

"We make the cinnamon syrup in-house," I said and set about making her drink.

"Sage, I'll see you later," Jackson said. "Remember what I said."

"Of course."

"And you're right. This Guatemalan coffee is fantastic. Please bring a pound or twenty of these beans home."

"I'll try."

My brother took off, and as I made the mocha, I thought about how being at a music festival hadn't budged Jackson's instinct to treat me like I was forever thirteen, frozen in time like amber.

"Is that your fella?" my VIP customer asked.

I shuddered, then laughed. "Nah, brother. And roommate. Thankfully he has impeccable taste in coffee, else I'd have to disown him."

Not long after my VIP pass/mocha aficionado left, a girl wearing a unicorn mask that covered her whole head walked up and ordered an iced coffee. When she walked off with her drink, she still wore the mask. A few people came up with cases of midday bed head, or maybe it was a tussled fashion look. One stood for a moment, holding his coffee and staring at the police tape by the barn, before shaking his head like he was trying to clear his vision and walking off. I wondered if they were musicians who'd been up most of the night jamming.

Then Nate walked up.

The singer had traded his black T-shirt in for a charcoal gray shirt with faint red writing on the chest that I couldn't make out. But otherwise, he looked the same as yesterday. Except for a tightness around his mouth, like it was harder for him to smile.

He handed over his festival mug. "My usual, please."

I thought back to yesterday and quickly said, "Iced latte?"

He smiled, and once again, his charm felt tangible in the way sunbeams on a hot day almost feel like something you can hold. "Right in one. You must have a fantastic memory."

As I ground beans for the espresso shots destined to go into

Nate's iced latte, he studied me intently. Or he'd perfected a blank look that felt like a soul-searching gaze.

As I tamped the freshly ground shot and twisted it into the espresso machine, Nate said, "You're going to get to know me this weekend. You're peddling my drug of choice."

"You're skipping out on the hard-living musician stereotype and sticking with coffee?" I asked.

"Too many of my idols OD'd, and smoking anything messes with my voice and makes me cough," Nate said. "Plus, I mostly cut out drinking last year. I'm not saying I won't have a beer once in a while, but I can't put away beers or shots during the whole festival as some people can, which was the silver lining of Maya leaving the band. That woman can put more whiskey down than your average sailor."

"Sailor? Interesting. I would've thought rum would be a sailor's tipple of choice. Although maybe that's pirates."

"Maya is definitely more of a pirate, always forcing me to walk the plank. Although she always wears cowboy boots, which is not pirate-chic, so you're right. I flopped instead of landing the joke." Nate's gaze suddenly changed, like he'd switched to a different plane of existence. "Hmm, emotionally walking the plank."

He pulled out his phone and starting yammering into a voice app.

I left him to write his song and pulled his shot, which I mixed with ice and milk in his tumbler.

When I handed it over, I said, "I'm sorry about your manager. You must be gutted about Ian."

As Nate looked down, he rubbed the back of his neck. "I'm going to miss him. He was a truly good guy, you know? We understood each other on a deep level."

Nate looked up at me. "But I'm going to look at it as an opportunity. Ian was too cautious, and if he'd been more aggressive, we might be headlining festivals instead of opening for bands we're superior to."

"Oh." I wasn't sure what to say. Maybe Nate's ego popping up was a protective measure? Everyone deals with grief in their own way and some people don't want to show strangers their metaphorical soft underbelly. Or the news might not have fully hit him yet.

But one question popped around my brain a few times: Could Nate really be this shallow?

Nate looked above my head, like he was seeing the future reflected in the ceiling of the coffee cart. "Ian had been distracted recently, and we need someone who is all in and has a grand vision. Don't get me wrong, I'm going to miss him. After all, he was the one who discovered us. He had a great eye for talent."

"But Maya didn't stick with Ian?" Or Ian didn't stick with Maya. I could almost still feel the simmering anger between the two from yesterday.

"Ian's one of the biggest reasons she left, along with her and Joe splitting up," Nate said. "It was for the best since Maya's meant to go solo. She's destined for the spotlight, versus being part of the supporting act."

I suspected he meant their egos clashed, and, in the ensuing battle over dominance, the band had stood behind Nate.

Or at least Ian had.

"I've heard Maya's new band is pretty good, so it all worked out," Nate said. He took a sip of his iced latte. "This is perfect. I'm going to have to check out your cart in Portland."

He walked away. I watched him go, trying to figure him out. He almost reminded me of a child. Maybe Ian had been the parental figure Nate had been rebelling against. But could that lead to murder?

Something brushed against my leg. I froze for a moment, then slowly looked down.

The orange cat turned and rubbed against my shins again. A motorboat purr thrummed through the air.

"Are you ready for a shot of espresso?" I asked the fluffy orange purring machine.

"Yes, I would like one. Double, actually," a voice answered, and I jumped.

A man stood outside the cart. Thankfully the cat hadn't spoken because that would've been weird.

The cat weaved a few figure eights around my legs as I pulled a straight double shot for the customer. But when I looked down, the cat was gone. Either he'd gone back to napping or he had an appointment somewhere on the festival grounds.

I served the espresso shot in a ceramic cup alongside a small glass of sparkling water. I'd packed the small collection of ceramic cups and shot-sized water glasses just in case a few people ordered straight espresso, and so far, I'd sold more than I'd expected.

"Cheers," the customer said. He motioned to the water. "It's good to see you serve club soda with espresso. I hate it when places hand over still water."

"I'm also on Team Fizzy Water," I said. I poured myself a glass of the Fred Meyer–house brand sparkling water. We'd debated stocking Topo Chico in the cart, which has a gentle flavor since it's natural mineral water. But I prefer the slight bite of the club soda, and since I tend to finish the cans once customers leave, paying less per can made sense.

He sipped his shot, which he took black. "This is delightfully well balanced. I like the dark fruit notes and the lingering sweet chocolate finish."

"You have accurate taste buds. I'm impressed."

"Do you sell beans?" He glanced into my cart.

I pulled a flyer out from under the counter. "Of course. We can ship the beans to you, or you can stop by our cart. We also sell at a co-op in Portland. If you want a bag to take with you now, I have twelve-ounce bags of our single-origin Honduras. It's grown in the Las Cabañas region, and it has delicious notes of brown sugar, marzipan, and apricot jam. I also have our house blend, Puddle Jumper, which is a medium roast of Bourbon and Caturra beans with notes of dark berries and spiced dates. We usually have more options, but I don't have a ton of space in the cart and didn't expect to sell many bags of whole beans at the festival."

By "many," I actually meant I didn't expect to sell any, but I'd picked them out of a sense of optimism, along with a few T-shirts.

"I'll take one of each," he said. I put both in a paper bag, and he tucked the flyer inside. He paid on the cart's tablet and slid his wallet back into his pocket. "I'm looking forward to trying out your other cart."

"Be sure to say hi when you come in," I said. "I put a coupon for a free drink at our regular cart in the bag with the beans."

"Coffee isn't too bad for something discovered by a goatherd," my customer said and left. I smiled, thinking of Kaldi, the legendary goatherd who supposedly discovered the best drink in the world. Stories say he noticed his goats were more energetic and danced after nibbling on the bright red berries of a plant. So he tried chewing them, too, which led to the discovery of the coffee bean. And after a few hundred years, Portland hipsters like me could drink beans sourced from all around the world.

A glance down at the new kitty nap spot showed me the orange cat hadn't left, but instead decided to visit dreamland in the cart he'd claimed as his own. "I shouldn't name you, but you'd make a nice Kaldi. Not that you need coffee, after all. You're a cat. Drinking some would get in the way of your sleep schedule."

The cat slumbered on, curled into an impossibly tiny ball once again. "Or you'd make a good Cafecito." I smiled, thinking of how the word translated to "small coffee."

And I laughed when I realized that, while crafting my festival plans, getting adopted by a tiny mascot hadn't even crossed my mind.

Chapter 7

After a series of mini-rushes, Logan, aka the festival head honcho, walked up looking like he needed an IV of coffee with an espresso chaser.

As he handed me his tumbler, I said, "Tough day?"

"You have no idea. Today is a nightmare and not just because someone we've worked with for years died," Logan said. "Drip coffee, please."

I filled his tumbler with house coffee, then handed it back along with a carafe of cream.

"Do you have oat milk?" he asked.

"Did you know Ian well?" I swapped out the cream for a container of my favorite barista-blend oat milk.

Logan shook the oat milk container as he nodded. "I heard you found the body. That must have been rough."

"It wasn't my idea of a good time."

"I'm glad you found him before most of our attendees arrived. If no one had noticed him until the festival opened, it could've been horrible."

Logan's words made me flinch. If I was going to rank how everything should have gone, Ian being alive and floating around, imitating a human mosquito, was first on my list. "Did you think about calling the festival off?"

"We're not the first music festival with a death. Look up Coachella," Logan said. I raised an eyebrow at him, and he let out a deep breath.

Logan's mouth scrunched in a grimace, then smoothed out. "I'm sorry. One thing I've kept up with over the years is disasters at festivals. From natural disasters, like flooding and mudslides, to one heartbreaking festival in Argentina when multiple people overdosed off a tainted drug. Of course, Alexis and I talked about that first thing and debated both the moral and logistical sides. The insurance implications of calling off the festival are just as complicated. If we did it incorrectly, it could bankrupt us, and that doesn't include the potential issues the death could have on our liability insurance if we're somehow responsible, although I don't see how we can be. I'm waiting to hear back from my lawyer, but we decided Ian would want the show to go on. So unless my attorney says to cancel everything, we're moving forward in Ian's honor."

"Good to know." Even though I was tempted to pack up, I was glad the decision—whether to cancel the entire festival—wasn't my responsibility. Part of me felt shaken that a death at a festival wasn't being treated as a big deal.

"Either decision would've been a massive headache. Not to mention the feeling here." Logan patted his chest to the side of his heart. "Campathon is my lifework. Someone dying here hurts. This weekend is supposed to celebrate music. And music is life."

"Do you guys have security cameras?" I asked. Hope bloomed inside me, like coffee grounds flushing with the first ounces of water. Maybe the case would be an easy open and shut.

"Yes, but not on that side of the barn, except for the door." Logan's voice was glum. "We have discreetly hidden cameras over the grounds for insurance purposes, but we don't have full coverage of every inch of the grounds."

"Too bad." Sort of. It would be creepy to know Big Brother Logan was watching all of the grounds.

"Maybe the detective in charge of the case will find something helpful in the footage we turned over. Ian deserves justice. I feel so bad for his family."

I nodded. Hopefully, the detective would crack the case and find the guilty. Although I still suspected the innocent were going to pay the price. "The dog days of summer . . ." I muttered.

"People keep saying that, and I don't know what it means." Logan looked at me like he knew I'd have the answer.

I couldn't disappoint him. "It's the time in the summer when the sun is in the same part of the sky as Sirius."

"Sirius? Like XM?"

"Not exactly. Sirius is a star. It's part of the Canis Major constellation, and it's the brightest star visible from any part of Earth."

"Canis Major, like a dog?" Logan asked.

Part of me wondered if Logan was teasing me or if he really didn't know. Instinctively, he felt honest. Like the sort of guy who struggles with white lies, let alone anything major. Like an overgrown frat boy version of my business partner, Harley. Except Harley is always jazzed on coffee, while Logan feels like he's permanently baked. "In Greek mythology, Sirius was Orion's dog."

"If I'm hearing you right, it's a weird saying everyone uses without really knowing what it means?"

"Maybe? I looked it up once when I saw a store advertising a 'dog days of summer' sale. I'd bet a bag of coffee beans that most people think it's just the hottest weeks of July and August. Although some people claim Sirius and the sun sharing space causes all sorts of astrological problems."

Logan's phone beeped. "I better get back to the grind."

As he left, the injustice of associating the unbearably hot days of summer with dogs hit me. Even if these are the sorts of days that make me want to nap in the shade with my brother's Australian shepherd. And the days are associated with bad luck, and everyone knows dogs are good luck charms. Or at least happiness charms.

★　★　★

The day picked up. A steady supply of drinks went out into the festival, held in either Campathon tumblers or a random collection of stainless steel water bottles and assorted cups. My favorite was a mason jar in a holder made out of a leather strap with an old bike chain repurposed as a handle.

After my fellow mason jar aficionado left, after promising to email me a link to the shop where he'd bought the holder in exchange for a free drink once he followed through, I noticed a woman. She stood, facing me, about ten feet away from the cart. She held something to her mouth, and she spoke into it like she was making notes. Her eyes kept studying my cart.

I picked up my phone and, even though I wasn't fully sure why, took a photo of her. The sunlight lit up her copper hair, and she was dressed sharper than most of the crowd, in a sleeveless gray button-down tucked into dark pants. But she wasn't as upscale as Faith the intern. This new woman stared at me through chunky black-framed glasses that reminded me of old photos of Buddy Holly. She'd paused when I'd taken the photo, like I'd thrown her off her game.

She walked up. She held out her phone, and I saw she was using a recording app. "I heard you found the body."

"Did you know there's an old radar station near the Cape Meares Lighthouse on the coast? It was used to spot planes during World War Two."

She lowered her phone and hit pause. Then she stared at me. "Who cares about some old radar station? Unless you're claiming it's relevant now?"

"You started with a random fact. I thought it was the game we were playing." I studied her face for a moment, taking in her hazel eyes, which narrowed as she looked at me. She looked to be about my age, so late twenties. She wore a lanyard, but whatever was on the end of it disappeared under her shirt.

"I have some questions for you to answer truthfully." Her words were curt like she had the right to demand answers from me. Which made my metaphorical hackles stand on end, like when my brother's dog sees an evil delivery truck. Or a scary cat. And if this Buddy Holly–glasses aficionado thought she could bully me, well, she didn't know who she was dealing with.

I made my voice sound bored. "Where's your police badge?"

"What are you talking about?"

"You haven't introduced yourself."

She breathed out loudly. "I'm Grace Taggart. I'm covering the festival for the Old Town music podcast and blog. See my press pass?"

"No."

Grace looked panicked, then pulled on her lanyard. Her face settled into a haughty line as she held her credentials out to me like it was a shield. It had the Campathon logo and said ALL-ACCESS PRESS PASS. A new thought invaded my brain: Would any local reporter show up at my cart, also looking for a scoop? I've heard any publicity is good. But I doubted seeing my mug splashed across the local news attached to a murder would help Ground Rules.

Another thought flashed in my brain. I doubted Grace's press pass allowed her to hassle the vendors, let alone record them.

"Good for you," I said.

She stopped recording on her phone, then clicked record again to start a new audio file. Her voice took a lower, more strident timbre. I guessed she was a fan of vocal fry. "I'm here at the Ground Rules coffee cart, which research has told me is owned by Sage Caplin and Harley Yamazaki. Are you Harley or Sage, or simply an employee of the company?"

Research? Like she'd read the About page of our website, but neglected to take in the photo? I stared at her.

After a long fifteen or so seconds, Grace practically growled into her phone. "For some reason, the coffee cart worker is unwilling to go on the record and talk about the tragic death of Ian Rabe, one of Portland's music visionaries. And let me be specific: Rabe was cruelly struck down and murdered at the world's premier eco-friendly music festival. One that I hold dear to my heart, as do many of my podcast listeners."

I tried to breathe in quietly but couldn't stop myself from snorting. Grace glared at me again, the black of her glasses making perfect picture frames around her hazel eyes, which had beautiful flecks of green. Which almost made me feel bad for wanting to yeet the blogger across the parking lot.

She paused her phone app. "Do you mind?"

Two women in crocheted bikini tops and jean shorts walked up, and I waved them around the music blogger. "What would you like?"

"Iced mocha for me," the first one said and handed over her festival tumbler.

"Ditto." The second girl handed her glass over.

"I really like your bikini tops," I said.

"Oh, thanks! I bought this from a woman who crochets them in Brazil, and I loved it so much I had to bring one back for my sister."

"And I adore it."

We chatted about travel as I filled their tumblers with ice and set about making their mochas. Grace glowered at me from the side of the cart. The sisters glanced at her occasionally with a "what's your problem?" look but otherwise ignored her. So I put extra care into crafting their drinks to show my approval, complete with a complimentary upgrade to an iced cinnamon mocha, which made them both happy.

"The only thing that would make this festival better is if it were on a beach like Trancoso," one of the sisters said.

"Yeah, yeah, you have to bring your trip to Brazil into everything," the other sister said, and they playfully bickered as they walked away.

Grace continued to stare at me as they headed toward the Pine Burrow stage. "Sure, you're friendly to them, but you ignored the free press."

"This is a coffee cart, and they were here for coffee. What'd you expect? Especially considering you just barged up and started demanding my time. You could at least buy a drink."

"Ian's death is going to be my ticket to stardom," Grace said. "I'm going to solve his murder and leverage it into something bigger. And now, given your attitude, you're my number one suspect."

Grace wheeled around and marked off.

"I'm glad to see you're mourning the death of one of Portland's music visionaries," I called after her. Her step faltered, but then she powered forward.

Maybe I'd played the showdown with the music blogger wrong. Perhaps going on the charm offensive would've been the smarter strategy. Get her on my side, like an annoying knight on a quest. But if someone had killed Ian, they'd probably be willing to take out a clueless podcaster with delusions of solving the murder. Unless she was secretly some sort of superhero masquerading as a mosquito. Hopefully she didn't have a huge social media following, or strong web-ranking analytics game, since the last thing I wanted was for Ground Rules to be associated with a murder at a music festival. If future event organizers searched for my company online, I didn't want the top rankings to be about death.

I searched for Grace's blog on my phone and found it ranked beneath an iconic local Portland brewery also called Old Town.

Her blog had a simple design, with her podcast's name written on Buddy Holly–style glasses identical to the pair she wore. Like the clunky frames were part of her brand identity. Every podcast was also available in a written transcript. She covered local shows and bands, ranging from tiny clubs to a handful of shows at the Moda Center, aka the biggest venue in Portland and the Trail Blazers' home court.

She'd interviewed Nate a few times, including the week before the Changelings performed on a late-night talk show. Which was easy to find because she'd reposted it repeatedly on Instagram and

Twitter. Interviewing Nate must have been a career highlight for Grace.

Or maybe she dug the guy. He was charismatic, even if I suspected he was shallow and self-absorbed. Unless I was overly harsh, as I'd only talked with Nate at my coffee cart. Maybe he was authentic, and I was cynical.

I skimmed the text of their interview.

What's the inspiration for your songs?

Life, mainly. I mean, sometimes I think about things that happen every day that, when you think about it, are weird, but we just accept it. And some of the best songs are about those small everyday moments. And the usual stuff, like heartbreak and love. And dusting yourself off to keep moving forward, even when life sucks.

What's the story behind "Mid-Morning Blues"?

The songs on the album are a mix of tunes written by Maya Oliveira or me and stuff we collaborated on. Maya wrote the first version of "Mid-Morning Blues," and we tweaked it into its current form together. I see it about that moment when you think you're in love with someone, but you're sitting together, drinking coffee, wondering if this is the one. Or just the one for now. It's basically a love song about a relationship that's over, but you haven't realized it yet.

That's deep.

It's life.

So who's Maya?

Maya's, well, a tornado. It's a long story, and Maya's not with the Changelings anymore, but she used to be the backup singer and played both guitar and piano. She's one of those people with, like, an encyclopedic knowledge of music, including music theory. I'm more of a learned to play guitar by ear, write what I feel in the moment sort of songwriter. She's more structured and plays a bazillion instruments. But we did some excellent collaborations together.

I look forward to hearing what she does with her next band. She's an amazing musician, even if she wasn't the right fit for the vibe we need for the Changelings.

I wished I could get the sense of Nate's tone, which didn't come through the transcript. I suspected it was layered with pretension since I was inclined to question Nate's motives about everything. But I did note Nate was open about Maya writing songs on the Changelings' album. I screen captured the interview and told myself to send it to Maya later.

I paused for a second. Regardless of what happened between them, Nate had spoken publicly about Maya with respect. That meant something. I tried to imagine what Maya would say about Nate in an interview. Would she shoot her mouth off and bag him? But maybe she'd be smart enough to stick to the sort of virtually meaningless PR speak professional athletes are trained to use. The type where you talk and seem honest without actually saying anything.

Maybe Nate was savvy enough to understand that praising Maya made him sound both honest and respectful of his former collaborator, so he wouldn't scare off potential future cowriters.

Or Nate was being honest and truly did value Maya, even if they couldn't work together long term. Chemistry matters, after all. Bax had talked about how difficult it can be to hire the right new staff members, since simply having the needed skills doesn't mean new coworkers will get along with the motley crew that works for his company. One bad apple makes life miserable for everyone.

Two women holding hands walked up, and I poured them a couple of iced cold brews with cinnamon syrup. And they were the first in a steady stream of customers, making me focus on the now and try to forget about Ian's death.

But that didn't stop the memory of finding him from hovering in the back of my mind all day, making me feel like the sword of Damocles hovered over Ground Rules, held up by a single hair, waiting to descend.

Chapter 8

Even though I offered to stay since he'd spent the morning in the cart, Kendall took over the end of the afternoon shift, although he promised to text if he got swamped or needed help closing.

After exchanging a flurry of "where are you and what's the meaning of life" texts with Bax, I headed toward the Pine Burrow stage. I followed a trail through the woods, passing by a mix of partially assembled tents and fully setup campsites. The first band of the festival was thanking the crowd for being awesome as I approached the stage.

The Pine Burrow stage was the smaller of the two main stages, and it was set up in a clearing in the forest. Trees towered above us, with the sun filtering through like dapples of joy. It looked like it belonged in the trees. Like the festival had happened upon a stage that had sprung up on its own, versus Logan's festival crew building it here.

Bax's text had said he was toward the back of the clearing, to the left when facing the stage, so I picked my way over, making sure not to step on anyone. Full-height chairs weren't allowed, and most of the crowd was either sprawled on blankets or in chairs that were only a few inches off the ground. Which reminded me that I'd left my chair in the tent.

Except Bax had brought it with him.

And Maya was sitting in my bright red camp chair, talking intently to Bax. He held a closed sketchbook in his hand. He'd been sketching a lot these days, working his way through an idea he said he wasn't ready to talk about. But now his eyes, and all of his attention, were focused intently on Maya's face. Like she was the only person in the world.

I forced myself to keep walking forward. Maya reached out and put her hand on Bax's knee. Maya's fingers were rangy and lean like the rest of her, with short, squared-off nails painted silver.

The water bottle clipped to the side of my bag clanked as I came to a stop.

Bax saw me and grinned. "Hey, stranger."

Maya looked over her shoulder. "Have the police been hassling you, too?"

I paused for a moment with my hands on my hips. "What do you mean?"

"I heard you found Ian's body. The police questioned me earlier today, and I was ready for them to drag me off to jail. They're acting like I murdered him." Maya was trying to sound nonchalant, but I could hear the fear layered deep underneath. Was she afraid because she was guilty? Or, like most people, because the thought of being arrested for something she didn't do terrified her? The same fear had circled through me on and off all day, muddled up with the rest of the emotions swirling in me.

Bax held a hand out to me, and I let him pull me down onto his lap. He nuzzled the back of my neck while I looked at Maya.

Her black cowboy boots had a layer of dust over the toes, and, like yesterday, she wore cutoff corduroy shorts, which she'd paired with a sleeveless black muscle tee. Her curly hair flowed over her shoulders. She looked effortlessly hip, except for the fear in her eyes.

"I talked with the police, but it wasn't a big deal," I said.

"Someone told them I had a beef with Ian," Maya said. She leaned over and examined her right cowboy boot. There was dried mud on the heel that flaked off as she brushed it with her fingers.

"Secrets always come out in a murder investigation," I said. "As do beefs, justified or not."

Bax shifted, and his arms tightened around my waist.

"Any beefs I had with Ian aren't the police's business." Maya's gaze at me asked if I could solve her problems. "What should I do?"

"It's not my place to give you advice, but whatever you do, don't lie. Refuse to answer questions unless you're accompanied by a lawyer. If they've heard about you having problems with Ian, they're going to keep asking you questions."

"Hopefully, they're done with all of us. It's not like any of us would've hurt Ian," Bax said. The three of us were silent for a moment. I almost told them Ian's death had the potential to hover over all our lives, casting shadows where they didn't belong if the truth didn't come out.

"My band is up next. I hope you'll stay and watch us." Maya bounced her knee and shook out her hands a few times. Her entire body showed she was a bundle of nerves. I wondered how many of the nerves were purely performance related, and how many were because of Ian's death.

"Why'd you think I'd staked my spot early?" Bax said. Maya looked up, and her whole body stilled for a moment as she smiled at Bax. She seemed slightly calmer for a few seconds, like she'd drawn strength from him.

"Sometimes, before I go on stage, I remember a quote from Dashiell Hammett. 'If you have a story that seems worth telling, and you think you can tell it worthily, then the thing for you to do is to tell it, regardless of whether it has to do with sex, sailors, or mounted policemen.' But it's hitting a bit too close to home this weekend," Maya said. Her hands twitched, and she was starting to turn into a whirlwind again a moment later when she stood up and headed backstage.

Between song lyrics and a seemingly endless supply of Dashiell Hammett quotes, I wondered if the inside of Maya's brain was a tangle of words, phrases, and music notes, all thrown together in a chaotic symphony that made sense to her but would drown anyone else.

Since Maya had left my chair, I shifted, preparing to stand up, but Bax's arm tightened around my waist, so I leaned back. For a moment, the world around me felt quiet as I chilled for a moment, trying to let the stress of the day wash away.

"You smell like espresso, Coffee Angel."

"You know I bathe in eau de caffeine each day." But his use of the Coffee Angel nickname made me feel fuzzy deep inside. I'd suspected I spent so much time at Ground Rules that our beans had invaded the pores of my body, soaking their ambiance through my skin into deep within my soul. I'd always smell like coffee now, forever marked, hopefully with notes of dark chocolate and stone fruit.

"Are you doing okay?" Bax asked. The tone of his voice had shifted, like he was worried about me. His breath tickled the hairs on the back of my neck.

The quip I wanted to make died on my lips since he felt serious, and he'd ignore any attempts to deflect with humor. "On the whole, I'm fine."

"You need to stop finding dead bodies. Wasn't one enough?" Bax's arms tightened around my waist for a moment.

"It's not like I want to. It's never part of my life plan." My next thought lingered in my brain for a while, although I couldn't talk about it with Bax, at least not now. As a child, my grifter mother had used me in several scams she'd run. Maybe my finding a second dead body was fate's way of punishing me. I still felt like I needed to atone, even if I'd been a pawn in my mother's games. But another worry, one that I kept telling myself was irrational, bubbled to the forefront of my mind. I tried to make my voice sound casual. "I take it you and Maya have been friends for a while? How'd you meet?"

"Maya dated a buddy of mine years ago when she was getting her master's in music. That's when I first heard Maya perform and got to know her. It felt like fate. She plays a bunch of instruments, and she's hard-core into video games. When I needed someone to score my first game for cheap, I asked her. She's been our go-to musician ever since. With an appropriate bump in pay, of course, 'cause she's more than worth it."

"She can be pretty dramatic." Part of me noted Bax's pride in paying his contractors well, which I knew carried over to how he treated his employees. He'd helped me research health insurance and other perks I wanted to set up for Ground Rules as we expanded. I hoped I could eventually match what he offered the Grumpy Sasquatch employees.

"Yet she's professional about work and never misses a deadline. She's a delightful paradox. Kind of like you."

Bax's words reminded me all people are contradictions. What were Ian's flaws and the unexpected twists of his personality?

It wasn't my problem, I told myself, even if I'd found his body.

Wait a minute. My back stiffened. "Why am I a paradox?"

"You look small and cuddly, so it's easy for people to assume you're as soft as cotton candy, but inside, you're pure steel. Hmm, or maybe saying you have a core of titanium is the better descriptor since it can handle extremes better than steel. Anyway, you're sharp and don't miss anything, but you're not judgmental about stupid stuff. But when someone crosses a line, I can practically see you pull on armor and leap into battle."

"Hmm." I definitely didn't see myself with a core of steel or titanium.

Another thought flitted across my brain. How profitable had Ian's business as a manager been? Would someone want to bump him off to take it over? If the Changelings were hitting it big, were they suddenly the sort of band someone would do anything to represent?

And what about the musicians? Maya freelanced for Bax. From what I'd heard from Bax when he'd talked about Maya and the few times we'd met, she had side hustles as both a bartender and an adjunct music instructor at one of the local colleges. And she'd mentioned doing some work for a nonprofit that gave free music lessons to underprivileged kids.

I'd guessed playing in a band was emotionally Maya's main gig, but maybe it was also a side hustle. Or she didn't have a dedicated primary job and cobbled together enough small gigs to live.

Bax's voice took me out of my thoughts. "By the way, Jackson's camped out over next to the jam section. I set up his tent while he set up one for a woman in his group. He called her Pip?"

"Pip? Piper Lacey? Seriously?" I twisted around to look at Bax's face.

Bax's head tilted slightly to the side, and his eyebrows scrunched together as he studied me. "You know her?"

"They dated back in law school, and he's always carried a flame for her. But she moved to Washington, DC, years ago." Memories of hanging out with Jackson and Piper flashed through my brain. Piper had tagged along some of the times Jackson had stayed with me when my father worked nights. We'd gone out to movies, played board games, and ganged up against my brother when he'd acted sanctimoniously. I'd stayed in touch with her for a while after she moved. Over time it slowly dwindled to the occasional "Happy birthday" or "Did you see there's a rumor about a new *Witcher* video game?" message.

"She's back in town. She seems hilarious. Jackson can't take his eyes off of her."

"Is she visiting?"

"I think she said she accepted a job as a district attorney? Maybe not in Portland, though."

"Interesting." I faced forward again. Bax's bromance with my brother had been an unexpected perk since he picked up life news my brother neglected to tell me. Although Jackson had gotten annoyed when I told him that. Probably because I called their conversation "gossiping." Piper moving back to town had the potential to be a big deal in my brother's life, providing his old flame was still single.

"There's something I need to talk to you about," Bax said. His back stiffened, making a spike of anxiety shoot through me.

"Okay." I didn't turn to face him, but I could feel as he drew in a breath, like he had something important to say.

But Alexis dropped into the chair Maya had vacated. Not just any chair, but my camp chair that I'd yet to sit in during the festival.

"This day," Alexis said. Her usually sleek bun looked messy, and a few tendrils of hair had escaped and framed her face. Her mouth was twisted to the side.

"You look like you've been put through the grinder," I said.

"I don't even have the words to explain how exhausted I am," Alexis said.

"How's the festival responding to the . . . you know, death?" Bax asked.

Alexis looked at the ground. "So far, we're saying the show must go on. Ian's bands know their time slots, and it's not like he attended all of their shows, anyway. They can perform without him. They're professionals, even if they're grieving."

"Still, it's rough," Bax said.

"Tell me about it. I've known Ian for years. His mom is going to be brokenhearted." Alexis clutched the silver medallion she wore around her neck. I'd caught a glimpse of it earlier and suspected it was a Catholic medal, but I'd yet to get a good look at it.

Alexis spoke again. "His poor mom. Ian's an only child, and he helped her out a lot. He always called her the hardest-working piano teacher in the world. Ian said their house was full of music as he grew up. He was a talented musician himself." She tucked her necklace back under her sleeveless button-down shirt.

"But Ian went into management?" I asked.

"He preferred the stability of managing other artists' careers, and he had a great ear for both talent and what would sell. But he'd been talking recently about recording some of his own original work 'cause he claimed his life was changing, although he wasn't sure his style was hip. He joked he wanted to be the next John Prine."

My head tilted as I looked at Alexis, and she must have read the confusion on my face.

Alexis sang a few lines about an angel who came from Montgomery. She then said, "Prine was a mail carrier who started out writing and performing music as a hobby until he was basically goaded into performing at an open mic night. That single performance led to paid gigs. His songwriting could be everything: funny, serious, heartbreaking. I swear half of the bios of the musicians here list Prine as an influence. His life story alone is amazing: think of being an army veteran turned mail carrier turned Grammy lifetime achievement award–winning musician. Ian was devastated when Prine passed away."

Alexis looked down as she rubbed her stomach. "I have to wonder if Ian could've made it as a musician. From the times I heard him, he had a ton of potential. If he could've made his own luck, maybe he would've been a star."

Alexis's phone beeped, and she sighed when she looked at it. "Running this festival is like herding a bunch of enormous, very confused cats who overreact to everything and get distracted by dangly objects."

"I guess if you're a cat, everything looks like a mouse?"

Bax snorted into the back of my neck. "A for effort, but maybe don't quit your day job to become a comedian."

Alexis half smiled as she stood up. "I'll see you tomorrow for more tea."

After she left, I started to ask Bax what he wanted to talk about, but Maya's band took the stage, so we climbed out of the camp chair and joined the crowd.

I'd never heard Maya perform live before, although I'd played the video games she'd scored for Bax's company. Her band—the Banshee Blues—was a trio with a drummer, Maya on guitar, and another woman holding an upright bass. There was a keyboard set up on stage as well, along with a guitar and banjo.

Listening to Maya made chills run down my spine. Her voice was powerful, and she felt like pure energy on stage. The crowd was in sync with her, dancing during the fast numbers and swaying when she went down-tempo, like she'd cast a spell on everyone.

Her final song was just her on the stage alone with the banjo, playing a stripped-down version of "Wayfaring Stranger." The lyrics felt weirdly appropriate today, talking about a soul's journey through life, hoping the afterlife will bring peace.

> *I know dark clouds will gather 'round me.*
> *I know my way is hard and steep.*

Something told me the next few days would be hard and steep for all of us as the police poked into our lives, looking to see if we were the murderer.

> *I'm going there to see my mother.*
> *She said she'd meet me when I come.*

Now that I'd seen death closer than I wanted to, my thoughts wanted to linger on what happened afterward. I'd seen the impact on families, but was there a final destination the soul headed toward? Or did we slowly vanish, like the last notes of Maya's song, as her voice and banjo faded? She bowed and walked off the stage while the crowd cheered and clapped for her.

The last lyrics echoed in my mind. *I'm just going over home.* I didn't want the song to end, but it's not like we could spend the rest of our lives here, stuck in this moment of time. Even if it felt like a single moment of spine-tingling perfection.

"I'm so glad there are a few more bands between us," a voice said behind me. "I'd hate to play directly after Maya."

"The crowd's warmed up."

"They're depressed now. Maya nailed that song. Gave me chills."

I glanced over my shoulder and saw two guys talking. More musicians, but I didn't recognize either of them.

"She's so versatile," the shorter of the two said.

"Which is one of her problems, since she jumps into too many genres, including in one set-list. But I could listen to her all day."

They walked away, and I glanced around the crowd, which was going back to their chairs or picnic blankets. The listeners who'd stayed seated on the gently rising hillside were relaxing. Like the performance was fleeting, even if I still had goose bumps that lingered, slowly disappearing in the afternoon warmth.

Later that evening, since he didn't have to get up at zero-dark-thirty to sell coffee to festivalgoers, I left Bax hanging out with Jackson, listening to a bluegrass band at the Pine Burrow stage, even though he offered to walk with me. Proper Boyfriend Behavior 101. And he trusted me when I said I didn't need his help, which showed he'd passed Proper Boyfriend Behavior 102 with flying colors. Even though I looked for her, I didn't see Piper, so I couldn't tell if Jackson was on his way to passing the boyfriend classes Bax had aced.

Winding through the festival grounds in the dark, under the trees, as faint strains of music wafted over me, felt comforting. There wasn't the sound of a revolution in the air, just the faint scent of pot. Long strands of LED lights were wound along the trails, helping attendees find their way around. I passed a girl wearing glow-in-the-dark fairy wings and it felt like she had wandered out of the forest, attracted by the music and energy of the festival attendees.

After double-checking that the cart was locked up for the night, I stopped by the Ground Rules Subaru, which was complete with a Ground Rules logo on the door and a sticker on the back that said JUST BREW IT. I'd left my weekender bag tucked behind the backseat, covered with a blanket. Now was as good a time as any to pack the clothes I needed for tomorrow's way-too-early wake-up call into my drawstring bag.

As I was checking my pack towel to make sure it was dry—it was—a couple of women walked past, heading toward the RV section where several bands had parked close together.

"Did you hear about how the Changelings' manager was killed?" the taller of the two asked. Her voice was high pitched, slightly Muppet-like.

"No, wait, you mean that Ian guy?" The dim light shone on her dark hair. She looked like a shadow moving across the evening landscape.

"That's the one. I mean, it sucks he died, and I feel sorry for his family, but he was such a creep."

"He wasn't that bad."

Their voices faded away, and I wanted to run after them and ask what they knew about Ian.

Focus on coffee, I told myself. Solving Ian's murder wasn't my job, and it's not like I had the experience to handle a criminal investigation. I took my bag and headed back to my tent.

But instead of charming, the looming shadows now felt threatening, reminding me anything could happen out here under the trees.

Chapter 9

Thankfully, my Saturday morning had a much smoother start. Even if Bianca of the Breakfast Bandit cart kept throwing me wide-eyed looks, like I was evil, if we came within ten feet of each other.

Thankfully, my too-early morning face wasn't that terrifying, especially since I'd managed a quick shower in the locker room, so at least my hair was tame. Added bonus: I smelled like vanilla deodorant, which doesn't clash with the aroma of coffee. By the end of the day, I'd smell like a vanilla latte.

A handful of early birds trickled in for coffee, all way too chirpy because being at a festival with night owls can't change the inherent properties of being a morning person. Although I was secretly satisfied when I saw one of my first customers' faces break into a wide yawn.

A handful of early-morning exercisers hustled by, one kicking up tracks of dust as he did a series of high knees and grapevines on the trail closest to the cart.

Still, it felt peaceful in the morning coolness to sip a cup of coffee, especially since I knew the day would heat up, both literally and figuratively.

Not long after I opened Ground Rules, my phone dinged with a text. My dad, who'd been up to greet the sunrise like normal. Because some things never change.

I clicked on the text to see a photo of my brother's Australian shepherd, Bentley. He was lying on his back on my dad's patio with all four paws splayed into the air. My dad had agreed to watch Bentley for the weekend since I wasn't home for dog-sitting duty.

I think I broke the dog.

I laughed and texted back. *Looks like Bentley's vacation is a hit.*

I paused then texted him a second time. *Btw, I found a dead body.*

My phone rang seconds later.

"Hi, Dad," I said.

"What's this about a dead body?"

Intermingled concern and curiosity came through in his voice, and he mainly listened as I explained the whole situation. But I could imagine his facial expressions: Briefly closed eyes showing horror that I'd come close to a dead body, since he hadn't wanted me to follow in his footsteps. Lips twisting in a grimace, showing a touch of annoyance that I hadn't already called him.

"What's the name of the investigating officer?"

"Trisha Adams."

"Adams . . . I think I met her a while back. About my height, brown hair? Incredibly tense?"

"That's the one. She recognized my last name and mentioned she'd met you."

"It's a good thing your brother is around in case you need legal help." Because Jackson's law practice focused on child advocacy, he'd spent some time around the criminal justice system, including representing clients in juvenile court.

As we talked, as if by mentioning her I'd summoned her, I saw Detective Adams. She walked up to Maya and tapped her on the shoulder as, I was willing to bet, the singer was on her way to my cart for coffee.

"Be sure to ask your brother to join you if the police question you again," my dad reminded me.

"Jackson said the same thing."

"Your brother has always been sensible," my dad said. "I'll tell Bentley hi from you."

"I'm sure he'll appreciate that." I laughed. "Bye, Dad."

"Bye, Pumpkin."

I hung up and watched Detective Adams and Maya continue to talk. Maya's hand gestures turned bigger, almost brash until Maya stormed away and headed straight to my cart. I ground a shot of espresso and got it ready to brew.

"The police asked me to go to their station," Maya said. "I refused. But this has to be a bad sign."

"If they arrest you, make sure you get a lawyer before talking to them," I said. I pulled the espresso shot, listening to the hum of the machine for a moment, and dumped it into a ceramic demitasse cup when it was done.

"I'm innocent."

I handed the shot to Maya. "Doesn't matter. Get a lawyer first. Honestly, even my dad would tell you that, and he's a detective with the local cold case unit. He even once told me to call an attorney before talking with one of his coworkers from the Portland police."

"I need to figure out how to clear my name. I know the police are looking at me. The detective practically tackled me." Maya looked down at the espresso as if she could read the future in the murky liquid. Some people read coffee grounds like tea leaves, but I knew the only thing this espresso could do is provide a delicious jolt of caffeine.

Although if I got bored, maybe I should pretend to read coffee grounds over the weekend for fun. While nothing in my body is psychic, I'm the daughter of a grifter, and I'd learned to cold-read people before I'd reached kindergarten age. Not that I'd gone to kindergarten; I'd been homeschooled until I'd moved in with my dad when I was thirteen. When I started public school, I'd been ahead in some subjects and behind in others. I'd never fully felt like I belonged, and I sometimes still felt like I was pretending.

And I'm pretty sure my childhood made me root for the underdog, although that's human nature. Who wants to support Goliath when you see David's struggle against impossible odds?

I eyed Maya. "What happened between you and the Changelings, anyway? I'm guessing the story is messy."

"If you want to hear the whole shebang, I'll need another espresso."

"Coming right up."

When I handed over a second demi-cup of liquid magic and an accompanying glass of sparkling water, Maya started to talk.

"I formed the Changelings with Joe, a wicked bass guitar player, and another longtime friend, Cam, as the drummer. But Cam quit the band about a year later when she moved to the East Coast. So we ended up bringing in Dev, a new drummer, who brought Nate with him. It seemed like a good balance for a while, with me and Nate trading off the lead on songs. Nate might be a twit, but his voice is golden." Maya looked up toward the sky like she was reading the past and seeing multiple wrong turns.

"But when Joe and I split up, everyone in the band turned against me. Ian and I agreed the Changelings could record the songs we'd been performing regardless of who wrote them, supposedly with compensation, of course. But giving up the band I created freaking killed me. It took me forever to pick up my guitar again."

"That's rough."

Maya pulled her hair back into a ponytail but then let it drop over her shoulders. "In a way, I have Bax to thank for getting me out of my pity party. He hired me to score a game, and the project helped. Creating something new and seeing it come to life reawakened part of my soul. I'll always owe Bax for that. But I'm going to be more careful with Banshee Blues. No bros like Nate allowed."

I wondered if Maya meant that, from now on, she was the designated front, the face, of any band she was in. After watching her last night, I couldn't imagine anyone being able to steal the limelight from her when performing. She was already the dominating force of any room she was in. Being on stage upped her magnetism by eight hundred million percent.

Alexis walked by and waved but hurried away from the food carts in the direction of the bathrooms. My gaze returned to Maya.

"Nate mentioned he's mostly sober," I said. Maya looked at me sharply, so I added, "He's turned into a regular at the cart this weekend. And he likes to talk. A lot."

Maya halfheartedly chuckled. "That boy never knows when to shut his gob. I will say this for Nate: He used to be a drunken jerk, but from what I heard, now he's just a jerk. Quitting the sauce was the right call since he slapped his ex-wife one evening when he was drunk."

We made eye contact, and I read more in her eyes than her words. Maya felt as disgusted as the anger inside me at the thought of Nate hitting his ex-wife.

"They split up when I was still with the band. Nate's ex was smart. She split with their kid and filed for divorce. Nate took anger management classes and quit drinking. He says he was only violent with her the one time, but he's always had a temper. He put his foot through an amp once, and Dev had to smooth everything over with the venue to hush it up. Alcohol might have been enough to help him lose control, but his anger was definitely there, simmering beneath the surface."

"Every time I've met him this weekend, he's acted all chummy and overgrown kid–like." And utterly self-absorbed.

"That's how he gets people to do what he wants. But, you know, everyone deals with life in their own way. I prefer to channel my anger and rage into my music," Maya said. She grinned at me. "Now love, for example, I like to express both musically and in-person using all five senses—if you get what I mean."

"Yeah, I get it." Even if I didn't want to.

"Nate's more like the Beatles, while I'm the Rolling Stones," Maya said. She grinned. "Would you let your daughter marry a Rolling Stone?"

"What?" I asked.

Maya's voice took on a lecture-ish quality, reminding me she had multiple degrees in music and, I suspected, an encyclopedic knowledge of music history. "Back in the sixties, during the height of the English music invasion of America, the Rolling Stones' manager—

Andrew Loog Oldham—decided the band needed a bad-boy image. He wanted to differentiate them from the Beatles and their boy-next-door-ish image, which wasn't remotely the truth. Which led to the famous 'Would you let your daughter marry a Rolling Stone?' headline."

"Aren't the Beatles more iconic?"

"For sure, and people argue they're the most influential band of all time, and I agree. But I'm not sure you realize how revolutionary the Stones were, Sage. They started out doing covers of American blues and rock and roll. But when they discovered their own voice and started writing their own music, they pulled in all sorts of influences—psychedelia, country, R&B, you name it. And I haven't even mentioned how their guitar players play both the rhythm and lead parts together, which is totally their trademark sound. They're like my musical idols. You know, I have a book I should lend you about the band."

I loved listening to the excitement in Maya's voice. At the unbridled passion layered throughout. Because I love seeing the unique interests that fuel people. There's something inside everyone that makes them tick. That makes them want to love life. And music clearly fueled Maya's soul.

Maya laughed. "And they've been making music together for over fifty years. Fifty! Imagine touring sold-out stadiums in your seventies. Imagine that many people loving your music."

"And you prefer them to the Beatles."

"Don't get me wrong, I love the Beatles as well. They were also incredibly innovative, and their albums kept evolving the longer they performed together. And it's not like the Stones were doing anything the Beatles weren't. I mean, they were all doing psychedelic drugs and living life as rock and roll gods. It's just the Stones had been marketed as bad boys."

"How is Nate like the Beatles, then?"

"He's way more boy next door, and I'm the scrappy underdog. But Nate's talented. Unfortunately. If anyone's going to hit it big, it'll be him. Not that he'll be Beatles big. No one is ever going to be that big again."

Alexis walked up, carrying her festival cup, which she handed over. "Can you do a mint tea? Or ginger?"

Alexis looked exhausted, like she'd been up late and woke up way too early. I sympathized, as I felt the same.

"How about a mint tea with a teaspoon of ginger simple syrup? Hot or cold?"

"That sounds fantastic. Hot, please."

Maya eyed Alexis, and I could tell the singer was concerned for her friend. "Are you doing okay? You look pale."

"I'm just tired and didn't sleep well last night."

I set Alexis's bag of mint tea to brew, then poured house coffees for a group of sweaty runners who walked up, making me miss Alexis and Maya's conversation. But I noticed that Maya put her hand on Alexis's arm. Like she cared deeply about Alexis. Yet Alexis had been quick to mention Maya to the police as a potential suspect. Did Alexis think the singer was a murderer, or did she want to direct the police's attention away from herself?

When Alexis's tea was finished brewing, I stirred in cart-made ginger simple syrup. As I handed her cup over, I said, "Careful, it's hot. This would've been a good time to use your Ground Rules mug since it's insulated. We have some knitted cup sleeves for sale if you want one."

Alexis took the cup and held it carefully. "You're right. This is gorgeously, wonderfully hot."

But she didn't say anything about her Ground Rules travel mug, and I wanted to push. Ask if it had ended up in Ian's hands, and how. Because there was something there, a thread sticking out that, if it was pulled correctly, might unravel the whole story. Except I wasn't sure how to get it started.

Alexis and Maya walked off together. But I didn't have long to brood over my lost opportunity to question Alexis since I was steadily busy.

Jackson stopped by the cart with a motley collection of coffee cups and asked for a round of house coffees to go. I showed him the photo of his dog at my dad's house. "I'm not sure you're getting your dog back."

"He must need someone to clean up after since you moved out."

"Ha-ha."

But then a willowy brunette, with her hair cut in a sleek bob, walked up. Her hands held a collection of mugs. "Jackson, we need to add three more coffees to the order."

I bounced on the balls of my feet and probably looked like an overexcited Labrador retriever. "Piper! I heard you were back in town."

"Hiya, Sage. Jackson's been gushing about how your coffee is the best in the city."

"Our goal is to be the best in the universe," I said. But I glanced at Jackson. Gushing? My brother? He'd flushed slightly. And his smile was a bit dopey. He'd hard-core fallen for Piper again, although something told me he'd never stopped. I mentally crossed my fingers that their relationship worked out, else my brother would be crushed. Again.

Piper somehow looked polished in a gray tank top and cutoff jean shorts. But she always looked poised.

"Well, if you're going to go big, go all the way." Piper smiled.

I wondered if she was going to apply that motto to her relationship with Jackson.

As I poured out the coffees, I asked, "I heard you're back in town for good?"

"I took a job with the US Attorney's office in Portland. I start next week," Piper said.

"Oh, exciting," I said. "How's the move been?"

"I found an apartment to rent in the Pearl District for now. It's not too far from your uncle's bar."

"We'll have to meet up for a drink once you get settled in," I said, knowing we'd end up at the Tav, aka the dive bar owned by my uncle Jimmy, who was also a silent partner in my coffee business. A voice in the back of my mind told me I should probably tell him I found a body since it was the sort of news he'd expect to hear from me first.

"I better get these coffees back to the crew before they all collapse from caffeine withdrawal," Piper said and picked up a batch of the mugs. She carried them away without spilling, showing off the ballet training from her childhood. Piper once told me she'd taken up yoga and aerial to de-stress during law school, and I guessed she'd been a regular at at least one fitness studio since I'd last seen her. She looked fantastic, and everything about her said her life was going well. Of course, some people are good at faking happiness, acting cheerful to hide the darkness inside. But something told me Piper really was happy. Fingers crossed part of that joy was because she lived in the same city as my brother.

Jackson watched her go, then turned and showed me his phone.

Uncle Jimmy had texted him: *I heard someone died at the music festival this weekend.*

My brother's reply: *Yes, that's true. Sage found the body.*

Uncle Jimmy: *Is it someone we know? Can you please keep Bug out of trouble?*

Uncle Jimmy couldn't be too mad if he'd called me Bug, aka the nickname I'd never outgrow. If he called me Sage, it meant the world might end. Or I was in serious trouble.

"I just realized I needed to call him," I said.

"He'd appreciate it. But more important, be sure to call me if the police interview you again."

"There's no way I'm a suspect. I didn't even know the guy. I just found his body."

"Just call me, okay? Now I need to get these coffees to the group before someone steals my breakfast burrito."

Jackson carried the rest of the cups away. I hoped he was simply being his usual cynical self. The criminal defense side of his practice—even if he only worked in juvenile court, which has an entirely different feel from the adult side—might make him see danger where none existed. Surely the police didn't think I could be a suspect?

But a sinking feeling in my heart told me Jackson was right. I'd noticed the way the detective eyed me. Hopefully she eyed everyone with the same level of suspicion.

Calling my uncle Jimmy sounded exhausting, so I sent him a quick text. *Talked with Jackson. Ground Rules is doing well this weekend.*

This cart needed to do well, since I really didn't want to have to tell my uncle, and mostly silent investor in Ground Rules, that the second cart was losing money.

Luckily my thoughts didn't have time to stew like over-brewed coffee since a steady stream of customers came up, needing to start their day right with a Ground Rules fix.

Then two women walked up and handed over travel mugs. I recognized one right away from her high-pitched voice: she'd called Ian a creep last night.

"You two are in one of the bands, right?" I asked as I poured out a couple of house coffees into their matching to-go cups that had a bird logo on the side.

"We're with the Waxwings. I'm the lead singer, and she's the drummer," the shorter woman said. Her low-pitched voice was mellow, versus the abrasive squeakiness of her drummer.

"I think last night I overheard you talking about the man who died," I said. I glanced at their logo, trying to remember what a waxwing looked like. The mental image of a bird with red feathers on the very tip of its wings like it had been dunked in sealing wax flitted across my mind.

"Ian Rabe?" Both of the women eyed me like I'd committed some sort of faux pas. I needed to gain their trust to get them to open up to me since I really wanted to know what they'd thought of Ian.

"Yeah." I made my voice sound sad. "I found his body, and I'm curious about him, you know? I didn't really know him. But now I'll always remember him."

"You were lucky you didn't know him," the Muppet-voiced drummer said.

They both stared at me again. Then the drummer's expression softened. "You know, you look like the woman from the bridal show ads a few years ago."

"She looks nothing like that model." The singer picked up her coffee like she wanted to go.

I laughed. "That was me. I'm surprised you remember." I told them about how one of my college BFFs was a professional photographer. She had convinced me to pose last minute for her when her original model for a local shop's petite wedding dress line had to cancel 'cause she was sick.

"I wouldn't have participated in the shoot if I'd known the photos were going to be plastered everywhere." It'd been partially flattering but mostly embarrassing, especially when taggers had redecorated one of the billboards.

"I knew it! I still have the flyer from the show in my wedding binder. I found my wedding dress at that show. You know, your photos were really charming. We talked about booking the photographer who took them, but she wasn't available."

"That's too bad. Erin's amazing."

"We should go," the singer said.

"Wait," the drummer said. She looked at me. "I can see why you're curious about Ian. Finding him must have been horrifying."

"I'm just trying to put it into context."

"In case this helps, back when we first started to perform, Ian approached me after one of our gigs. He flattered me, said the band had real potential. But then I felt like he was hinting I should sleep with him, and he skeeved me out. I've seen him pull the same trick on other female musicians, especially the young ones, as long as they're pretty," the drummer said.

"He was a legit manager, though—look at the bands he repped. I'd love to be where the Changelings are now, especially since our songs are way better. Plus Ian's always been nice to me," the singer said.

"Doesn't mean he wasn't a creep. And I know he didn't take the calls of at least one musician after he slept with her."

"Whatever, Ian said he was planning to settle down," the singer said.

"What? When?" the drummer asked.

"He joined us outside the bus after the Thursday night barbecue. He wasn't weird or skeevy. Just normal."

"So you talked with him the night before he died. Wicked."

"It's creepy when you put it that way."

They walked away with their coffees.

Maybe the drummer was right. If Ian used his career as a pickup line on aspiring musicians, he'd preyed on the dreams of numerous women. And no one likes to have their dreams crushed.

And maybe he'd slept with the wrong musician.

Chapter 10

Like every time I'd seen him, Logan was decked out in a Campathon shirt; today's represented the current festival. I wondered if it was a subtle sales tactic to move T-shirts. This year's shirt, featuring an image of trees and an old-school tent with Mt. Hood in the background, was charming.

Or maybe Logan didn't have anything but festival T-shirts in his wardrobe. Maybe he kept the ones that didn't sell instead of buying new clothes.

Logan looked tired as he walked up and put his Campathon tumbler on the cart's counter, along with his VIP pass to scan. "Coffee, stat, please."

"Because you said *please*." I scanned his card and gave it back, then filled his cup with house coffee, which I handed over along with the carton of oat milk.

"Thanks for remembering that dairy kills me," Logan said.

I flinched at his words.

He cringed. "I shouldn't have said that. But it's not a real Campathon if I don't stick my foot in my mouth at least five times. It's one of the reasons I'm so thankful to have Alexis onboard since she excels at smoothing things over in my wake."

"Have you known each other long?" I asked. Behind my hopefully pleasant façade, my brain was whirling. Was Alexis used to smoothing things over? To tamping her own emotions down so she could fix everyone else's messes?

"She's like family. Our parents are friends, so I've known her since she was a baby. Alexis started at Campathon as an intern when she was in college and came on part-time as she finished her degree, then full-time when she graduated. Whenever I gave her more responsibility, she rose to the challenge and became my second-in-command. I couldn't run the festival without Alexis."

"You're lucky to have her." Unless she killed Ian. Alexis always seemed so calm and collected, but maybe she was one of those people who control their temper until it erupts in a volcano of anger, destroying everything in its wake.

"I need to make sure I'm not overworking her this year," Logan said, but it sounded like he was talking to himself. He pulled out his phone, signaling our conversation was over.

As Logan walked away, I realized he had several twigs caught in his ponytail. Like he'd been skulking around in the bushes, or maybe trees.

Or maybe Ian's death had made me see everyone in a negative light. Perhaps Logan had taken a shortcut across the grounds versus creeping through bushes for some nefarious purpose. He must know the grounds like the back of his hand, so he didn't need to follow the trails to find his way around.

The thought made me shiver.

As the morning traffic continued, with steady sales of coffee, I fell into a rhythm. French presses of house coffee. Pouring morning cold brews with the gooseneck kettle. Pulling espressos for serious coffee drinkers who needed their morning—or rather midmorning—fix. I even sold a few coffee sodas, even though I saw them as an afternoon drink.

My phone beeped with a text while I was serving up a round of drinks. I checked it once I had a gap of time.

My uncle Jimmy. *Follow Jackson's advice. Call me if you need me.*

Of course he was on the "listen to your lawyer older brother" train.

Detective Adams walked up as I was handing over a couple of cold brews to a group of hungover-looking fortysomethings.

"I have to remember to stop drinking like I'm still twenty," one of the forty-year-olds said as they stumbled away.

"Try to remember that when you hit the beer garden tonight," his buddy groused.

"Do you have a moment?" the detective asked.

As I finished wiping down the espresso machine, I glanced at my phone. I should call Jackson. Instead, I turned to the detective. "Unless more customers come, yes, I have a moment."

I grabbed a bottle of water and stepped outside the cart. When the weather broke after the heat wave, I thought it would be a good omen for the festival. But now, I was dealing with a different type of heat. And hydration and shade weren't going to help me here, although they couldn't hurt. After all, I'd learned Life Lesson 101: Stay Hydrated years ago.

The detective had forgone her suit today for stodgy khakis and a polo shirt. Which would've made her stick out in the festival crowd even if her shirt didn't say MULTNOMAH COUNTY SHERIFF'S OFFICE on the chest. She had a gun on the belt on her hip, along with her gold shield.

She stood a little too close to me in the shade of the cart, staring down at me. Reminding me she didn't just wear a badge, but she was bigger than me, too. Of course, most adults are taller than me, along with the occasional ten-year-old.

"I have a few more questions about yesterday."

"I'm all ears." I stared back, hoping my expression was bored. Impassive. I locked my desire to shove her away deep inside me.

"Tell me about how you found the body again."

As I told the detective about how I'd taken several trips to fill the cart's water tanks, Bianca from the Breakfast Bandits walked by, glaring at me again. Something in her face told me she wanted me to be dragged away in handcuffs.

I looked back at the detective. "If I'd ignored the orange color in the bushes, someone else would've found him." And I wouldn't have to deal with any of this.

"You're still claiming you just met Ian Rabe this weekend? You didn't know him before?"

"Like I said, I met him for the first time on Thursday afternoon."

"What about Maya Oliveira? How long have you been friends with her?"

"She's really more of Bax's friend. But she works for him as a freelancer, so I'm not really sure if 'friend' is the right word. More of a work colleague, maybe." I hoped. "I wouldn't say I know her exceptionally well."

I remembered the first time I'd met Maya. Bax's video game studio is in the same building as the coffee roastery part of Ground Rules, and I'd stopped by after a long day working the cart. I'd found them sitting on the couch in front of the studio, side by side, joking around. Bax's eyes had lit up when he saw me, and he'd jumped up, grabbed my hand, and pulled me over to introduce me to Maya as his girlfriend. Maya had smiled when she saw me and said, "So this is the woman Bax keeps yammering on about." And then she smiled and looked mysterious like she had secret thoughts she wasn't willing to share.

The detective's words broke me out of my memory.

"I heard Maya got you into the festival."

I nodded. "Maya did, through her connection to Alexis. From what I heard, it was chance that Maya and Alexis were together when Alexis found out the original coffee vendor needed to cancel. It was lucky for me that the spot opened up and that my employee and I were able to rearrange our schedules to be here."

"I heard your company is overly ambitious."

I adjusted my ponytail to give myself a moment to think. "What's that supposed to mean? We're working hard to produce the best coffee in Portland, but it's not like we're trying to shake down other shops or trample them into submission. And I'm not going to apologize for us having ambitions. It'd be ridiculous to be a business owner and not want to flourish."

"Hmm." The detective eyed me. I wondered if she thought she'd hit a nerve.

I wondered if being called overly ambitious bothered me or if I was just annoyed with the detective on principle. While I wanted Ground Rules to grow, I also knew Harley and I weren't cutthroat about it. We weren't going to bust the kneecaps of our competitors or aggressively put them out of business. We just wanted to lure regulars to our cart and soon-to-be shop with the best coffee in the world. If that was too ambitious, I didn't want to know what the detective would call someone who actually acted aggressively.

"You know, gossiping about me and my cart isn't going to help you solve this case." I knew I'd made a mistake as soon as the words left my mouth.

The detective stepped closer to me, making the molecules of personal space between us vibrate with tension. My fists started to clench, so I made myself relax. My hands opened. I relaxed my shoulders and focused on dissipating the ball of anxiety hovering around the midpoint of my spine.

I let out a deep breath. "Listen. I want you to solve Ian's murder. But I don't know how I can help you. I didn't know him. I had the misfortune to stumble upon his body, but that's it. And I only found it because I was one of the first people awake." Maybe I should've started an evening business, as all of the bodies I'd found had been early in the morning, before most of the world woke up.

"Have you ever studied martial arts?" the detective asked.

I looked at her. Was she implying I was a secret warrior, able to take down a man a foot taller than me? Although maybe I should have felt proud that the detective thought I was capable of being a secret assassin. Even in the movies, the improbably good female fighters are usually taller than 5'1".

A couple of twentysomething guys dressed like they'd escaped from the 1970s walked up to my cart.

"Hey, look, customers," I said and bolted into the cart. The detective stood still for a second, then strode off through the trees. Like she had more people to hassle.

As I crafted a couple of iced drinks, resisting the urge to ask the guys if they'd fallen out of a time warp since who wants to wear shorts that short, I realized I should've listened to my brother. If the police asked to talk to me yet again, I'd call him.

I should've called him earlier. Talking to the detective alone was a mistake I should've been smart enough not to make. Life Lesson 102: Use Common Sense When Talking to the Police.

"Meow?" a small voice asked. The orange cat was back. It jumped into the cart and headed to the now-official kitty nap spot.

Bax ambled up for his morning coffee, which I handed him with a smile along with a mason jar of chia-seed pudding from the cart's fridge. He looked like he knew something was wrong in my world, but a group walked up before he had a chance to ask.

I forced myself to smile and not brood as I resumed making coffees, enjoying the steady flow of business since it kept me from spiraling into a storm of thought. The comforting aroma of coffee surrounded me, telling me the world would be all right.

"Dad!"

The chirpy voice sounded familiar, and I wasn't surprised to see Bax's son, Niko, sprint up to his dad. Niko wore a green T-shirt promoting *Dreamside Quest*, which is one of Bax's best-selling games. Niko's mother, Laurel, followed behind, carrying a bag over one shoulder, her six-months-pregnant belly leading the way. Her husband, Ryan, followed, hauling a couple of chairs with a bulging backpack over his shoulders. Everything they needed for a blended-family day of festival fun.

The only weird thing about Laurel is that she looked like my prettier older sister. Her blond hair was a shade darker, and she was about five inches taller, with green eyes that were almost as brilliant as her brain. She'd earned her PhD in population genomics when she was pregnant with Niko and now did research at a local university. Her husband was also a professor, with a focus on biostatistics.

"Sage!" Niko ran my way as soon as he saw me standing by the door of the cart. He crashed into me, and his arms circled me.

"Did you ask Sage if you can give her a hug?" Laurel asked as she followed in her son's wake.

"Sage always lets me give her one," Niko said. "But I can't jump on her."

I laughed. "It's fine, Laurel. He asked if he can hug me hello a few months ago, and we set up our ground rules."

Laurel smiled at me, and, as always, I felt like she was legitimately happy to see me.

Niko pulled on my arm. Green eyes like his mom's looked up at me from a face shaped like his dad's, complete with the sort of chin dimple you see on heroes in Disney films. "Did you know my mom's going to Trinidad and Tobago? But they don't have any blue-footed boobies there because those mostly live in the Galápagos Islands. So I don't mind that I'm not going," Niko said.

I glanced at Laurel, who was smiling at her son.

"The blue-footed boobies do a dance like this," Niko said. He bowed with arms out and his back arched, and then started bringing his knees up and stamping down purposefully.

Laurel laughed. "I just found out yesterday that I received funding for a research project, so Ryan and I are going next year for about six months."

"With the baby, I'm guessing."

"Because an infant's the one thing you absolutely need for international research projects." Laurel laughed. "My mom's planning to come with us to help with the baby. And Niko will visit, of course."

But, I realized, Bax would take over full-time Niko care, at least for most of the time Laurel and her husband were out of the country.

Laurel kept talking. "They have some lovely beaches, if you and Bax want to drop by for a relaxing holiday."

A penny dropped in my mind. She was inviting me in case Bax took Niko abroad to visit his mom. My back straightened, and I felt a bit lighter.

"Thanks for the invitation," I said. "Would you like something to drink?"

Laurel looked wistful. "I can't even explain to you how much I miss coffee."

"We have some caffeine-free specials," I said, and told her about my favorites, and she ordered a peach and lemon iced herbal tea, along with one of the Ground Rules mugs. She chose the camp-style cup, aka the one I picked out.

"I'd like a lemonade," Niko said.

"What's the magic word, Nikolaus?" his mom asked.

"Abracadabra?" Niko laughed. He looked at me. "Please, Sage."

"Regular or peach?" I asked.

His head tilted slightly as he debated. "Peach, please."

"Coming right up as long as you bring me a cup." Niko raced over to his stepdad to rummage around in their festival backpack.

Alexis walked up, and I ended up making a peach and lemon iced tea for her, too. They chatted, and I noticed Alexis eyeing where Laurel's belly button popped out on her baby bump.

"Thanks," Alexis said and hustled off with her drink.

Niko thanked me when I handed over his stainless steel water bottle, now filled with peach lemonade. He rushed back to his dad.

I handed Laurel her drink.

"Any word on when your store will open? I can't wait to try the new place. I'm so impressed you're expanding."

"It's the next step in my plan for world coffee domination. But construction is just getting started, so we'll see when we're finally ready to open."

"Starbucks better watch out." Laurel laughed.

My VIP coffee addict popped up for her fix, and as I made her iced mocha, Laurel rejoined her husband, son, and Bax. I felt a bit weird as I watched Bax walk off with Niko, Laurel, and Laurel's husband in an extended family mishmash. It's not like I was jealous since clearly, the Laurel-Bax ship had sailed long before I entered the scene. And even if they argued occasionally, Bax and Laurel had committed to co-parenting. And I'd been impressed. The first time I heard them disagree about which elementary school to send their son to, they'd kept their argument focused on the topic. Which turned out to be their usual communication style. I'd taken it as a good omen.

Maya walked up. "I scored *Dreamside Quest*," she said.

I leaned forward against the cart, propping myself up on my elbows. "Okay?"

Maya laughed. "Bax's son is wearing one of the game's promo shirts."

"Oh, yeah. I noticed the shirt earlier."

As I made Maya an iced espresso, a guy who looked familiar walked up. I scoped him out. Shaved head. Tight black T-shirt and boot-cut jeans. He looked like he lifted weights. He either had a dedicated tanning habit, or India showed up on his family tree, as he sort of resembled actor Rahul Kohli.

"Oh, hi, Dev," Maya said. Her voice was unenthusiastic.

Dev? Like one of the members of the Changelings? The drummer who'd brought in Nate? I eyed his muscles again, guessing he did a lot of the heavy lifting on tour. But Maya seemed immune to his charms, based on the way she'd tensed up.

"I heard this cart is one of the best coffee options in town," Dev said.

"And the only one at this festival," I said. I handed Maya the short glass of iced espresso.

"I can't imagine anything better than an iced espresso right now," Maya said and looked at her glass like it was full of gold dust.

Dev stared at it. "You have cold brew, right? Why drink iced espresso instead?"

"That's a loaded question," Maya said. She sounded angry. "The drinks are a totally different experience."

I had the feeling Maya wasn't only talking about the coffee. "Maya's right. Coffee brewed in hot water is more acidic, and some people find those notes become harsh as the coffee cools. One of the advantages of cold brew is that it's smoother because of the lack of acids."

"But it just doesn't taste as colorful," Maya said.

"That's the factor I'd call brightness," I said. "It's why we offer both since cold brew is consistently more stable. And we can pull a shot for anyone who prefers iced espresso. But we sell more cold brews since when you add a bit of cream, it's the perfect slightly sweet summer drink."

"Which do you prefer?" Dev asked me. Then he glanced at Maya like he wanted to talk to her. But she kept her gaze snapped forward. She downed her espresso like it was a shot of tequila.

"I'll see you later, Sage," Maya said and strode away. I snagged her empty glass off the counter and put it in my dishwashing sink.

"It depends on my mood," I explained to Dev. "I go through huge cold brew kicks, but like Maya, I like the brightness of iced espresso. We're also offering coffee sodas if you want something a bit sweeter and carbonated."

Dev handed over his Campathon tumbler. "I'll go with a cold brew."

"How are you doing with everything that happened? This weekend must be unbelievably rough for you and your band," I said as I filled his tumbler with ice.

"It sucks. Ian deserved a full life." Dev looked down.

"I'm sorry for your loss."

"I wish we knew what had happened," Dev said. "The police talked to all of us, but they didn't tell us anything. All I know is Ian died. And since he was a gym rat with a recent clean physical, we assume something bad happened."

I poured water and cold brew concentrate into Dev's tumbler. "Sometimes, just being close to death is hard, right? There's the whole sense of mortality and fleetingness of life. Especially when it's unexpected." I noted Dev's comment about Ian being a gym rat.

"I keep circling between grief and fear for the future. Someone's going to need to go through all of Ian's emails and files to see what balls he had in the air for us. But then I feel guilty worrying about the future when there's Ian's family and what they're probably going through. But it's not like Ian and I were close. Our relationship was professional."

I handed Dev his cold brew and the container of half-and-half. "Did Ian book gigs and such without asking you?" Unless Dev meant something else by "balls in the air." If they didn't have much of a personal relationship, then the only balls in the air would be gigs, right?

"Not exactly. I mean, we'd have strategy sessions, and we'd talk about when we wanted to tour and our availability for gigs. Ian did so much for us, but he didn't always keep all of us in the loop. For example, we're working on our second album. He said he might have some awesome studio for us to record at that would help us get into 'the perfect Changelings groove.' Whatever that meant. But he didn't go into specifics. I have no idea if he booked something for us, or if it fell through. Maybe the record company knows."

"Working on your sophomore album must be scary."

"You have no idea. Writing this album is hard. The best tracks of our debut were based on Maya's songs, even if she wasn't around when we recorded it. So it feels like we're discovering who we are all over again. But I'm ignored when I bring this up because what would I know? I'm just the drummer."

The air was starting to feel heavy, so I racked my brain for a way to lighten it. "Didn't the Foo Fighters' singer start out as a drummer?"

"He did. But I'm no Dave Grohl." Dev glanced at my face, then purposefully looked at my hands. "I take it you live in Portland?"

I folded my hands together. My work jewelry is always minimal, including no rings, which is the prudent choice around food service, since the last thing I wanted to do was hand out E. coli or some other foodborne pathogen with espresso 'cause it'd gotten trapped under bling on my fingers. And I didn't have an engagement ring or wedding band to show off—or to tell potential suitors I'd already staked my claim with someone fantastic. "Yep, I'm local."

"Want to go out sometime?" His face slowly split into a warm smile.

"I'm involved with someone."

"Too bad." Dev's smile showed he was a tad disappointed. As he walked away with his cold brew, I wondered what I would've said if I'd been single.

And I wondered how many people he asked out each gig. Something told me he had plenty of admirers, even if he was competing with Nate for attention. But I bet there were enough fans to go around.

Chapter 11

A woman walked up, looking like she was ready to dropkick the day into the sun. I sympathized since the festival had taken a left turn and chugged full steam ahead away from my expectations.

"You okay?" I asked her.

She folded her arms and rested them on the counter, then put her head down on top of them. "No."

"Want to talk about it?" People confess all sorts of misdeeds to bartenders and priests and, I've found, their baristas.

Her voice was slightly muffled. "My ex-fiancé is here with his new wife, and when I saw him, I stared and didn't look where I was going. I ran full speed into a garbage can in front of them. And I was supposed to come to Campathon with my new boyfriend, but he dumped me last week. I gave my little sister his ticket, and we were supposed to have a sisters weekend. But she hooked up with some rando last night, and she's been ignoring me all day. Today sucks the big one."

"I'm sorry. If it makes you feel any better, while I'm working, my boyfriend is hanging out with his pregnant ex, their kid together, and her new husband."

She looked up and smiled. But her eyes were still grim. "Sounds like a good time."

"It's a barrel of laughs," I said. I didn't mention the gorgeous whirlwind of a musician who was hovering around the edges this weekend, maybe threatening to blow up my relationship with Bax like a tornado. Or maybe I was just jumping at shadows. Silver lining: at least I hadn't run into any garbage cans.

At least not yet. The festival was still young.

"Maybe some coffee will help. It can't make things worse." Her voice wasn't quite as dark.

"Coffee always makes the world brighter," I said. Something about her expression, maybe the glimpses of humor despite her pain, made me like her.

"I wish I could see the future and know this misery will end," she said.

"You know, I could always read your coffee grounds for you," I offered.

"Huh?"

"You know how people read tea leaves? I can read your future in coffee grounds."

"Really." Her brown eyes narrowed slightly as her eyebrows lowered. But a smile also slipped across her face, and it filtered all the way up to her eyes. "If I cross your palm with silver, I assume."

"You'll have nothing to lose since this is on the house. No silver required."

I ground a tablespoon of our Puddle Jumper blend, then mixed it with hot water in an eight-ounce ceramic cup.

"Let it sit for about four minutes to brew," I said. "Then drink it but be careful because the grounds aren't filtered. So don't drink to the last drop, you dig?"

"Like Turkish coffee," she said. "You don't want to drink the dregs at the bottom of the cup else you'll end up with a mouthful of grit."

"That's right, except I'm not boiling this multiple times."

Her eyebrows furrowed as she looked at me. So I explained how when you make Turkish coffee, you bring the water, coffee, and sugar mixture barely to a boil three or four times before serving.

"Three or four, huh?"

"It depends on who you talk to. Everyone has their own take on the proper way to brew it. Some people also add rose water, although the best version I've tried included a pinch of ground cardamom. Dang, I wish I'd brought an ibrik so I could make Turkish coffee." Plus a hot plate for the ibrik.

As she sipped at her coffee, trying to avoid the grounds, a twenty-something in a rainbow-striped T-shirt came up and ordered an iced latte. But before I could make it, my first customer handed her cup over to me when it was mostly empty, other than a collection of grounds at the bottom.

I twisted the cup, watching a drop of coffee wind through the grinds. "Hmm. It looks like what you're secretly looking for is on its way to meet you, but you'll be surprised because you won't expect it when it comes, and it'll be different than you expect. Because often-times what we desire and what we need don't match up. But for now, you should focus on yourself. Work on being the best version of you, and it'll lead you home."

"Does this mean I'm done running into garbage cans?"

"I'm sorry, the fates aren't that specific." We both laughed.

"Wicked," the rainbow-striped twentysomething said. "I want you to read my future!"

After selling a Ground Rules mug and cold brew to the original woman, I brewed another cup of coffee-and-grounds and put it in front of the twentysomething, then made her cinnamon latte. She sipped at her latte as her coffee cooled. A couple of her friends, also in their early twenties, joined us.

"She's going to read my coffee grounds!"

"What? No way," the one wearing an orange string bikini top said.

The third woman looked at me skeptically and folded her arms across the Portland Thorns logo splashed across her shirt.

"No, coffee grounds!" Rainbow-stripes acted like she didn't drink caffeine, ever, based on how she vibrated in place.

"How much to read?" the woman in the Thorns shirt asked. She seemed like one who would ask, "Are you sure?" when one of her friends said, "Hold my kombucha."

"It's free, as long as you buy a coffee to go," I said. The newcomers ordered a couple of iced cold brews with caramel syrup.

Faith walked up and held out her coffee cup without saying anything. Like she was desperate for coffee. And maybe a bit of sympathy.

The rainbow-striped girl turned to her. "Want to get your coffee grounds read, too?"

Faith barely paused, then said in a gracious voice, "Why not? As long as I can get a cold brew as well."

I made a collection of cowboy coffees and put them in front of my growing group of young twentysomethings. I noted the three friends were at least twenty-one since they wore the official wristbands that would allow them into the beer tent.

"You look nice," Rainbow-stripes said to Faith as I poured out the intern's cold brew over ice and diluted it with water.

"So polished," Bikini-top added. "Those earrings are fab."

"I'm here on my summer internship." Faith glanced down like she was embarrassed by their praise. But then she brushed a few specks of dust off of her dress. Somehow, she still looked fresh and pristine. Like staying clean was her secret superpower.

"Wicked! We're all going into our final year," Rainbow-stripes said and name-dropped a local university. "I volunteered with the Innocence Project last spring and interned part-time this summer. But I spent most of my time bartending at a pub since I need to save for the next school year."

"I had an offer to intern for an environmental group this summer, but I dropped it to go surf in Mexico all summer," Bikini-top said. That explained her golden tan and sculpted arms.

The girl in the Thorns jersey stayed quiet. I put Faith's cold brew down on the counter, then glanced at the Thorns girl. "Did you go to any of the games this summer?"

Bikini-top laughed. "Any game? Try every home game, ever. She's like their biggest fan."

Rainbow-stripes looked at me. "Rosa honestly is their biggest fan. She even applied for a job with them."

"Nothing wrong with that," I said. I smiled at Rosa, but her answering half smile was wary, like she suspected I was making fun of her.

Rainbow-stripes handed me her coffee cup, which was mostly empty except for the grounds and a few droplets of coffee. I eyed it like I was reading the future. I ran through what I knew about Rainbow-stripes, like her being a student and interning the Innocence Project, which advocated for those wrongly—at least allegedly—convicted of crimes. The local chapter had been in the news recently when they'd overturned a high-profile conviction. Anyone they accepted as an intern would be on the top of her game. She must be smart and dedicated with unlimited potential.

"Hmm, I see an owl in your grounds," I said. "Like you're on a quest for wisdom."

The girl's eyes widened, and her bikini-top friend said, "Oh, maybe she'll be able to tell if you should apply to law school!"

"And the grounds say you should follow your heart, since ultimately, only you know the best path for your own journey."

"But what about the loans?"

I put the cup down. "Scholarships? You know, if you're debating law school, you should set up some informational interviews with lawyers if you haven't already."

"What do you mean?"

"Call some law firms and set up times to chat with attorneys and ask them about their careers. When my brother was applying to law school, he set up informational interviews. Multiple lawyers took him out to dinner since they could expense the meal to their firms."

"Do you just, like, call up the firms and ask?"

"Let me give you my brother's card, and yeah, just email him. Say you're applying for law school, and ask for fifteen minutes of his time. Be concise, which will hint you'll respect his time, and tell him that Sage sent you."

I pulled out my wallet and extracted one of Jackson's cards. I'd taken to carrying a couple around, since I run into homeless teens often at the Rail Yard.

"Oh, cool, child advocacy," Rainbow-stripes said as she read Jackson's card.

"My turn!" Bikini-top shoved her cup over. She'd left a bit more coffee behind, but I could still see the grounds. I thought about her skipping an internship to surf.

"Hmm, the hummingbird in the middle of your cup says to be careful about being too impulsive. Passion is good, but sometimes, especially in the near future, be aware when you're acting too hasty. You're going to have a big decision soon, and you should consider taking the time to weigh your options instead of committing rashly."

"Oh, that's so true, Erica. You always jump into things and then complain when you get bored, or you hate the project." Rainbow-stripes laughed. Bikini-top shrugged her shoulders, then smiled.

"I need to get back to work," Faith said.

"Wait, make sure she reads your grounds," Bikini-top said. She handed me Faith's cup.

I could feel Faith's level gaze on me as I looked into her cup. "Hmm, I see a tiger, which is an animal that's patient. You know what you need to do. But keep debating the best path forward, although you'll know when the right option emerges."

"She's not just a tiger, but one with impeccable stripes," Bikini-top said.

"Thanks, I think," Faith said and left with her cold brew. I noticed Grace, the music blogger, watching us from behind a tree.

Rosa pushed her cup toward me. I eyed her for a second, noting her quiet skepticism. But she had interests and desires, as you don't go to all of a team's games without some serious passion.

"Hmm, I see a dolphin. You're grounded and serious, but you have a fun side you let your friends see, even if you hide it from the world. But you don't need their approval since you know what you want to do."

"I told you that you shouldn't have let your sister talk you out of taking the job at the biology lab," Erica, aka the one in the bikini top, said.

"Sounds kind of generic," Rosa said. She tugged at the bottom of her jersey.

I smiled and shrugged. "Maybe the coffee grounds read your skepticism. Or, you know, this is just for fun, and you shouldn't put faith into fortune-tellers. Since you control your own fate."

For the first time since she'd walked up to the cart, Rosa smiled for real. Her face lightened, and I saw the light inside her that had drawn her friends.

After picking up their drinks, two of the girls walked away, but Rosa paused.

"Reading coffee grounds is just a game, right?" Rosa asked.

"Yeah, it's just for fun. If anyone takes this too seriously, I'd suggest professional help."

"And you stuck to simple advice. But you should know Erica's going to tell everyone about how this amazing psychic read her coffee grounds and totally changed her life. You're going to become the Campathon guru in her life story."

"People frequently hear what they want to," I said.

"Erica always does," Rosa said. She walked off with her cold brew. She'd known I wasn't really psychic, which reminded me that fortune-telling only works because people hear what they want to hear, especially if they're desperate for help. Which meant my internal sense of justice said it was okay to joke around and read coffee grounds, but I'd never do it for someone who thought I could contact a dead spouse, for example. That'd cross a line I needed to respect. Although it sure would be useful to contact Ian from across the veil and ask him what happened.

Grace, the music blogger, stalked up. She held her phone up like she was recording. "Is this why you killed Ian? He was in on your scam? How much have you defrauded the music fans of Cam-pathon?"

"Do you want a coffee or something? Nice classic shot of espresso? Or velvety smooth cold brew?" I picked up a cleaning rag and wiped down the ordering counter. Sugar seems to magically float out of the jars to coat the counter no matter how often I wipe it down.

"Did Ian find you fleecing people out of money? So you had to kill him to protect your scam?" Grace stared at me through her vintage-inspired glasses. I held back a groan and shoved down the tiny tendrils of anger that started to build inside me.

Alexis walked up, holding her festival mug.

"Hi, Alexis. Can you help me with something? This blogger is hassling me."

"She was reading coffee grounds," Grace said. "I have video proof."

Alexis blinked hard and then looked at me.

"Some college girls and I were goofing off. Which is tangential to the harassment. And she hasn't bought anything despite coming up and demanding my time."

"Yeah? How much did you charge them to be scammed?" Grace held her phone out again, clearly filming me. I made myself sound calm.

"Umm, nothing? I mean, they paid for their cold brews. But you know, I have to wonder if you recording attendees buying coffee is good for the festival. It's one thing to photograph a band but record-ing people at the food carts seems like an invasion of their privacy." I looked at Alexis. "Filming me while I work definitely feels like an in-fringement on mine."

Alexis briefly looked angry, then took a breath. She turned to Grace. "Your contract says photographs of performances only and in-terviews with willing musicians and audience members. No videos."

"But the videos aren't of a band performing, which is what you said I couldn't do. You didn't say anything about not filming the food carts." Grace crossed her arms over her chest.

"Do you think that makes it any better? I didn't think I'd need to specify, but I'll know to update next year's contracts to spell out no videos anywhere on the festival grounds, period. Erase the videos you've taken this year, or I'll have security kick you out. And I need to see you delete them now."

"Make sure she fully erases the videos and doesn't just move them to her phone's deleted items folders 'cause those can be brought back," I said. Grace glared at me, and I let myself smirk back.

Alexis nodded and watched as Grace deleted multiple videos from the festival, including several of me. In one, I stood outside the cart, finger-combing my hair while redoing my ponytail. Totes suspicious if messy hair is a crime against humanity.

"If I hear you're causing any more problems, you're out," Alexis said. She stared at Grace, reminding me of a high school teacher threatening to give a sophomore detention.

"You think Logan will let you do that? He said my blog would be good publicity for the festival." Grace sounded whiny.

"My boss trusts me, so yes, he'll back me up. Especially when I tell him about you hassling our beloved vendors and recording stalkerish videos." Alexis continued to glare at Grace. Seeing this side of Alexis impressed me since I'd suspected she had a spine of steel behind the calm, collected façade. She could pour oil on troubled waters, but she was more than capable of lighting the oil on fire when needed.

Grace turned and stared at me. "You won't get away with this. You and Kendall are the worst. You'll regret this when my podcast tells the world about your sketchy behavior," she hissed at me, then stomped away. Alexis stared at the music blogger as she faded into the trees.

Kendall? What did my employee have to do with my reading coffee grounds and, according to Grace, fleecing customers? Hopefully she was smart enough not to slander me, and Ground Rules, on her podcast or blog. Else she'd have a serious problem on her hands.

Alexis turned to me. Her head tilted slightly as she looked at me like she was trying to read me. "I'm sorry about that. I was hesitant to give her a press pass, but Logan thought as long as Grace bought an entry pass, we should upgrade her since her podcast isn't terrible and some of her interviews are decent. We're always looking for media coverage, which has been hard to get from the local papers, other than a few short pieces saying that we're still around."

She looked down for a moment. I wondered if the stress of keeping the festival felt heavy, like it was shoving her to the ground. She looked up with a grin. "So, can you read decaf coffee grounds?"

I laughed. "I'm not psychic."

"But you read coffee grounds for some girls?"

"Yes, but as a game. I didn't charge them anything. I basically told them what they wanted to hear. So they got a good value for their free reading."

"It's too bad you're not psychic or willing to fake it on my behalf, as I could use some good news," Alexis said. "Barring that, I'd love an iced lemon verbena and mint tea."

"Trouble with the festival?" I poured her drink.

"The festival is okay. Logan's a great boss and running this is more than a job for me. It's a calling. I love seeing the happy faces of the crowd, and being able to support the bands means something. But my personal life is crashing and burning. I've been able to push it aside and focus on the festival, but next week is going to be rough."

Alexis's phone beeped, and she pinched her lips as she read it. She picked up her tea. "Duty calls," she said and rushed away.

During a quiet moment, I texted my dad. *Would it be weird if I described the body I found to you to see if you might know how he died?*

My phone rang a minute later.

"You're going to need to explain your text," my dad said. I told him I wondered if Ian had been murdered, or if it could've been natural causes. Or some sort of freaky accident.

All of the nerves running throughout my too-tense body desperately hoped it was an unforeseeable accident.

"Fine. Tell me about what you saw," my dad said. But he sounded hesitant, and I couldn't blame him. This wasn't the usual sort of father-daughter bonding phone call he wants to receive. When I was done, he was silent for a moment, no doubt digging through his experience as a detective with the Portland Police, currently with the cold case unit.

"What I tell you goes no further, right?" my dad said.

"I'll only tell Jackson if it becomes necessary. I won't tell Bax, let alone anyone else."

"This isn't an official diagnosis, and whatever you do, don't quote me. But if I responded to the scene, the victim's red eyes would stand out. It could be a sign of strangulation."

"It almost looked like he'd been crying," I said. The cloudy redness of Ian's eyes was going to feature in one of my nightmares someday.

"It's one of the signs we train responders to look for in domestic violence situations." My dad's voice was grim. "It's important anyone who has been strangled gets prompt medical care because victims can collapse later from swelling or respiratory distress."

"Does that mean Ian could've stumbled away from an attack and collapsed later?" I asked.

"I have no way of answering that question," my dad said.

"I was just spitballing ideas."

"But I can tell you that yes, it's possible for a strangulation victim to suffocate later. And I should remind you there's a perfectly competent detective on site who knows more about this than you do, and is trained to handle crime."

"It's hard to forget about what I saw."

"If the death is bothering you, and it should, you can close up the cart and go home. You don't need to be at the festival. Especially if you think you could be in danger."

"I know. But it's not like I'm investigating. People just tell me things." Especially if I played my cards right and, usually, just look at people sympathetically. "And I doubt I'm in danger."

"That's a problem if people tell you things and put you in danger."

My VIP customer walked up. She'd changed into a dark purple tank that looked fab with her burgundy hair.

"I need to go. Customer."

"Stay safe." The undercurrent of frustration came through in his voice, although he sounded patient as always. Like he wished he could order me to go home. But he'd learned pretty early on that while coaxing or convincing with logic works with me, a blind directive makes me want to do the opposite on principle.

"I will. See you next week."

I hung up my phone and smiled at the VIP. "I love that color on you."

She glanced down at her tank. "I spilled lemonade on the shirt I was wearing earlier, so I had to change."

"Oh, you know, when life spills lemonade, switch to an awesome shirt." Lemonade? I wondered which cart she'd seen behind my back.

As I made the VIP's mint coffee soda, I said, "I'm guessing you're a regular Campathon attendee?"

"This is my fifth year. Coming is like art therapy for me," she said. "It's always fun to see the different bands they book each year, along with some old favorites. I even rented a camper van so I could sleep in comfort."

"This is my first time, although my brother has been a regular for years." Although I wasn't sure if the music or his friends brought him back each year. Maybe both.

"I'm so jealous of musicians. You know the old cliché 'can't carry a tune in a bucket'? That's me."

"Music isn't on my list of accomplishments, either," I said. I looked at my VIP, with her professionally dyed hair, friendly face, and exceptionally smart eyes. Like she was used to making quick, usually right assessments, even while drinking copious amounts of caffeine. More than me, and I practically submerged myself in coffee each day. So I asked, "What do you do when you're not a VIP concertgoer?"

"I'm a nurse anesthetist," she said and explained how she administered anesthesia during surgeries for a local hospital. "Sometimes I work with an anesthesiologist, and sometimes I'm solo."

I grinned. "So you're saying that you're good at knocking people out?"

She laughed. "As long as they tell me their prior conditions and let me put drugs in their IV."

"I'm guessing someone lying about their health could be deadly in your line of work?" A thought started rankling the back of my brain, but I couldn't bring it into focus.

"Definitely. Like if someone drinks a lot more alcohol than they admit, that can lead to complications. So while you should always be honest with your doctor, never, ever lie to your anesthesiologist or nurse anesthetist. Unless you want to risk life-or-death complications."

Her words made me wonder: Could Ian's death have been an assault turned deadly?

"Even for healthy people, losing consciousness is dangerous, right?"

"Of course, which is why surgery should always be a calculated risk. Anesthesia is fairly safe nowadays, but it used to be more dangerous."

She sounded cheerful, like this was something normal to her. Like she was discussing the merits of Ethiopian versus Guatemalan coffees. Which made sense since she dealt with it all the time.

I handed over her drink, which she waved at me like a toast before sauntering off.

Could Ian have been knocked out somehow and just never woke

up? And my father had mentioned that people can collapse later after being strangled. Maybe Ian had been in some sort of fight, walked away, and paid the ultimate price later.

My back muscles tightened as Detective Adams walked up. She carried a can of iced espresso from a national company, so she wasn't on the hunt for caffeine. She must've brought the canned drink with her 'cause she was afraid I'd poison her or something.

Part of me wondered why the detective was skulking around the festival. Before she had a chance to say something, I went ahead and asked. "So why are you hanging out here?"

"Virtually everyone I want to interrogate is here, and they won't visit my station for an interview," she said. "This case is annoying, and I feel like the solution is here, somewhere."

"Hmm, if Ian was strangled . . ." I started to say, but my words faltered when the detective's gaze snapped my way.

Her eyes were practically Superman's heat vision. "How do you know that?"

I forced myself to shrug and told myself to quit talking to the detective. But I couldn't help but say, "His eyes were red, and I've heard that's a sign of being choked. But who knows? Maybe he left his contacts in too long or he'd caught pink eye or something. Or I remember wrong. I'm not used to analyzing crime scenes or dead bodies." And I wished I could scrub the memory of Ian's body from my brain.

The detective continued to stare at me. "Are you working with Maya Oliveira?"

Working with? Like in cahoots? "My business partner is Harley Yamazaki. You can look up the business records with the county if you'd like, or just check our website. Our bio photo is pretty awesome since one of my best friends is a photographer, and she took some stellar photos of us at our first cart." As I prattled on pointlessly about photography, thoughts twirled through my mind, almost making me dizzy. My guess that Ian had been strangled must be right, considering how seriously the detective was looking at me, like she wanted to arrest me. Or I'd stumbled close enough to her leading theory to make her suspicious.

"Where were you on Thursday evening, again? Hanging out at the jam session?" The detective eyed me like she was trying to catch me out in a lie. Since I'd already told her I'd gotten an early night.

I did my best to give the detective a bright smile. "If you want to interview me again, I'll need to call my lawyer. He's at the festival, so, as long as he checks his phone promptly, it won't take him long to stroll over here."

Detective Adams's look was full of frustration intertwined with skepticism. "You just happen to have a lawyer on retainer?"

If by "retainer" she meant bound together by blood and, more important, respect, love, and a regular heaping of annoyance, then yes. But all I said was, "Fortunately, yes. Would you like me to call him?"

"No, we're done here." The detective strode away, off to kick over a few more rocks to solve her case.

I just hoped she'd find a new theory and would quit trying to lob pebbles in my direction.

"It's all about obsession," Maya said. "My focus is on writing from the heart and turning it into something greater than simply my own emotions."

"I wonder if all artists feel that way," I said. I took a sip of water while Maya held a tumbler of cold brew. She took it black, just like her espresso. Some days, I wonder if how people drink their coffee reflects something about their fundamental nature. My weekend VIP liked her coffee plentiful and sweet, although she was willing to experiment. Harley is a purist, able to articulate minute nuances of different beans and blends, and able to taste way more than me, although I'm no slouch. Neither my business partner nor I are fans of sweet coffee, with Harley drinking it straight while I prefer a splash of cream. Although I've developed a palate over the years for what will appeal to our customers and am proud of the sweet coffee drink recipes I've created.

"Music is the perfect metaphor for life," Maya said as if I hadn't spoken. "The highs and lows. Celebrating triumphs and heartbreak, sometimes in the same verse. Because our lives exist in fragments, you know. Or at least our memories do."

I knew what she meant. And some people lived in the margins. And sometimes, those were the most dangerous spots to be.

"So, are you good friends with Alexis? You seem tight," I said. "I'm still thankful you helped us get into Campathon." Despite everything that had happened this weekend. And despite the last forty-eight hours feeling like they'd lasted longer than a month.

Maya blinked, like I'd taken her out of a train of thought, and then nodded. "When I was in grad school, Alexis came to me after an open mic night and said she dug my song. We started hanging out. When I formed the Changelings, she actually introduced me to Ian. Who acted like he adored my musical vision. Well, maybe he did because while he ultimately didn't back me personally, he did champion my music. And look what the band has done with it without me."

I heard a note in the undertone of Maya's voice before. Agony. Maybe intertwined with a touch of jealousy. Because her songs had received rave reviews, but with Nate as the voice. Maya as Ariel, having sold her voice to Ursula the sea witch, crossed my mind again.

I wondered if Harley ever felt that way about Ground Rules, since ultimately her roasting skills are the bedrock of our business, with me the public face. But she always says partnering with me allowed her to focus on what she loves. And while she fills in as barista sometimes, like this weekend, she spends most of her time in the roastery and filling wholesale orders.

"Did you always see yourself in a band, or did you ever consider the songwriter route? That's a career path, right? Someone who writes songs for other musicians?"

"I've thought of it all. Teaching. Music production. But performing live completes my soul. That being said, Bax bringing me onboard his studio, as I've said before, both helped me out of a dark spot and kept the wolf from the door. And if another door opened, like say as a songwriter, I'd stick my head through it and scope out the other side."

As if she'd summoned him, Bax walked up, accompanied by his son. Bax grinned when he saw us. Niko chatted animatedly as he hopped along next to his dad, taking a mix of steps and skips. The sight made me smile while reminding me the kid had only two speeds: full-blast and asleep.

"Two of my favorite people!" Bax said when he saw us.

"What about me?" Niko asked.

"I said two of, not all of. You're definitely in the top three, buddy." Bax grinned at his son, and I hoped Niko understood the teasing note.

"Top three?" Niko sounded mock-outraged, and I let out a breath in relief. He knew.

"Okay, buddy, you're at the top."

"Is Sage second?" Niko asked.

"Maybe. But that's not a discussion we should have lightly," Bax said.

"I think she is!" Niko said.

I felt myself blush. And I really hoped I was in the top two of Bax's list, since he was definitely on the top of mine.

Bax leaned over and whispered something to Niko.

Watching Bax with his son reminded me how, of my friends, Bax feels like the most "adult." I mean, we're all adults. But Bax owns a house in a city getting more expensive by the day, and a successful business, while raising a fantastic kid. Most of my friends have one of those three things, like a job they're passionate about. But they don't have it all together in the way Bax does. They have roommates while paying off student loans, or a job that pays the bills but a hobby or secondary endeavor that fuels them creatively, not unlike Maya and her music. But my friends don't have all the pieces put together yet, although we're all trying.

"Maya, want to get a burrito with us?" Niko asked. He looked up at her, and I wondered how well they knew each other.

"Sure." She leaned over and took his hand. And Niko grinned.

"Want us to bring something back for you?" Bax asked me.

I tried to smile, feeling like an afterthought. "Nah, I'm okay. I'd rather wait to eat until I'm done here."

"Come find us when you're off," Bax said, and the three of them walked off with Niko in the center.

They headed to the burrito cart, and I made myself look away. Instead of feeling sorry for myself, I arranged one of the Ground Rules mugs on the counter and took a photo of it with trees blurry in the background. It wasn't my best effort, but it was good enough for an Insta post once I added a caption.

Remember, we're at #Campathon this weekend! And our regular cart at the Rail Yard is open for all your coffee needs. #JustBrewIt #GroundRules #Campathon #CoffeeIsLife #RailYardPDX

I scrolled through our mentions, seeing us tagged in a few posts from the Rail Yard, which is always a happening destination during the peak of the summer since it's on the tourist map. The photos looked like a typical day of iced drinks, tacos, and the sort of summer vibes that made me feel homesick even though I was only fifteen miles away.

I texted Harley. *Looks like business is happening at the Rail Yard!*

Harley texted me back promptly. *OMG I've been working my tail off! Emma just gave me some jojos, so I'm fueled to run today's numbers. We're up from earlier in the summer, so being open all weekend is paying off for now. #ToldYouSo*

I grinned and texted back. *Awesome. See you on the flip side. #WhoUsesHashtagsInTextsAnyway*

She responded by texting me a gif of a vinyl record and *#Coffee-IsLife*, and I tucked my phone back in my pocket. No matter what happened this weekend, at least both Ground Rules carts were doing well. And it looked like Harley's world was untouched by Ian's death. A small flicker of jealousy flinted inside me. My weekend should've felt carefree, instead of tinged with sadness and grief.

Niko skipped up and shoved something into my hands. "I

bought you a chocolate chip cookie! It has oats in it, which I know is your fave!"

His hands looked dirty, but I still smiled as I took the cookie.

"Thanks, Niko!"

Niko turned and dashed back in the direction of the burrito carts, leaving a small trail of dust in his wake. I grinned and put the cookie down on the counter. But the feeling of doubt resettled down on me.

But thankfully someone on a coffee mission walked up, so I had a reason to escape out of my own head for a few minutes.

Chapter 12

I glanced at the clock. Kendall was due to join me in a few minutes. Most of me was done with the festival. Going home sounded like the best idea possible. I reminded myself this was an excellent opportunity for the business. Quitting now would say we'd failed. But like many things, the reality of being here had been so different from the dream. And while I'd made all sorts of contingency plans in case things went wrong during the festival, I wasn't sure how well I'd dealt with the not-so-minor problem that popped up.

I forced a smile on my face as two women holding hands walked up to my cart. They looked happy. Like the weekend was going exactly as they hoped. And they deserved to have a fantastic time, and that included service with a smile. My internal pep talk made the smile on my face turn real. Well, mostly natural, although, I assumed, tinged with sadness.

As I handed over their iced oat milk lattes in their festival cups, I caught a glimpse of a woman in Buddy Holly–style glasses recording my cart with her phone.

Grace.

Again.

Such the wrong name. Annoying felt more accurate. Or irritating. Thoughtless. I debated texting Alexis to complain about Grace, but I figured the music blogger was steadily digging her own grave. I did snap a quick photo of her filming the cart since Alexis had already warned her. Grace either wanted to get kicked out of the festival, or she didn't think Alexis was serious. In this fight, she was a fool to underestimate Alexis. I'd clocked the steely look in the festival organizer's eyes.

Grace walked up toward the cart, eyeing me like I was a rabid wildebeest ready to attack. Or maybe flee. I didn't know the usual MO of a wildebeest. But, I decided, she reminded me of an anteater. She was digging in the ground, looking for more small bits she could turn into a meal. I'd read once that anteaters rely on their sense of smell, and Grace was following the wrong trail if she thought I was the path she needed to scour to find the truth.

I went ahead and texted Alexis the photo of Grace with her camera pointed at my cart along with the words *Guess who's back?*

But before Grace had a chance to say anything, the VIP-pass woman walked up for her hourly coffee. As always, she held up her pass as she approached the cart. Like I'd forget who she was or that she had access to all she could drink if she didn't display it.

"I want to try something new!" the woman roared. She looked more amped than usual, like the caffeine she'd drunk an hour ago was actually hitting her bloodstream.

Grace stared at her like the woman had said something outrageous. So I gave my VIP a wide smile.

"Anything for one of my best customers. Maybe one of the teas?"

"No, one of your coffee options. But something I haven't tried."

As I suggested a coffee soda flavor she hadn't tried, Grace melted away. But when I handed over the drink, I noticed Grace was talking to Bianca of the Breakfast Bandits. And both were staring at me like they expected me to murder someone at any moment.

Like I serve up shots of pure death at the cart.

Kendall showed up exactly on time. As he pulled on his apron, I asked, "Do you know the music blogger stalking the cart? Grace Taggart?"

Kendall's shoulders stiffened. "Grace? Seriously?"

"That's a yes." I leaned against the cart and watched Kendall as he slowly turned and faced me.

"Grace and my sister Dagny were friends in college," he said carefully.

"Oh." I could already fill in some story gaps. I'd known Dagny when we were high school students together, although we hadn't been close. She'd gotten an academic scholarship to a local university but dropped out after a rock-climbing accident. Her rope broke, and she fell. She'd spent a while in a rehabilitation facility for a traumatic brain injury, and she'd never fully recovered. Kendall had moved home to help his parents care for Dagny, and he was just now getting back into the swing of school and his own life.

"Grace used to come around some when Dagny first came back home. She stuck around a while, unlike most of Dagny's old friends." Kendall's voice was bitter. "But Grace posted photos of Dagny all over her social media feed, even though we asked her not to."

"Why?"

"Sympathy. Grace kept talking about how much Dagny changed. She said she was bringing awareness to TBIs, but she was clearly enjoying all of the people telling her how kind she was to visit her poor, damaged friend."

"I'm sorry."

"Seeing my sister used for likes and attention on social media . . ." Kendall's voice trailed off and I saw an undercurrent of highly controlled anger in his face. Anger I'd never seen before. But I understood. Grace's desire to play Nancy Drew took on a new shade. Was she the type of person to do anything for fame?

A customer strolled up, so I left the cart in Kendall's hands and headed to Slice, Slice Baby for a piece of their veggie special pizza, complete with fresh arugula and olive oil drizzled on top. Then I decided to treat myself: a stop by the Complementary Chocolate cart was exactly the sort of pick-me-up I needed.

I laughed to myself as I read their menu. Then debated between a Has Anyone Told You Recently That You Have a Beautiful Soul fudgesicle or a Your Smile Lights Up the Room chocolate truffle cupcake. Everything on their menu sounded like a chocoholic version of heaven.

"I'm happy to answer any questions," the girl working behind the cart said. She was a teenager, maybe sixteen, with a warm, slightly crooked smile. The other woman working in the truck looked like an older version of her, so I bet they were a mother-daughter duo.

"What's your favorite dessert on your menu?"

"My current obsession rotates between the chocolate cheesecake bites with strawberry surprise and the chocolate chip mini-pies, which are basically like chocolate chip cookies in pie form. But we always have the mini-pies, while the cheesecakes are seasonal, if that helps."

"Hmm, tough decision." I ordered the mini cheesecake bites and paid on their cart's tablet. They used the same system we had at Ground Rules.

"You're one of the people at the coffee cart, right?" the Complementary Chocolate teenager asked as she handed over my dessert. Which ended up being three truffle-sized dark chocolate–coated pieces of cheesecake with a freeze-dried strawberry on top. They came with a mini-flag stuck into the center cake that said HAS ANY-ONE EVER TOLD YOU THAT YOU'RE AN EXCELLENT LISTENER?

"Yep. I'm one of the Ground Rules owners."

"Bianca from Breakfast Bandits said you killed someone yesterday, but I told her she has to be wrong since you're here."

I closed my eyes for a second. It's not like food cart owners gossiping like stereotypical middle schoolers was a surprise; my fellow owners are humans, after all. But Bianca had an extra seasoning of bitterness. "I found the body the other morning, but I didn't have anything to do with his death."

"Most people here will be smart enough to know Bianca's always full of it. She's just nervous people will prefer your coffee to her cart."

"We're not even competition this weekend, since getting our usual pastry delivery was too much of a pain. We only have packaged biscotti and vegan energy bars."

"I guess someone could bring something cold for breakfast and skip her cart because they can just get coffee at Ground Rules, but that's a stretch. But you know how it goes. Most of us support each other, but there are always a few bad apples in every bunch. We're definitely on Team Ground Rules."

The older woman showed up in the order window. "Are you talking about our neighbor, Backstabbing Bianca? That woman's always out to make trouble."

"You know her?" I watched as the woman's eyes flickered up and then back, like a series of annoying memories was invading her thoughts.

"We were in a pod together in downtown Stumptown for a while. My first food cart focused on dumplings, including a breakfast bao that was popular for a while. She flipped out over the competition and tried to start a bunch of rumors. She claimed my vegan bao had pork, and my pork bao put someone in the hospital with trichinosis."

"Trichina-what?" the teenager asked.

Her mother half smiled when she looked at her. "Trichinosis. It's an illness you get from undercooked pork."

The teen's nose wrinkled. "Gross."

"That's terrible. Are you still food cart neighbors?" I asked.

The mom shook her head. "The lot we were in redeveloped, and instead of finding a new full-time spot, I rebranded to chocolate and desserts. I mainly work festivals and events now, so it worked out. I don't miss the daily grind. Although weddings can be a trip."

I nodded and asked, "Do you bake wedding cakes?" before taking my first bite of the cheesecake. The taste covered my tongue like little pips of sunlight and rainbows.

"Absolutely not. Wedding cakes are, honestly, the absolute worst. And they rarely taste that great. But dessert stations have been popular recently, with a wide range of options instead of a single cake. You should look at the photos on our website, 'cause we've done some beautiful displays."

I nodded, focusing on the flavors of the truffle as she talked. The crisp dark chocolate coating gave way to soft chocolate cheesecake inside, along with a hint of strawberry. I looked inside the remaining cheesecake half and saw the strawberry was swirled throughout the bite. The chocolate shortcake crust added an almost salty depth.

"This tastes like heaven," I said, and the mother-daughter duo smiled. "I really appreciate how you've doubled down on chocolate and happiness, theme-wise."

"In a way, I can thank Bianca for inspiring the name of my cart. After dealing with her for three years, I decided I want to put some good back into the world."

"And she took a job at my high school," the teen said.

"In a cafeteria?"

"No way. I'm almost like a social worker for a youth transition program based in her high school. I help students with disabilities find employment and career-related education so they'll be successful when they graduate. It's unbelievably rewarding. Having the food cart as a side business is now more like a hobby combined with a summer job."

"And I get to eat chocolate." The teen grinned, like eating dessert was the most critical part of the arrangement. Which made sense to me, but then, I'd built part of my life on a foundation of coffee.

The mom's smile toward her daughter mixed exasperation with affection. I wondered what it'd be like to work a legit, honest job with my mother. Which made the devil in the back of my mind snort. I couldn't see my mother baking cookies, as that's something you can order from a bakery, or willingly doing a job that involved serving the public versus fleecing them.

"Thanks," I said.

"We'll definitely come by for coffee later!" The teenager waved at me as I left.

Bianca stared at me as I carried my two remaining truffles past her cart. Kendall needed to try one, so I decided to sacrifice one of my truffles for my employee.

Could Bianca have killed Ian to frame me? But why? And the festival was only a long weekend. It's not like I'd stolen her primo placement on a busy street corner or food cart pod. And it's not like our raw, vegan quinoa and goji berry bars from a friend's small Portland-based company were legit competition for her breakfast burritos and sandwiches. And the primary reason why I carried the bars—which were surprisingly tasty—was to support my friend who'd started the company when he decided his falafel cart wasn't a long-term prospect. Thankfully the bars made an excellent emergency breakfast and snack for desperate vegans who showed up sometimes with low blood sugar, on the search for the former vegan falafel cart.

But, after glancing at Bianca again, I decided to stick with the chia-seed pudding I'd brought for my breakfasts during the festival just in case.

Chapter 13

Kendall gave me an exasperated look as I approached the cart. He crossed his arms over his chest, covering up the Portland Timbers logo on his T-shirt.

"Uh-oh, what I'd do?" I asked. I put the plate of cheesecake bites on the counter.

"Some girls came up and asked me to read their coffee grounds."

I laughed. "Did you?"

"Why would I? I just stared at them, wondering if they were pranking me until one said she'd heard the psychic was blond. And female. Then the coffee bean dropped, and I knew you'd been up to something. Again." Thankfully, Kendall didn't sound mad, just mock-exasperated. And he was trying hard not to smile.

"Which made your crystal ball become less murky." I told Kendall about my morning reading coffee grounds.

"You've never offered to read mine," he said. "Which beans would create a more accurate future: a blend or a single-origin bean?"

"I'm not psychic." While I'd told Harley about my mother in the early days of starting Ground Rules, Kendall didn't know about my grifter roots, and the lines I'd tried to avoid crossing.

"Oh, I guessed. And I've seen you cold-read customers before. How'd you get to be so good at it?"

I offered Kendall a cheesecake bite. "I just observe people. What they're wearing. What they're talking about. The first woman whose grounds I read was basically looking for hope, like most people, so I focused on that. You can learn a lot about a person by watching their body language and the involuntary movement of their facial muscles. And I acted confident, even if my reading was an educated guess that could've been absolutely wrong. Because bravado makes people think I'm telling the truth."

Kendall swallowed a bite of dessert. "What am I thinking now?"

"That you love the cheesecake bite."

"You're right, but how did you know?" His gaze in my direction had the studious note I'd seen in his eyes whenever he'd faced something new.

I half smiled. "You closed your eyes after you bit into the truffle, which is something people do when they want to block out their other senses and enjoy the flavor of what they're eating. I see you do it all the time when sampling coffee. If you'd wrinkled your nose or scrunched your lips, I would've known you didn't like it."

"You make it sound easy. Like it's just stating the obvious." He took another small bite of the cheesecake truffle. I'd admired his restraint; I'd wanted to shove the whole bite in my mouth in an overload of flavor.

"It's not rocket science. You just need to observe the small details. Most of life is lived in the small details, even if we focus on the big moments." I knew I wasn't talking about cold-reading customers, but I don't think Kendall noticed. Mainly because he was eyeing the dessert again.

"Maybe you should stock desserts like this in the shop," he said, his eyes going dreamy as he took a third tiny bite.

"It's a good idea if we want to turn into a dessert destination," I said, although I liked the daydream. And offering delicacies like this could open up a whole new business line of paired coffee and desserts. But Harley and I had long ago decided Ground Rules' focus was coffee, and we didn't want to get distracted by food. While both of us loved to eat, it wasn't what we saw as our core competency.

Plus, our new shop was at a micro-restaurant development with excellent chefs. Customers could carry food from the other restaurants into our shop or the communal seating area. Which meant they could also bring along our coffee drinks when ordering, or eating, food in the other cafés. We'd offer pastries from my favorite bakery, but that was it. (And it was mainly to maintain regular access to their salted vanilla pear muffins, aka my usual Friday-morning treat for slogging it through another week. And because none of the other restaurants opened for breakfast.)

My VIP customer stopped by for her hourly coffee. "I'd like to try a cappuccino this time around," she said. "I need to slow down on sugar."

Considering the number of drinks she'd consumed, that sounded reasonable to me, and I almost asked if we should switch her to half decaf. I wondered if she'd actually sleep tonight, or if she'd spend the entire festival awake, jazzed on caffeine, heading toward a crash on Sunday when the music stopped.

"Dry or wet?" Kendall straightened up, ready to shift into his suave barista mode.

"Let's split the difference and go medium wet."

"Is it okay if I use one of our cups since you won't really get the full experience in your travel mug?"

"Oh, that sounds fancy."

Kendall made the medium-wet cappuccino in the usual smooth, perfect style I'd taught him, crafting a leaf in the microfoam in one of our white ceramic cups. He sprinkled it with our "magic dust," aka our "proprietary" blend of sugar, cinnamon, and cocoa powder, to finish it.

"Heaven," the VIP said after taking a sip. She stood at the corner of the cart's order window, taking slow sips like she was savoring each moment. I ate my final cheesecake truffle, even though Kendall gave me puppy dog eyes when I didn't share it.

"I bet that look usually gets you what you want from girls," I said.

Kendall laughed. "You're a stronger woman than most. But you haven't seen the smirk."

"Smirk?"

"Oh, it's saved for the special moments when I know a girl is into me but is playing hard to get. The smirk says I know, while not being too aggressive. The girls come running."

"Keep telling yourself that, sweetheart," the VIP customer said.

Laughter burst out of me before I could rein it in. Kendall blushed slightly, then smiled.

"And I'd like an iced coffee, please," the VIP added. She handed over her pass again, along with her well-used travel mug.

As our VIP got her cappuccino chaser with a splash of cream and sauntered off, I still mentally laughed, since she'd said what I'd wanted to say. And Kendall, thankfully, rolled with it.

"By nightfall, she'll be vibrating hard enough to charge the battery of a campervan after the sheer amount of coffee she's drunk," I said.

"How do you know she's staying in a campervan?" In approved barista mode, Kendall started cleaning. Either he'd taken one of my lessons to heart—never leave the cart dirty between customers if you can help it—or he was hyperaware his boss stood a few feet away.

"People tell me things."

"That literally never happens to me," Kendall said.

I pushed myself away from the cart to leave, but Alexis walked up and ordered a lemon verbena and mint iced tea, which I suspected was her favorite drink of the weekend. She looked slightly frazzled but also determined. "I've hit the halfway point of the festival. It's all downhill from here."

As Alexis bustled off, Nate showed up, so I stayed at my post by the front counter of the cart. After ordering his drink and handing over his mug to Kendall, whom he barely looked at, Nate turned to me, like, of course, I wanted to chat with him.

And he wasn't totally wrong, since I did wonder if he could've murdered his manager. And this was as safe a place as any to find out more about the singer.

"Alexis sure left in a hurry," Nate said. He stared after her. Like he was surprised the gravity of his existence hadn't drawn her into his orbit. Like it should keep her at the coffee cart, hovering over his every word like he was an oracle.

"Well, she's busy," I said. The stress running through Alexis was almost palpable on the air around her. Part of me thought I needed to do some yoga poses or meditate to shake off the tension Alexis had left behind.

"How's Alexis taking Ian's death?" Nate's voice seemed fake casual, but maybe because he always sounded that way when talking about other people.

"I have no idea. It must make Alexis's job managing the festival more challenging." I moved the sugar container, reusable spoons, cup for dirty silverware, and other coffee supplies to the side. I swept some spilled sugar off the cart window. I reached inside and grabbed a bar towel to wipe it down as Kendall made Nate's drink.

"I just can't get over Ian's death. We were going to be dads together, you know?"

My hands stilled. "Dads?"

"Yeah, Ian's having a kid with someone."

"Who is the mom?"

Nate shook his head. "I don't remember. He didn't say, or if he did, it didn't register in my brain."

I moved the sugar container and coffee supplies back to their usual spots instead of replying. Was this a relevant detail? Maybe he'd slept with a married woman, and her spouse saw Ian at the festival and lost control.

Or maybe the whole world is a soap opera. I told myself to get a grip.

Nate spoke again. "It's not like either of us are married. We both knocked up one of our rotations, if you know what I mean."

I should've pointed out to Kendall how my eyes scrunched and my lips pursed together showed I was appalled and disgusted but trying to hide it.

Nate continued talking. "Neither of us are meant to be tied down. Yet here we are."

I wasn't sure what to say, especially since Maya had already mentioned Nate having a kid and an ex-wife, so I settled on, "So you're going to be a dad." Again.

"Yep, baby girl Green will make her debut in about three months." He blinked quickly before looking down at the ground. "I really need the band to do well, else I'll have to get a day job to take care of my kids. Ian's death really sucks for me."

Ian's death wasn't so great for Ian, either, echoed in my head. But I kept the words inside. Instead, I asked one of the questions that'd been rattling around my skull for a while. "What exactly does a band manager like Ian do?"

"Ian handled everything on the business side so the band and I can focus on the music. He scheduled our tour and shows and negotiated all of our contracts, including with our label. We had a contract booking agent and a freelance publicist on our last tour, but they worked under Ian. He excelled at handling the small details while keeping the big picture in mind."

"Did you pay him for help?"

"He got ten percent of everything we earn, so he has—had—the incentive for us to earn as much as possible."

"Do all managers represent multiple bands?"

Nate frowned. "It depends. Hypothetically a manager could only rep one band if the band did well enough. Ian said he signed another band a few months ago, but he might've been trying to rile me up. He'd do that sometimes. He thought it was funny."

"That sounds mean."

"He said I write my best music when I'm off-kilter," Nate said.

"He also sounds manipulative," I said.

Nate looked thoughtful. "Maybe a little, but that's one of the things that made him such a great manager, you know? He was shrewd and covered all of the angles. Nothing could go wrong around him because he always had plans B, C, and D ready to go. And I knew he always had my back."

Even if he was also sticking a knife in it? I wondered. Except maybe Ian had treated Nate well and just had problems with Maya. I was predisposed to be on Team Maya, but whenever I talked to Nate, I could feel his magnetism as well. Maybe the two were like flip sides of a magnet, unable to share a stage. Maybe Ian had seen Nate as the better long-term financial bet. Or he'd just liked him more. Their personalities meshed.

Or maybe Ian thought he could keep a handle on Nate, while Maya is an unstoppable force.

Kendall put Nate's drink down on the cart's ordering window. The singer looked wistful as he picked up his latte.

"I better go meditate for a while, so I'm ready to perform," he said. His steps dragged as he walked away.

Kendall leaned his elbows down against the counter and looked at me. "Is he for real, or what?"

"I don't know," I said, watching Nate walk away. "I feel like he's all froth and no espresso, you know? But maybe he just rubs me the wrong way."

Since the cart was in Kendall's more than capable hands, I knew I should head to the children's stage to find Bax and company. But instead, I stopped by the side of the barn where I'd found Ian.

I turned so my back was to the barn. To the left, I could see the parking lot where the vendors could park. There was a loading zone next to the door to the barn's commercial kitchen. I remembered seeing a photo of a wedding held at the barn. The Pembroke family seemed to have found a way to make their farm into an event destination for quirky events, with Campathon being the crowning jewel. Which gave Logan a checkmark in the innocent column, since the death could harm more than the festival.

If I turned to face right, I could see the back of the food carts. If

I faced straight ahead, through the trees, I caught a glimpse of the driveway the vendors used to access the parking lot. We had a different entrance from the main Campathon gate.

Why had Ian been here the night he died? Could he have met someone in the parking lot?

Or he'd been on his way to the bathrooms. Or he'd been out for a nighttime stroll, communing with the trees before the masses descended.

Maybe if I could figure out why Ian had been out here, I could figure out what happened to him.

Which, dollars to donuts, was already on Detective Adams's list of action items.

Motion in my peripheral vision caught my attention, and I saw Grace peeking around the corner of the barn, staring at me. Like she was following me across the festival grounds. She ducked behind the building.

"Have fun, Harriet the Spy," I muttered, and walked away in the direction of the children's stage. But my feet slowed when I heard a couple of women chatting. I walked behind them, hoping they wouldn't notice me blatantly eavesdropping. They were both dressed in jean shorts and tank tops. One of the women wore the sort of purple-and-green boho headwrap beloved by yoga enthusiasts, while the other sported a hip pixie cut.

"I'm still amazed Alexis gave us such a fantastic spot in the lineup."

"Did you, like, blackmail her or something?" Pixie Cut turned her head, and I caught a glimpse of dyed blue bangs.

"No, but not long before the schedule came out, I saw Alexis at the coffee shop in my neighborhood with the guy, Ian, who died. You heard about that, right?"

"Wait, that rumor is true?"

"Sadly. I checked with Alexis and yeah, it's true. But back to the coffee shop, 'cause this is strange. I used to see Ian there often, so he must've lived nearby. But it was really early in the morning. So was

Alexis with him? Maybe she was subtly buying my silence with our lineup spot."

"Were they, like, together, together?"

"I don't know, but six is pretty early for a business meeting."

"Six a.m.? What were you doing up that early?"

"I had to drive to Seattle for a stupid family thing . . ."

Their voices faded away as they turned left, when I needed to keep going straight.

Ian and Alexis.

Alexis had said she'd known Ian for years. Maybe they'd just been getting an early morning coffee together. But six a.m.? That's the kind of early coffee you grab with a boyfriend or spouse as you're both on your way out to start the day. Although maybe there were secretly a bunch of morning birds who met at zero-dark-thirty over coffee. Perhaps I'd meet all of them when we opened the new shop.

I thought back to Ian and Alexis. They hadn't seemed lover-like. In fact, she'd seemed annoyed by him. And if they'd been a couple, wouldn't she have given his bands prime spots during the festival? Ian had complained that his bands' time slots weren't good enough.

Although, Alexis had gotten one of his bands in even though they were brand new. Was that weird? Or just a bit unusual? Or a sign of a festival organizer who trusted a manager she'd worked with before? I mean, if a trusted industry friend said I needed to try out the new almond milk heading to the coffee world because it blew the other nondairy options out of the water, I'd take them seriously. I'd order a case and experiment.

My phone beeped. A text from my friend Manny, who'd talked about coming to the festival. But he hadn't pulled the trigger on buying tickets, which hadn't stopped him from texting complaints about not coming this weekend.

Did you see this photo of you on Instagram? his text read, along with a link. Which I clicked.

My breath drew in as I scanned a photo of me handing a drink to a guy with Willie Nelson braids. I had a dopey smile on my face. I read the caption. *OMG, this cart has the best apricot coffee drink ever! Who would've thought apricot juice and coffee even mixed?!? #OMG, #Weird-TasteButILikeIt #PDXFoodCarts #Believe #Blessed #Campathon.*

I clicked on the Campathon hashtag. Colorful photos filled my feed. I took in snaps of the bands, of the gorgeous Pine Burrow stage, of a child around six years old dancing with the No Drama Llama behind him. One peak hipster shot of a woman's back as she sat on the hillside, the City Lights stage far below her. Her back tattoo read "Prone to Wander."

I scrolled through a few, noting one of the cheesecake bites at Complementary Chocolate. The poster had adored the cheesecake as much as Kendall and I had. I stopped at one that showed one of our lattes next to the Campathon schedule displayed on someone's phone. *This is the best sort of to-do list!!! #Campathon #Festival #Tunes #Grooving.*

I scrolled through a few more band photos and paused at one of Maya on stage. I read the caption: *A goddess among us. #BansheeBabes #moderngoddess.*

On stage, Maya did feel like she should be an old-school goddess of music. Like her songs had the power to bestow pain or pleasure depending upon her whim.

After a few more scrolls, I paused. There was a snap of Nate with his arm around a dude with a goofy-looking smile. The caption told me the man was a Changelings megafan who couldn't believe he'd met his idol.

But the background was what kept my attention: Ian and Alexis stood squared off like they were arguing. Alexis's eyes were narrowed, and her arms were crossed over her chest. But something about him said annoyed lover. Like this was a tiff between intimate friends. Maybe it was the way he leaned in slightly, with his hand on her arm.

I screen-captured the photo. There was definitely something more than a festival organizer-band manager relationship going on.

But was Alexis a killer? She looked kind of physically frail. When she'd confronted Grace, she'd had more of an "I'll call security and kick you out" vibe than "I'm going to pummel you."

But Ian had been holding a Ground Rules coffee cup, and I hadn't sold him one. But I'd sold one to Alexis.

Who knew what Alexis would've done if she'd been pushed too far?

And based on what Nate said, it sounded like Ian enjoyed pushing people's buttons.

Chapter 14

On my way to the kids' area, I passed by a cluster of four tents grouped together, with a hammock hanging in the middle. Collapsing in a hammock and napping sounded so tempting I wanted to commandeer the campsite.

I'd thought this weekend would be a mix of stressful and fun controlled chaos, balanced with mornings of hard work and evenings spent relaxing and listening to music. Now, I felt like I'd need a vacation just to recover from the festival.

I walked up behind two women, maybe in their early twenties, dawdling along the path. I was going to pass them until I heard one say:

"Did you hear about the dead guy? I know why someone offed him."

"Really? Why?"

"He threw a plastic fork on the ground. Plastic. I mean, who does that?"

"Maybe Gaia struck him down."

I passed them, holding in a laugh. If only Ian's murder was something so simple. Guilt hit me in the gut, telling me I shouldn't laugh. Someone had died. I might not have liked Ian and suspected he was hinky, but Alexis had said he'd been a good son. I'd heard some fondness in the undercurrent of her voice when she talked about him, mixed with frustration.

Like Bax's ex, Laurel, Alexis wasn't drinking caffeine, although she clearly missed it. She'd looked sick both mornings, and she'd been in a hurry to get into the bathroom Friday morning.

My pace faltered a half step, as if my brain needed the energy to plop a connection into place that clicked together and felt right.

Had Alexis looked sick because she was pregnant or because she'd just killed Ian?

Or both?

Nate claimed Ian was going to be a dad.

Could Alexis be pregnant with Ian's baby?

As I approached the clearing with the stage, I slowed down and looked around. Bax should be here, somewhere. There was no sign of him.

But I did spot someone I recognized.

Faith.

She was holding a tablet in her hand, with a frustrated look on her face.

"Are you doing okay?" I asked her.

"I have no idea how Ian kept all of his musicians on track. Is it really hard to look at the festival's schedule and write down the times they're supposed to perform? Maybe enter them onto their phone calendars? I'm starting to think I should have brought Sharpies so I could write 'If found, please send to the Pine Burrow stage by four p.m.' or whenever, across their foreheads."

"Who's missing?"

"Half of Waffle Twaddle. They're pretty new. Ian claimed this is a great opportunity for them since they should be a big hit with the five-year-old demographic, which is evidentially represented well at the festival. But hey, maybe they can go on-stage without a drummer and bass player."

"It'll be a shame if they don't play." A man and a woman started waving in Faith's direction.

"It'll be their own fault."

"Are those your wayward musicians?" I motioned.

Faith looked over. The couple waved again and skipped backstage. "Yep. Okay, now if I can make sure the Changelings show up for their seven o'clock slot, I'll be done for the day."

"It's nice you're taking care of Ian's musicians this weekend," I said.

"He wouldn't have wanted their dreams derailed. But I can't believe the festival didn't cancel because of Ian's death." Faith looked like she was barely holding on; in her place, I would've felt outraged the organizers had decided to keep the show going.

"Are you going to go into the music business, too?" I asked.

Faith snorted and the angry vibe around her faded, replaced by confidence that rang through the air. "No way. I'm applying to a joint law school and MBA program next year, and then joining the family business as corporate counsel before working my way up to CEO. This internship was supposed to look stellar on my grad school applications."

Faith told me that her grandparents started a regional financial services firm. I recognized the name. "Since I'm the only grandchild left, I need to help out with the family business."

"Only one left?"

Faith pulled at her braid as she frowned. "My cousin passed away a few years ago. Car accident."

"I'm sorry." First a cousin, now Ian. Faith's family was going through an extended tough time.

"My dad's devastated about Ian. I spoke with him earlier, and he's spiraling with guilt."

Talking about loss supposedly helps with grief, and I was feeling nosy, so I asked, "You said you didn't grow up with your brother?"

Faith brushed off the hip of her dress, like it was dusty. But it looked surprisingly pristine to me. "It's a long story. The short version is my dad and his college girlfriend broke up a week before graduation, and he left town to backpack across the world for a year before law school. She didn't tell him that she was pregnant. She raised Ian on her own. No one knew about Ian until about nine months ago when my dad ran into his ex-girlfriend and Ian in a café."

Not telling someone about their child didn't sit right with me unless there was a solid reason. Like a woman fleeing from abuse. Which didn't sound like the case here.

"My grandfather and dad were so happy to have a boy in the family again. They were really impressed by Ian's drive. That he built his music business from scratch without having the advantages of 'privilege and private schools,'" Faith said, and it sounded like she was quoting her family. "Bit hypocritical of my dad, since he had the sort of cushy background that's the opposite of Ian's. And it's the sort of life he would've given Ian if he'd had the chance."

"Like yours?" I asked, suspecting this was a sore spot for Faith. But it was fascinating. After my nomadic early childhood, the life of a privileged teen almost felt like a novel.

"My parents sprung for private schools, but they were all about me learning the value of money. For example, I had to get a job and pay to maintain my own car if I wanted to drive, although they bought me a preowned Acura, at least. Once I started high school, they set me up with internships each summer. And I tried to do boy things to bond with my dad."

"Boy things?" The words felt like nails on chalkboards to me.

"Fly fishing, camping. Stuff like that. Oh, he was excited when I played varsity golf in high school, and we still golf sometimes."

"Adding a brother must've been interesting."

"Like I said, my dad was over the moon. My mother wasn't exactly thrilled with Ian popping up, but it's not like she could complain. She met my dad in law school after Ian was born. If my dad had known he had a son back then, he would've wanted to marry Ian's mom."

Faith's smile was sad. "My dad would've had Ian, but he wouldn't have had me."

"I'm sorry." I could practically taste the grief that rolled off Faith. It reminded me of ashes and copper.

"My poor grandfather. He's really going to be devastated. And he's not doing well."

I looked at Faith. Her clear brown eyes met mine.

"Cancer," she said. "Stage-four pancreatic. It's rough."

We stood for a moment. Even if Ian had gotten on my nerves the few times I'd seen him, he didn't deserve this, nor did his newfound family. The thought of losing Jackson caused an ache to form deep inside. I couldn't imagine losing my brother while a beloved family member was also dying.

"I'm sorry to be such a bummer," Faith said.

"You're not. I wish I could explain how much I feel for you. And your family." The words came out of my mouth automatically, but I meant them.

"I really want to think about something else." She tried to smile, but her lips didn't want to cooperate.

The quiet between us hurt, like someone was screaming, so I asked, "This is random, but do you know anything about how the Changelings' songs were copyrighted? Is that something the label did? Or did Ian take care of them?"

"Why?" Faith asked. Something told me she'd appreciated the change in subject, so I told her about Maya and her missing song royalties.

"That must be why they were arguing. I wondered, but Ian didn't want to talk about it. Let me check his emails." Faith scrolled through the tablet. She looked up at me. "The songs are registered to Nate."

She replaced the cover on the tablet and slid it into her tote bag.

"That's weird. I heard Ian tell Maya he'd get it all straightened out."

"That is—that was—Ian speak for buzz off," Faith said. She looked thoughtful.

"Hmm."

"But I'm pretty sure Maya knows," Faith said. "I think this is why she and Ian were arguing on Thursday night."

"You mean Thursday afternoon at the coffee cart?"

"Nah, they got into it outside of the Changelings' RV. They had a pretty big crowd by the end. I didn't hear much 'cause I had my earbuds in for most of it, but Maya yelled that Ian would pay for disrespecting her, before she stormed off."

Faith's phone beeped. "Of course, a band needs to know if they're scheduled for three p.m. or seven p.m., and they can't check the schedule. Excuse me."

I watched her stride off for a moment, noting how capable Faith was. The bands were lucky she'd stepped up to help them since no one would've blamed her for falling into a well of grief. Something told me she'd collapse later when the reality fully sunk in on her.

I made a note on my phone to ask Jackson if any of his law school friends had gone into entertainment law and could help Maya. Although considering her loud fight with Ian, she probably needed a criminal attorney as well, unless the police found a better suspect.

As I scanned the crowd, I didn't see Bax, but I did see another familiar face. Alexis was leaning against the fence on the edge of the children's area, watching a group of toddlers dance to the band. They looked like very drunk, tiny adults. I made my way over to her, pausing for a moment when a small blond girl raced by me, followed by a man who looked like he needed a Rip Van Winkle–style nap.

I studied Alexis's face as I stopped by her. Tears shone in her brown eyes. She looked pale.

"Alexis." My voice trailed off, and I took a deep breath for courage before finally asking, "Are you pregnant?"

She looked at me with wide eyes, the way a deer startles in place when caught in headlights. "Why do you . . . How did you figure it out?"

"No caffeine. You've looked pretty off in the mornings. It seemed logical." Plus I'd seen her race to the bathroom, either because she had morning sickness or because she'd just killed the father of her fetus. The thought made shivers run down my back.

"You do know this is none of your business," Alexis said.

"If I'm right about who the father is, then while it might not be my business, it will be significant to many people. Including the police."

Alexis glared at me. "Surely you don't think I killed Ian? Why would I off the father of my child?"

I told the smug feeling deep inside my chest to go away. I was right about Alexis's pregnancy, but I didn't need to gloat. "If you haven't mentioned it to the police, they will think it's strange." At least I assumed they would. Not that it was my business to tell them. But someone might figure it out, and they'd wonder why Alexis hid it.

Alexis looked down as her brief moment of fight fled. "It's no one's business, except mine. I'm not even three months along yet. Ian's the only one who knows. I mean, who knew, and I don't know if he told anyone, like his mom."

Should I tell Alexis that Nate knew? At least, Nate knew Ian had a child on the way, and I assumed he was referring to Alexis. Something told me Nate would've happily blabbed the name of the mother if he'd known. Which might be why Ian hadn't told him. If Maya was a deep river, Nate seemed like a babbling brook with a layer of faux-broodiness.

I took a deep breath and told myself to project calmness. "What are you going to do now?"

Her shoulders hunched. "Have a baby. I wasn't planning on being a single mom, but if that's the hand fate has dealt me, I'll figure it out. It's not like I thought Ian was magically going to turn into husband material. He claimed he'd take care of us, but he promised a lot of things. I pretended to believe him because I loved him, even though he always ruined everything. But he sure could daydream."

"Had you two dated long?"

Alexis's laugh made the hairs on the back of my neck stand up.

"Dating is too strong of a word. We tried to be exclusive in college, but he kept cheating on me. So I moved on, or at least I tried to. He was like an itch that I'd periodically scratch. He offered to change for me. Said he'd do the monogamy thing. He even asked to marry me last month. Claimed he'd figured out how we could make the whole house with a picket fence dream come true. He acted like he'd found the perfect score."

Alexis half smiled, and the tears were back in her eyes. "You know, it was a nice dream. And I knew he wanted to change, even if he was deluding himself."

A small cough made me turn my head. Faith stood behind us, her shoulders slumped instead of held in her usual straight posture. "I'm sorry to bother you, Alexis, but I have a question."

Alexis rubbed her eyes. "Of course, I'll do whatever I can to help," she said. "Walk with me to the bathroom, and we'll talk on the way."

The intern and the organizer walked away together.

Several people had mentioned Ian having some sort of big score on the horizon. Could they mean an inheritance from the grandfather he barely knew? Or was he embezzling from Maya?

"Sage!"

I turned as a tornado in a green shirt crashed into me, followed by a handsome face that still made small butterflies flutter in my stomach.

"Are you having a fun time, Niko?" I asked. Bax paused a few steps away. A stuffed llama wearing a miniature top hat peeked out of the bag over his shoulder.

Niko told me about his day, about petting the No Drama Llama and getting a stuffed llama for his new little brother, and the bands he'd seen. All somehow without taking a breath.

Bax grinned at me from over his son's head. "We're going to walk over to the Pine Burrow stage to find Laurel, if you want to join us."

But on our trek to the Pine Burrow stage, my phone beeped. Kendall. *I need help.*

"I gotta go help Kendall," I said. I left Bax and Niko, wishing I could stay with them since Niko's happiness felt like lemonade on a blisteringly hot day. But Kendall wouldn't have asked for help if he didn't desperately need it.

Chapter 15

The line at Ground Rules was longer than I would have expected, hence the text for help, so I metaphorically rolled up my T-shirt sleeves and jumped into the cart. The aroma of freshly ground beans made me feel like I'd come home.

Kendall pulled shots of espresso and crafted drinks while I took orders and poured out cold brews and iced teas. We worked seamlessly together, barely needing to talk. We were like dancers who'd figured out the funky beat of our workflow.

The coffee VIP walked up toward the end of the rush. Her burgundy hair looked a little mussed, like she'd been dancing wildly. "A time like this calls for an iced mocha," she said.

"Oh yeah?"

She nodded. "I need an energy boost for the Renegade Snugglers. They're my favorite."

After the VIP walked away, Kendall said, "I'm still shocked she's able to stop by hourly. My heart would explode."

"She's getting her money's worth from her VIP pass. Although I'm not sure how she's not vibrating in place given the amount of coffee she's consumed. We'll have to figure out what percentage of our sales this weekend were her drinks."

Kendall laughed. "I'm guessing ten percent, minimum."

"I'm guessing at least twenty percent."

The man I'd bought pizza from at Slice, Slice Baby walked up. "Can I offer you guys a trade? A slice of pizza for a cold brew."

"Of course." He handed over a pint glass with the Slice, Slice Baby logo etched on it.

"It looks like you've been doing well this weekend," he said.

"We can't complain. How have pizza sales been?" I mixed water, ice, and cold brew concentrate in his glass like it was a magic potion.

"Steady. But business is always brisk at Campathon. This is my fifth time at the festival and it's always been a moneymaker. We were concerned when we heard about the death, but it doesn't seem to have affected the crowd much. I'm pretty sure most of the people here don't even know about it."

Had the local news posted much about the death? I handed over his coffee, and he gave me a coupon for a free slice of pizza.

"So why does Bianca have such a beef with you?" he asked. "She warned me to stay away."

"I assume she thinks I have a major case of cooties."

He chuckled and took a sip of his coffee. "This is excellent," he said. "Bianca also has it out for the Kauai Vibes cart, which is hilarious, since he's the chillest food cart owner I've ever met."

"His chicken teriyaki is fantastic." And the Kauai Vibes owner had been calm when Bianca had tried to go full-force road rage on him, which made me want to like him.

"Try the pork katsu next time. The sauce it comes with is out of this world."

As he walked away, I handed the pizza coupon to Kendall. "I've already eaten at Slice, Slice Baby. You should try it."

"Thanks." He tucked it into his pocket.

I opened up the browser on my phone and checked out a few local news sites. They mentioned Ian's death but were hazy on the details. "Hmm," I said.

"What?" Kendall asked.

"From an article about Campathon: Police haven't announced the name of the person who died, saying they need to notify the family. They also haven't announced the cause of death, including whether it was an accident. But get this: Six years ago, a construction worker died of a heart attack while dismantling one of the festival's stages. His family's wrongful death lawsuit against Campathon was thrown out. To quote organizer Logan Pembroke, 'Legally the festival had no liability in the unfortunate death. But our thoughts and prayers are with his family.' Many have asked if Campathon will survive a second death onsite."

"I hadn't heard about the death six years ago," Kendall said. He prepared a cold brew in a mason jar, complete with a splash of mint simple syrup, and took a sip. I hadn't realized the budding actuary was a mint fan.

"Two deaths definitely feels unlucky." If Ian had died of natural causes, then Campathon might pay a heartbreaking price for bad timing, except other music festivals had dealt with sudden deaths, including a sad number of overdoses, and disasters without folding. If Logan had been the victim, part of me would've wondered if the heart attack victim's family snuck onsite. But I couldn't see a connection to Ian.

"Incoming," Kendall said.

I looked up to see Grace striding up to the cart. She held her phone by the side, and I was willing to bet an espresso and a pony she'd already started recording us but was trying to hide it.

"Let me guess. You'd like a mocha? Maybe with a shot of cinnamon to jazz it up?" I said. I realized I'd made a strategic error this weekend: I should've given the drinks silly music-related names on the Campathon menu. Maybe next year. If the festival, and Ground Rules, survived.

Grace's steps slowed suddenly. "What?"

"If you're not a chocolate fan, I recommend an iced cinnamon oat milk latte. Oat milk might sound strange, but it's by far the best nondairy substitute we offer, and even people who drink regular cow's milk tend to like it. And it's always fun to mix some plant-based products into our diets."

Grace's face scrunched in confusion as she looked at me. A muffled noise made me glance at Kendall, and he turned away from the music blogger quickly, trying not to laugh.

"Coffee is gross," Grace finally said. "But I do have some more questions for you and Kendall."

Her voice took on a slightly angry note when she said my barista's name. Not unlike the furious undercurrent I'd heard in his voice when he'd told me about Grace and his sister, Dagny.

"Just go away, Grace," Kendall said.

Her eyes narrowed as she looked at him. "You've always talked a good game, but you're the least supportive person I know. Even to people you supposedly care about."

I glanced at Kendall. There was an undercurrent between my barista and the blogger that felt strained and not just because of Kendall's sister.

"Where were you at the time of the murder?" Grace asked Kendall. A woman with long wavy brown hair, maybe about twenty-four, in a yellow-striped crop top and high waist "cheeky" jean shorts walked up.

"Kendall was with me," she said. "We stayed in all night."

"You must be Kendall's friend from Colorado. I'm Sage, it's nice to meet you." I smiled at her and gave her heart-shaped face a quick scan.

"Kendall raves about you all the time," she said. "I feel like I know you already."

I didn't have the heart to tell her that Kendall hadn't even told me her name.

Colorado girl looked at Kendall. "Sweetheart, I was going to grab a burrito. Can I get something for you?"

"I'm fine for now." He tried to smile at Colorado girl, but it looked forced. His eyes darted back to Grace.

Colorado girl sashayed away, and Grace's gaze followed her.

"Grace," I said, and she jumped as she looked at me. "Leave. Or I'll call Alexis and tell her you've been hassling me again."

"Is that the same sort of lie you told that led you to kill Ian Rabe?" she asked, but quickly scurried away. She ducked behind a tree but I could still partially see her as she spoke into her phone.

I glanced at Kendall. "Grace was just your sister's friend, huh?"

Kendall flushed slightly. "We might've gone on a few dates."

"Is *dates* a euphemism in this instance for something more intimate?"

"Yes, but we did physically go out to dinner a few times, too."

"Where you showed her your smirk," I said, and Kendall blushed again. Making him blush might turn into my new favorite hobby.

"She seemed cool at first, but she really did break a ton of boundaries by posting about my sister when my family asked her to respect Dagny's privacy," Kendall said. "And she, well, became way too intense. Scary, even. Because when she obsesses over something, she loses all sense of proportion. I had to change my phone number after I called it quits."

Interesting.

More important, I wondered how far the blogger would go for a story.

A few more groups walked up, but the afternoon pace continued to be mellow.

"You should go," Kendall said.

"You sure you don't want me to stick around?" I asked. I'd already wiped down the front counter and refilled the sugar and cinnamon containers while Kendall had scrubbed down the espresso back counter after the surprise rush.

"Go find Bax. I'll be fine. It's not that long before we close, anyway." Kendall made a shooing motion with his hand. "I'm sure he's pining without you."

"I'm sure he's fine." Maya's face flashed through my mind.

Kendall laughed. "You haven't noticed the way he looks at you."

"Is it similar to the way Colorado girl looks at you?"

To my delight, Kendall blushed. Again. Which felt the perfect time to make an exit. I snagged the mostly full bag of compost and headed on my way.

"I could've gotten that when I close!" Kendall called after me.

As I dumped the compost in the bin, I knew Ground Rules was building into something special. Kendall was a fantastic employee, and he brought a freshness that complemented Harley and me. We all worked together well as a team, with all of us pulling our own weight. Our skills overlapped in the right spots, like while working together in the cart. But also when looking at the big picture, like when Harley and I looked at expanding our wholesale business while maintaining our food cart and soon-to-open brick-and-mortar shop. Working with my team felt like it was all meant to be. Fated. Like how life usually felt with Bax.

Feeling hope for the future made a tinge of guilt flip through me, given this weekend, when I thought of Faith's family and Ian's mom. And a snake of fear reminded me that a murder investigation hanging over Ground Rules could also reduce our plans to bitter dust.

When I closed the compost bit and then turned, the woman walking up with her own bag of compost jumped. Like she'd come face-to-face with the worst serial killer in the world.

"Hi, Bianca." I stood still, between her and the compost bin, as she looked at me with wild eyes. "How's business? We've been hopping, and it looks like you've been selling a metric ton of breakfast burritos."

"You're in my way," she said. Her breathing was still too fast.

"I'll move as soon as you tell me why you're spreading rumors about me. I mean, I thought I'd left petty rumors behind in middle school. Along with acne, and thankfully adult acne is a rare problem for me as long as I moisturize."

My babbling made her freeze. Like the silly words were hidden threats, hitting the spot deep in her thalamus, flooding her body with glutamate, aka the brain chemical behind fear. I paused myself, trying to remember when I'd learned that. We must have looked like we were playing statues or freeze tag next to the compost bin.

I let a sly half smile cover my face as I stared at her, and she shifted. She finally muttered, "When you're found standing over a dead body, you shouldn't be allowed to stay at a festival."

"Finding a body wasn't my fault. If you want to be mad at someone, consider this: the festival decided to continue despite a tragic, onsite death." I looked at her, my eyes flicking to the salsa stain on her light green Breakfast Bandits T-shirt.

At least I hoped it was salsa and not blood. I spoke again. "You must be terrified of my cart's competition if you're trying to scare people away from us. Which is silly since we only have coffee, and we're not even offering pastries this weekend." Only because getting them delivered was a pain, but I didn't need to tell her that. Let her think we weren't offering food as a nod toward team spirit. After staring at Bianca a moment longer, I sauntered away. Behind me, I heard the thud of what I assumed was Bianca throwing her compost into the bin.

She couldn't be jealous of my cart, could she? If anything, our products were complementary, just like chocolate at my favorite food vendor of the weekend.

And I really wished I'd figured out a way to offer our usual muffins, croissants, and cookies at the festival. We would've sold them during the breakfast rush. And having met Bianca, I wouldn't feel guilty about upping the competition.

As I strolled along the walkway next to the barn stage, I paused.

Jackson and Piper walked toward me. My brother had a smile on his face, versus his usual resting scowl, and he leaned over and touched Piper's lower back as they walked, making her turn to him with a grin. She leaned toward him slightly.

My brother's smile faltered when he looked forward and saw me. Worry took over his relaxed expression.

"Are you staying out of trouble?" Jackson asked me. Like I was a teenager he suspected had been raiding the liquor cabinet again. (I mean, I'd only liberated a bottle of rum once. I'd been nineteen, and I'd paid him back. It's not like I'd purloined a top-shelf bottle of scotch and then ruined it by using it as a base for sweet cocktails.)

The words *the detective has been sniffing around* formed in my brain, but I swallowed them before they left my mouth. The last thing I needed was a Jackson lecture.

"The cart's doing well. You should've seen the line of customers a while ago. Totally slammed."

Jackson's look my way told me he suspected I was hiding something he deserved to know about. But that could've been years of guilt from a brother who acts like he's still my babysitter, even though I've legally been an adult for a decade.

Piper looked at me and raised her eyebrows. "Jackson told me about yesterday morning. Are you doing okay?"

As I said I was fine, a large group walked toward us, so we moved off the path, under the canopy of the trees. The group passed by, leaving the lingering herby note of pot on the air behind them.

Piper waved her hand in front of her nose, clearing the air.

"Must be interesting working for the federal government when ganja's illegal federally, but legal at the state level," I said. And she must need to look the other way often during the festival.

"It's a cluster-duck," she said, taking care to emphasize the D.

"You can swear in front of me," I said. Piper's answering grin split the seriousness of her face in half, reminding me why I'd always liked her. And not just because of her unexpected sense of humor, which I appreciated. But because you could tell, if she asked a question, she cared about the answer. She wasn't the best at small talk, but she was definitely the person you wanted watching your back in a fight.

"I've spent too much time with my three-year-old niece."

We chatted for a few moments, with Piper telling me about how her older sister's family lived in a town about thirty minutes from Portland, and she'd stayed with them while finding an apartment.

"It was such a relief to move into my own place," Piper said. "And to not have a three-year-old wake me up every morning at five a.m. to ask me if I know where water comes from. The answer, according to my niece, is the tap."

Jackson interrupted our small talk. "Is the detective still hanging around?"

"Yes."

Jackson looked at me like he expected me to say more.

"Fine. The detective said some of the people she wants to interview are here and won't leave the festival."

"Makes sense. As you know, never talk to a cop without your lawyer present." Jackson looked at me like he suspected I was spilling all sorts of secrets to the detective. The words that I didn't have anything to hide bubbled in my brain. But they died before they made their way out to my lips since I knew my brother had a point.

"We're not all the enemy," Piper said.

"If you wanted to interview one of my clients, I'd tell them to stay silent," Jackson said.

"Good thing I specialize in white-collar crime. I've yet to come across a twelve-year-old who's been accused of insider trading." Piper's tone was tart, but it didn't feel personal. Although I wondered how this would affect them long-term since they were on opposite sides of the courtroom, even if they practiced in different courts.

I laughed. "I read a *New York Times* article years ago about a fifteen-year-old who orchestrated some sort of stock scam online using chat rooms."

"Who uses chat rooms these days?" Piper asked.

"If he did it now, he'd be on Discord or Reddit or something. But this was pre–social media as we know it. Around 2000, I think.

He'd buy a stock low and give out fake stock predictions on message boards and drive the stock price up. Then he'd sell, and he made a ton of money before he was caught. The real question is who based their stock picks off of anonymous online advice?"

Jackson laughed. "She just lawyered you."

Piper mock growled. "The two of you have the weirdest memories. Jackson never remembers my birthday, but he can recite a quote from a law journal he read over a decade ago while hungover."

"How many times do I have to remind you, law journals are not my hangover cure."

Seeing my brother laugh made my day feel a tad bit brighter. We made plans to meet up later, and as I walked away, I thought about truth versus appearance. And I wondered about the people who'd accepted a hot stock tip online and invested, confident they were on to a sure thing, only to find out they'd been duped by a high school student who'd figured out an "easy" way to make money. Years ago, I'd learned from the master that the easy route is usually a con. Or it'll come with too high a price.

My steps paused for a second, like I couldn't walk and think at the same time. I remembered a podcast I'd listened to while making syrups back in the kitchen at Ground Rules' roastery and office. My favorite history podcast had played an episode from a new podcast that talked about William Moulton Marston, who had tried to invent the first lie detector test using blood pressure. Once, he'd been leading a class on Legal Psychology in front of a bunch of lawyers. He had an actor come in and bring him an envelope. The students didn't know it was a test. The actor had been carrying books, spoke with a Texas twang, and sharpened a knife against a leather glove. When the actor left, the professor gave his students one minute to write down everything they'd seen. Of the 147 "clues" the class could have observed, between them, they'd only noticed thirty-four, and no one had noticed the knife. The podcast host talked about how a key part of being a historian is looking for the assumptions you make when analyzing historical records. You need to make sure you're not blinded by what you want to see. Aka what most people naturally do is only look for evidence that supports their pet hypothesis.

What assumptions had I made this weekend? And what assumptions were I making now? Was there a metaphorical knife we'd all missed?

Marston's lie detector test was thrown out of the first criminal trial he tried to use it in. But in a left turn, he later went on to create the character Wonder Woman, and he based her personality on his psychological theories.

What would a psychologist think of Maya? She was passionate and forthright, but there was nuance beneath her exterior. Part of me wondered how much of her forthrightness was secretly a defense mechanism. While Nate came off as shallow and self-absorbed, but maybe that was his protective shell. Maybe Nate was a metaphorical onion with something sweet in his center. I suspected he mainly caused tears if you took the time to try to peel back his layers.

And what would a professional think of me? A barista sticking her nose into a murder that didn't concern her? I should stick to crafting espresso drinks to be a small bright spot in someone's day. Because coffee can make anything better, at least for a short while.

I pulled out my phone, googled "Alexis Amari," and found her listing on Campathon's website, which included her social media links. All of which led to the official festival accounts. If she had personal accounts, she'd kept them locked down.

But someone had tagged both her and Logan on the festival's Instagram account, which led me to her personal account.

Which was private and didn't use her real name, although it did use her photo. I clicked FOLLOW, curious if she'd accept my request. Because while we felt friendly, she had to rank as a business relationship first. At least for now. Who knew what we'd think about each other in a few weeks when the festival was in our collective rearview mirrors? For all I knew, she'd hate me if we hung out away from the festival. Or vice versa.

But thankfully, not all of Alexis's friends locked down their profiles and, after a few searches, I found her tagged in photos online on multiple platforms. A snap of her standing outside Portland Center Stage at The Armory with a couple of women made me pause. According to the caption, they'd been going to an Austen adaptation, which made the poster ecstatically happy based on the number of exclamation points she used. All of them were stylish in trendy cocktail dresses and slinky shoes like they were making a girls' night of it.

All of the posts Alexis was tagged in showed her out, doing things. But that made sense. Maybe her personal profile showed a series of bread photos or at-home hobbies. The sort of details you curate to show the world. A funhouse mirror that showed a happy life instead of real gritty details.

I went back and clicked on Logan's account, which was entirely photos of the festival and the Campathon grounds. Including one of the barn during sunset with the caption *A quiet spot that's going to rock in just two weeks!*

My breath caught.

Ian had commented. *Looking forward to it!*

Which wasn't particularly wise or insightful. How many people post something simple as their last written words?

Granted, if Ian had known this was destined to be his final post, maybe he would've gone philosophical. Or made different decisions. And for all I knew, he'd posted a boatload of clever comments since then, including last Thursday evening.

By following the social media rabbit hole, I found Ian's personal profile, which included a link to his professional website. His content revolved around the bands he managed. Like he spent his life entirely focused on his job. Which made sense since he was using social media to represent his work, not himself. I wondered if he had a private friends-only account full of images and comments that made Ian seem like a real person with secret desires and goals. Something that showed his personality versus a persona. But getting to the heart of a person through social media is always tricky. People only post what they want the outside world to see, versus the secret self they keep hidden deep within.

Detective Adams's face flashed through my mind. I bet she suspected my hidden self as a dark chasm since she was investigating me for murder. And it wasn't like I could claim it was really a spot of rainbows and unicorns. Like everyone, there were moments of my past that rankled like blisters, even if I told myself I'd owned up to my mistakes. I'd like to think my hidden self was the same as my public persona, but that was as believable as an influencer's social media account. Everyone has secrets they try to hide.

I clicked on a Campathon hashtag and smiled as I scrolled through a collection of photos. People gathered today under the trees, enjoying the music and friendship. And good food.

But then I felt cold.

Someone had posted a photo of the stage, but they'd caught Maya and Bax hugging on the side of the photo.

Maya's hand was nestled on the small of his back. She'd tucked her face into his neck like he was a lifeline in a once-in-a-century storm. Her eyes were shut like she was lost in the moment. I couldn't see Bax's face. But the photo looked tender.

Or maybe Maya's eyes were shut because she blinked during a quick hug, versus closing them while in the grip of a deep emotion. I told myself that while a picture might be worth a thousand words, it can also be misleading. Mistaken moments in time. And Bax gives out hugs freely to friends.

But a wary feeling still set up in my heart, making me feel sick.

To distract my brain, I pulled up Piper's account since we'd been online friends for years, even after she moved, although we hadn't stayed in close contact. A photo from yesterday of her standing with

Jackson and a couple of their mutual friends caught my eye. Jackson stood next to her, and she leaned toward him. Granted, like the photo of Bax and Maya, it was just a small, singular moment. But if Piper wanted to show the world her subtle lean-in to my brother, it boded well for their combined future.

Fingers crossed something good would come out of this weekend.

Chapter 16

Instead of heading to find Bax and the crew, I went for a walk down one of the paths. The photo of Bax and Maya weighed on me. I felt like someone was watching me, but a quick glance back didn't show anything. Maybe Grace's general presence had fired my brain into paranoia mode.

But the grounds were full of sunlight filtering through trees, and snatches of music and glimpses of people. The whirling emotions inside me settled down, and I felt like I was coming back into myself. I paused when I caught the glimpse of a fairy statue off one side of the path. Someone had put a crown of flowers on her ceramic head. There were multiple statues hidden around the grounds, with the difficult-to-find life-size centaur being an Instagram favorite of the few who'd managed to find it. The path I was on curved to meet Campathon's main entrance and long driveway that led from the highway to the barn stage. The fields closest to the road had been turned into a couple of gravel parking lots. One held cars, and another had rows of filled-to-capacity bike racks. The festival encouraged attendees to not drive and charged more to park than it cost to hear the music. The festival was on a county bus route and Campathon organized a bike ride from Portland, and several from a light rail park-and-ride about five miles from the festival. I missed my bicycle, since commuting to work on it is one of the ways I clear my head.

Along the driveway, about halfway between parking lots and the barn stage, the festival had a designated "merch" area. A row of long tables nestled beneath cheerful red canopies.

When I walked by, one of the bands was signing. The other tables were filled with a selection of band merchandise with handmade signs saying which band's gear was available at each table, along with a time frame. The mix of items made me smile, from trucker hats to beer cozies, T-shirts to CDs and LPs. Campathon had its own table at the far end, with branded merchandise frequently sporting the tent-and-music-themed logo. There was a white shed behind the tables with a bright red door.

I paused when a bird logo on a ringer T-shirt caught my eye. It was the same logo one of the Waxwings members had on their travel coffee mug.

"You a fan of the Waxwings?" a woman with silky black hair asked, and I realized she was wearing one of the ringer shirts. Her blunt-cut bangs reminded me of one of Harley's past hairstyles.

"Honestly, I like their logo. I need to make a point of hearing them." It was mostly drawn in black and white, except the bird's wingtips were red. If Bax's ex, Laurel, were here, I'm sure she'd know why the bird had colorful feathers at the ends of its wings. There had to be an evolutionary reason for it, other than the bird wanted to look hip.

"If you decide you want one, I'm here for another hour."

"You're not set up here all day?"

"The bands trade-off times. It's kind of chaotic, but it works."

That explained the signage. I picked up a Waxwings coffee cup and checked the manufacturer. I held back a smile when I saw it was one of the cheapest options we'd avoided when creating Ground Rules' merchandise. We hadn't had faith in the cup's longevity and didn't want something mediocre to sport our logo. I pictured the woman muscling Rubbermaid bins across the festival grounds. "Do you have to lug your gear here every time you go to sell?"

She jerked her chin toward the shed. "We can store our merch in the shed. The festival sends someone out to unlock it each day, and only lets approved people enter it all day, before locking it at night."

Which explained the college-age kid sitting on a stool in the shade by the barn door. Interning at Campathon would look good on his résumé. Even if he'd spent the day bored out of his skull since the merch tables were far from the music and the pulse of the festival.

The woman seemed happy to talk with me, like she was lonely working the tent by herself, so I asked, "Are you with the band?"

"My husband's the bass player for the Waxwings. I always take care of their merch table on tour. We're going home next week, and I'm so excited to have a few weeks in one place, even if it's the granny suite in my sister's house."

I raised an eyebrow at the Waxwings wife. Who definitely looked like she wanted to talk. The words poured out of her mouth like a friendly torrent.

"We used to rent our own apartment, but we're on the road so much it wasn't really worth it. When my sister bought a house with a stand-alone basement apartment, we ended up moving in. Her wife wanted to put it up as a short-term rental, but this works out well for all of us. We pay them rent year-round, and it's less than our old place. They get their privacy most of the year since we travel so much. So it's a win-win situation, even if some people think it's weird I technically live with my sister."

"It's not strange at all. I live with my brother."

We paused for a second. Since starting Ground Rules, I'd come to love opening the cart early in the morning and being done slinging coffee by midafternoon. Although I almost always spent a few hours working in the warehouse. And not just because it gave me a window to drop by and say hi to Bax since his video game development studio was Ground Rules' next-door neighbor. We sometimes did a fitness class together at the studio tucked in the back of our building.

I'd come to like the routine. The expectedness. Although maybe I'd become too complacent.

Too boring.

I smiled at the Waxwings wife. "Going on a tour must be rough."

"You have no idea. Half the time, I'm not even sure we do. We do a show, get on the tour bus, and wake up in a new place. And I don't sleep that well on the bus, so I feel like I exist in this weird fugue state. But it's not all bad. I love my husband's band, even if we get on each other's nerves occasionally. You learn a lot about someone's character when you spend days and weeks in a small space with them. And we sometimes have time to explore, and I've seen a lot of great places. And we meet all sorts of interesting people. I keep debating grad school or a full-time job that pays more than peanuts, but it'd be hard to forego the nomad life."

"You acclimated once to living an entirely different type of life, so you can do it again if you want." The first half of my childhood had felt nomadic, and the stability of living full-time with my father had been hard to accept at first. Now, I wouldn't change it for the world.

"Exactly. I'll need to make the switch eventually, but it's hard to think about a nine-to-five existence again." She paused for a second. "Of course, the festival has a weird vibe this year. Did you hear about the Changelings' manager dying?"

I nodded. "A little. It's kind of creepy. What'd you hear about it?"

"There's a lot of rumors going around like maybe he OD'd, although someone else said he was a pretty straight arrow, if you know what I mean. I know I saw him argue with that singer that used to be with the Changelings. What's her name? Maria? The tall drink of water."

Her words made something in my brain stand up straight like it had been called to attention. "I think I know who you mean."

"They were by the RV area late Thursday night. I saw him walk away, and she stopped by the fake bonfire like she was going to join us, but then she stalked into the woods."

Maya walking into the forest like a vengeful dryad crossed through my mind, and I wondered if I'd been spending too much time playing video games with Bax. Besides, based on her band name, she probably thought of herself as a banshee.

Banshee. The Changelings. Both of the band names screamed Maya. And why she wanted to work with Bax suddenly made more sense. It explained why she and Bax clicked so well. Most of his games had a fantasy element.

"You okay? You went silent." The woman studied me like she was reading something deeper in my face than I wanted.

I forced myself to smile. "Sorry, I just realized how tired I am. I was up way too early, especially for someone sleeping in a tent."

"I can't handle sleeping on the ground," she laughed. We talked for a few more minutes, and I ended up buying a Waxwings beanie I definitely didn't need but thought might make a good gift, before walking away. I should find Bax, and his last text said he was at the Pine Burrow stage.

Chapter 17

On my way to the Pine Burrow stage, I detoured through the RV area. Unlike the free-for-all in the grounds for tents, anyone who'd brought an RV had been assigned a spot in a series of orderly rows. Which hadn't stopped the spaces between the RVs from turning into a hodgepodge of camp chairs, canopies, and folding tables. Alexis had mentioned she'd even worked out a detailed plan since one of the bands needed to leave early, and she'd set them up with a spot where they could easily split when needed. Which wasn't too difficult to plan since there was a paved road on either side of the lot used for RVs.

Maya and Ian had argued loudly here on Thursday night. Could the singer have killed Ian? She had the best motive I'd heard, but something told me Maya wasn't the culprit. She lived emotionally in the moment, but she didn't feel violent. Just passionate.

I paused for a moment. When had Ian died? He'd felt cool to my touch. I closed my eyes, trying to remember if he'd been sprinkled with early morning dew. Had he been damp? But I'd only touched his neck. My stomach flipped over at the memory.

If Ian had followed Maya after their argument, had it continued until they were next to the barn, and Maya ended it?

Or had Ian come face-to-face with Alexis? Maybe he'd already been in an angry mood and argued with his lover?

Nate's face flashed through my mind. Could his manager have pushed him too far? He supposedly had a temper.

A man hopped out of a tour bus in the row farthest from the entrance. His name clicked in my mind.

Dev, the drummer from the Changelings. He was smoother than a cup of cold brew coffee without being weak or mild. Perfectly brewed, at least for someone not named Sage.

We made eye contact, and he smiled. "Coffee deliveries?" he asked.

I laughed. "Just on my way to the Pine Burrow stage."

Nate popped out of the bus next. "Hey, it's the coffee girl. Sarah?"

I hate it when people call me "girl," but I let the word wash over me without touching me. "Sage."

"Sorry, Sage."

"I take it that's your home for the weekend?" I nodded at the RV.

"Yep. The band's home away from home for the past few months. At least until I have to return it to my friend next week," Nate said.

"The band and one grumpy intern," Dev said. His deep voice took on a sarcastic note.

"She's trying her best," Nate said.

"Yeah, no. Faith has a good game face, but she's in over her head."

"Well, if Ian had said he'd rent a camper and then told me last minute I was sharing with a band, I'd be obnoxious, too." Nate looked off into the distance. "I can't believe the cops took all of Ian's stuff."

"I'm surprised the police didn't take the whole RV," Dev muttered. He glanced at me. "Have you ever explored the inside of a tour bus?"

"Nope, I haven't," I said. While I was curious what the interior looked like, nothing could make me follow Dev and Nate onboard. And not just because one of them could be a murderer.

Faith walking up made a few notes of tension creeping on my spine settle down. She looked uncharacteristically untidy, with a smudge of dirt on her cheekbone.

Nate put his hand up, and Faith stopped, looking like she was one stupid comment away from ripping Nate's head off.

"You've got a little something on your face." Nate rubbed the dirt off her cheek in a move that was almost the way a parent would clean off the face of a child, but his hand lingered a touch too long and was a tad too gentle. "That's better."

Faith smiled warmly at Nate like he was giving her relaxing energy by touching her face. "The kids' area is intense."

"Sounds about right. My kid bounces off the wall when there's live music. He's totally going to follow in my footsteps," Nate said. "It almost makes up for how expensive child support is. Kids are ridiculously spendy, you know."

Dev made eye contact with me. "Some of us are totally single and child free."

I laughed. "My boyfriend has a son."

"Too bad. About having a boyfriend, I mean," Dev said.

This conversational path felt like it was fraught with landmines, but Dev seemed relaxed about it. Maybe he flirts instinctively with anyone he finds vaguely attractive.

Nate's voice was a murmur, but Faith's voice came through loud and clear as she pulled out her iPad. "Let me make sure I don't need to be somewhere else."

The iPad had a tattered Rabe Music Management decal on the back. Not the sort of graphic I'd think the polished twenty-year-old would use.

But I could see the owner of a music management company putting it on his own tablet.

Nate had said the police had taken all of Ian's belongings, although Faith had been carrying stuff around for Ian, so had they missed anything? This iPad looked a bit beaten up, like it had been in use for years, so maybe he'd bought a new one and handed over the old device as a backup to his intern.

"You up for another poker game tonight?" Nate asked Faith. She was still eyeing the tablet screen.

She looked up, looked him straight in the eyes, and smiled mischievously. "You want to lose more of your money to me?"

"You wish." Nate's eyes never left her face. Like she was the only person who existed in his world. Part of me wanted to ask about his baby mama.

But then the poker chip by Ian's body flashed through my mind, making my stomach feel sick. I glanced at Dev. "You guys play poker often?"

"Sometimes. Also, hearts and rummy. Pretty much anything to make the hours go by. Ian was a phenom at poker, so we really should've played hearts or something with lower stakes. Seriously, that guy could've gone pro. His poker face is world class, and I swear he can count cards. Not that he cheats. He doesn't need to."

I noticed Dev's switch into present tense when talking about Ian, and a flicker of grief flashed across his face like he realized what he said, too. I asked, "Did you guys play poker Thursday night?"

Dev's half smile felt as charming as Nate's usual aura, but also more authentic. "Ian proposed a game of good ole Texas Hold'em. I didn't join the band since they wanted to play for actual money this time around."

"Do you usually play for Jolly Ranchers or something?" As I spoke, Faith hopped aboard the tour bus.

Dev laughed. "You're funny. We play for pennies, mostly. Candy isn't a bad idea except I'd eat all of it. But I don't gamble with real money since I don't want to throw it away. It's why I rarely drink on the road, too."

I hadn't realized Nate had been paying attention to our conversation and decided to be his bandmate's wingman. "You should see this guy on tour. He can turn anything into a workout."

"Parkour and free running," Dev said. "And yoga videos on YouTube. You should join me, Nate, since age is going to catch up with you soon."

"A new parkour gym opened up in southeast Portland," I said. I'd noticed the sign when I was biking to the Ground Rules roastery.

"My buddy owns it. Let me know if you want a friends-and-family discount. I'd happily hook you up." Dev's look my way was flirty, again, but not creepy, so it was easy to laugh. Although my feet itched to continue on across the festival grounds.

"I don't know if jumping over walls is really my thing." I stepped backward, trying to subtly show I was moving on.

"Oh, it's way more than that," Dev said. Nate's eyes glazed over, and he leaned against the RV while looking at his phone. Dev's face brightened as he talked about functional fitness. His voice became more passionate until he finally stopped with a rueful laugh. "I'm sorry, this is definitely my soapbox."

"I gathered." But I smiled at him. "My dad's hard core into cycling and I'm used to people being passionate about fitness." I didn't mention that Bax had a serious workout routine, and everyone else at Ground Rules was a soccer addict.

"I swear we're more entertaining when we play poker," Dev said. I started to edge away, long past ready to make my goodbyes.

Nate started singing "The Gambler," but stopped when a woman walked up. "Oh, hey, I know you!"

Grace stood a few feet away. She smiled at Nate. "I interviewed you once."

"Yeah, I remember. For a blog?"

"For an up-and-coming podcast." Grace adjusted her glasses. "We're really starting to take off."

"That's fantastic."

"I'd love to talk to you and your band about Campathon, and your fallen manager. This weekend must be devastating for you."

"Yeah, it's tough, but we're rallying in Ian's memory." Nate sounded soulful.

As Grace started to interview Nate, I waved and made my escape. What would it have been like to meet Dev when I was single? Although he wasn't really my type. Not anymore. Once, he would've been the sort of mistake I would've loved to make. All my past romances had been fun but short. Bax was a break from the norm, the person I felt like I fit with for the long term. Someone I clicked with on a deep, fundamental level, even if I couldn't always articulate why.

Although based on the photo I'd seen of Bax and Maya, maybe I'd be solo again soon. My smile fled, and the thought felt like a punch to the solar plexus.

"Hey, Sage."

My back muscles tightened briefly until I realized the voice was feminine.

Faith.

"The guys can be a bit much, huh?" she said. She matched her pace to mine. "They were talking to some weird chick when I left."

"A music blogger turned wannabe Nancy Drew," I said. A quick glance told me Faith had reapplied her makeup, and her hair was neatly braided again. She looked like a glamorous social media influencer who'd wandered into the festival on her way to an upscale tea at the Heathman in downtown Portland.

"Huh?"

"They're talking to Grace Taggart. She's a music blogger but thinks solving your brother's murder could be her big break."

"Hopefully someone figures out what happened," Faith said.

"So you like poker?" I asked. I pictured Ian, Faith, and the musicians around a table, with cigars, cards, and a bottle of whiskey. Not unlike the painting of dogs playing poker.

"Not really, 'cause gambling isn't my thing. My philosophy is more 'slow and steady wins the race' and make smart choices. But it was fun, especially since Ian was so into it. And he turned bluffing into an art form."

Faith's voice sounded wistful by the end.

"So, Ian won big?" I asked.

Faith's smile was tinged in sadness. "Depends. Is twenty dollars big? I walked away with ten, and Ian stopped the game when Nate wanted to write an IOU. Ian was really smooth about it. He broke up with the game by claiming he needed to talk to Alexis, but it was obvious he wanted to keep Nate out of trouble. I expect he did that a lot."

"Did the whole band play poker?" I asked. But a voice in the back of my mind asked about Ian visiting Alexis.

"All except Dev, who disappeared somewhere and didn't come back until two a.m. He woke me up when he stumbled back into the RV. He's such a jerk."

"Dev?" He hadn't mentioned leaving or being out, but it's not like I asked. But had Dev and Ian both been gone at the same time, and only one returned? My heart thudded a few times as I wondered if a murderer had just been trying to flirt with me.

"Yeah, he's full of himself. Be careful if you go out with him." Faith's serious tone made me lock eyes with her.

"Oh, that's not going to happen."

"Good." The note of relief in Faith's voice made some of the weariness of the day slip off my shoulders.

"I noticed your iPad earlier—" I started to say.

"Ian's old iPad. Mine is nicer, but I wasn't about to bring it to a grungy festival. Besides, this is synced with Ian's calendar and contacts, which is the only reason I've been able to keep the bands on schedule."

"Did he have anything scheduled last night?"

Faith stopped and looked at me. I kept my gaze level as I looked her in the eyes. "The police keep sniffing around me because I found your half brother. I'd love to see justice served, and not only because the detective in charge of the case is wasting her time suspecting me."

Faith pulled the iPad out of her tote bag. After a few swipes, she handed it to me. She'd launched Ian's schedule, and I skimmed it.

Festival Check-in: Thursday after 3
Barbecue: Thursday after 7
Glisan Street Duel. Friday at 12 P.M.
Waffle Twaddle. Friday at 2 P.M.
Glisan Street Duel. Saturday at 3 P.M.
Changelings. Friday, 7 P.M.
Changelings. Sunday, 3 P.M.

The only other entry said, *Meet with A, beer tent. Saturday, 9 P.M.* But when I clicked it, there wasn't any additional information.

Was "A" Alexis? Or one of his musicians?

I scrolled back a week. Ian had blocks of time marked out as M and C, PT, and a single half-hour GL. But nothing that screamed out why someone would want to kill him. And when I clicked on the calendar listings, he didn't have anything extra included, like addresses or notes. Would it have killed the guy to make his calendar easier for a stranger to read?

More important, Ian didn't have anything planned for the night he died, other than the barbecue. No midnight trips to stargaze scheduled.

I handed the iPad back.

"Sorry it's not helpful," Faith said.

"Thanks for letting me be nosy."

"I think I'd do anything to bring Ian's killer to light," Faith said. She looked younger than normal, like her true self had peeked out from the polished façade. "It's just . . . you can't understand how devastating Ian's death is, especially to me."

"I'm sorry. Truly."

She nodded at me. "I need to go check on a band," she said and strode briskly away. She wiped her face like she'd dealt with a few of the renegade tears she'd been pushing off since hearing the news.

Something told me Faith was focusing on the bands and the festival to avoid dealing with the sinking mass of loss swirling around inside her. But she wouldn't be able to put it off forever, and I hoped she'd be okay when it finally hit.

Chapter 18

Finally, I made it to the Pine Burrow stage.

"Sage!" Maya flagged me down. "I need your help."

"I was just looking for Bax." I rescanned the crowd again.

"You just missed him. He went back to the kids' stage with Niko and Laurel," Maya said.

I groaned internally.

"Trust me, what I need you for is way more interesting than watching a bunch of halflings fawn over llamas. C'mon." She grabbed my hand.

I felt like Maya's words hypnotized me in a daze, and I let her pull me backstage. Or maybe I was just tired from a long day and ready to follow someone else's lead for a while.

"One of my go-go dancers couldn't make it, and I need a replacement, stat."

The words made my thoughts sharpen like I'd been doused in ice water. "Go-go dancer? What?"

"Don't worry, it's just for a few minutes. I just need you to rock out on stage for a song. You'll be perfect. I hope you know you're adorable, and you have the perfect look for what I need."

I glanced down at my Ground Rules T-shirt and shorts. "Umm . . ."

Maya laughed. "Don't worry, I have clothes you can borrow. And I'm talking like a nineteen sixties' go-go dancer, not one you'd find in a nightclub now. And I promise this is important."

I started walking forward again. "If I see any feathers, I'm running away. And please explain to me how it's possible to have a go-go dancer emergency."

Which is how, half an hour later, I ended up on stage wearing a waist-length bright red wig, white go-go boots, and sparkly silver tank dress that ended mid-thigh, with a thick belt around my hips. I looked like a cheesy Halloween take on the 1970s. The other dancers were dressed similarly, except one was decked in red sequins and the other in gold. Both were also topped off with wigs, one black and the other silver.

I forced a smile on my face and grooved out during the song, thinking to myself that I really needed to learn how to say no when people asked me to dress up. A photographer wearing a press badge took photos, which Maya planned to use on her next album cover. Although she'd been a bit vague on how go-go dancers meshed with the name Banshee Blues.

The other dancers and I linked arms and bowed at the end of the song, and I'm pretty sure my whole body was blushing. I bet I looked like a tomato under the stage lights.

"Thank you!" Maya said as we sauntered off the stage.

"At least these boots were made for walking," I said to the dancer in gold, and she looked at me like I'd just spouted a second head. I didn't explain I was quoting a song. I followed the other two dancers off the stage.

Maya's trio started their next song, and I paused on the step down from the stage when the dancer in front of me stopped. Bax stood at the side of the stage. He stared at me with a weird look in his eyes. I blushed, and he grinned slowly, but it felt like he was seeing something other than me.

A voice caught my attention, and my gaze snapped to the bottom of the stairs. "Gorgeous, I'm not letting you by until you agree to

join me for a drink. Or two. We could have a beautiful evening together."

The dancer in red looked frozen, and the guy blocking her way
down the stairs basically oozed primordial sludge.

Or maybe I was projecting.

"Excuse me," I said in my best "can I talk to your manager?"
voice. I pushed past the gold-dress dancer and stepped in front of her.
"Dude bro, get out of the way. And leave this poor girl alone."

His eyes flicked my way but returned to the dancer in red. She
looked young to me, maybe still a teenager. And from the way she
was still frozen, she had no idea how to handle the situation. Bax was
heading our way, ready to play knight in shining armor.

But I've been a bartender. I put a don't-even-think-of-arguing-
with-me tone in my voice. "Do we need to bring out a fire hose or
something to wash you off the pavement? Move it."

My tone must've set off the backstage security guard's radar since
he walked over, his arms held at his sides like he was ready for anything. "Is there a problem here?"

"This guy's a wannabe fire hazard," I said. "And he's harassing
this dancer."

The dude bro sputtered. "I'm not hassling anyone."

"Not letting someone pass by you unless she agrees to get a drink
is harassment. You should be ashamed of yourself." The dude bro
tried to glare at me, but I gave it back as good as I got. He looked
away first.

"We have a strict no-harassment policy at the festival. Come
with me."

The security guard made the dude bro walk away with him despite his protest that we'd overreacted. The girl in red gave me a look
of pure gratitude. "Thanks," she whispered and then bolted away.

I walked over to Bax, who eyed me again, and it was different
from usual, like when I'd been walking off the stage. It was like he
was seeing me, but also something that wasn't there.

"Are you okay for now?" I asked Bax.

"Just dandy. I'll wait for you here while you change. Although I won't complain if you stay in the outfit for the rest of the night."

"Yeah, no way." I headed back to where I'd left my clothes. Pulling my Ground Rules shirt and jean shorts back on felt like I was coming back to myself.

When I returned, Bax was sketching in the book he always carries around with him. He looked intense, so I felt a bit guilty when I talked.

"Where's Niko?" I asked.

"He left with his mom just a bit ago," Bax said. His voice sounded distracted, so I didn't tell him I was sad I didn't get a chance to say goodbye to his son.

Although if Bax had full-time custody, at least while his ex was abroad, I'd end up spending plenty of time with Niko if I wanted to see Bax. They'd always be a package deal. Except Niko spent half of his time with his mom, so it normally wasn't a daily package deal, barring emergencies. I legitimately adored Niko. He was a tornado of random facts, perpetual energy, and relentless curiosity. But how would Niko being around full-time change things between Bax and me? The last thing I'd want to do is make Niko feel unwelcome at his dad's house, especially since he had more of a right to be there than me.

Bax was still focused on his sketchbook, and I recognized the look in his eyes. He'd thought of something, probably video-game related, and he was sketching it out. Bax rarely talks about his ideas until he's had time to let them marinate in his brain. And I knew he'd been playing around with new ideas for a while but hadn't found a game idea that he'd felt passionate about. Which hadn't stopped his studio from developing a couple of games that, he said, were doing well. Even if they hadn't fully sparked his imagination.

"Give me a minute, and I'll put this away," Bax murmured. Like he could feel my eyes studying him, even if his own never left the sketchpad.

I checked my phone. Nothing from Harley, so the cart at the

Rail Yard was fine, although a few friends had texted. My buddy Manny had sent me a photo of the view of Mt. Hood from his new apartment. My former food cart neighbor, Zarek, had sent me a snap of my Ground Rules cart in the Rail Yard, aka the food cart pod we'd been at for over a year, with a line of customers. I texted him back, *Your bars are selling well!* He responded promptly with a heart emoji.

"Sorry about that." Bax put his arm over my shoulder and led me away.

"It's okay. Inspiration struck, right?"

"Something like that. I wish you could have seen you staring that guy down from above. If you'd been a Greek goddess, you would've turned him into a toad or something."

"It wouldn't have been much of a change for him."

"That poor girl he was hitting on looked frozen."

"Learning how to deal with jerks can be a tough skill to develop. It's easier to back down or give in."

"Not backing down when you know you're right is generally an admirable quality," Bax said.

"Generally?"

"I'd hate to see you get hurt by standing up to a biker gang instead of, say, calling 911, but it's one of the many things I admire about you."

I laughed. "Oh yeah? What else do you admire?"

"Now you're just fishing for compliments, Coffee Angel." Bax rested his hand against the small of my back.

We moved into the crowd to watch the Banshee Blues perform. Like yesterday, Maya was like a magnetic force drawing the listeners to the stage. Listening to Maya made me feel like we were in the presence of greatness.

After the final notes of Maya's set faded away, and the crowd slowly started to disperse, Bax asked, "You hungry? After chasing Niko around all day, I'm starved."

I patted his mostly muscular torso. "I wouldn't want this wasting away, so let's hunt down some food."

"Did Niko have a good time?" I asked as we walked toward the food zone.

"He had a blast. He started to have a meltdown when Laurel made him leave, but he catapulted early 'cause he was beat. He's going to sleep well tonight."

Ground Rules and the Breakfast Bandits were both closed, but the rest of the carts had short lines. But the man who worked at the Breakfast Bandits with Bianca was outside their cart. He glared at me as we walked past.

Bax looked at me. "What's with him?"

"The breakfast war is getting real, yo. The Breakfast Bandits are on the front lines of the battle."

"Are you saying they're jealous of your coffee?"

"That's my assumption since I don't think I've given them an actual reason to hate me." Except for winning a staring contest with Bianca, but they'd started glaring at me long before that, in retrospect, an absolutely ridiculous moment on my part.

We paused for a second, and I scanned the carts. I'd already eaten at Slice, Slice Baby today. Yesterday, I'd had lunch from Kauai Vibes and dinner from the Burrito Bus.

"Maybe a savory pie from I Only Have Pies For You?" I said.

"The carnitas burrito is calling my name," Bax said.

We split up to grab dinner, and we met back up. I carried a slice of chicken pot pie with a side of arugula salad on the camp plate I'd brought with me, while Bax had a burrito about the size of his head. He scoped out my pie, and I twisted it to my side. "Mine."

"I'll share some of my carnitas burrito."

"Well, if you put it that way."

We made our way to the City Lights stage and settled down with our food in the back of the meadow, looking downhill at the stage and the swaying crowd in front. A girl twirled past us, not quite in time with the music, but with a beatific smile across her face.

This was what I'd daydreamed about when I'd agreed to work at the festival. An almost perfect moment, just me and Bax, listening to music. Warm but not unbearably hot weather, relaxing after a great meal. But Ian's death continued to hover. If this were a painting, there'd be black shading on the edges, adding pending darkness to a tranquil image.

After the band played their final song, I asked Bax one of the questions that'd been floating in my mind. "You know all the investigation about Ian's death? Do you think there's any chance, even small, that Maya's involved? Or Alexis?"

Bax's forehead wrinkled as he frowned at me. "How can you ask that?"

"I'm not accusing anyone. But you know Maya better than me, and Alexis, too."

"I don't really know Alexis." He pulled his sketchbook out of his bag.

"But you know Maya fairly well." Maybe too well.

"Maya wouldn't go beyond telling Ian he was a jerk to his face. She's passionate, but she'd never hurt anyone," Bax said. He opened his sketchbook and turned to it.

Conversation over. Should I poke, at least verbally, at him? But maybe I should take everything he said at face value. Everything about Maya told me she was direct. She didn't hide behind social niceties. She wouldn't have skulked around and attacked Ian in the dark. But what if they'd run into each other and started arguing?

My thoughts felt like they were running in circles so I pulled out my phone and did the usual thing people do to fill random time gaps.

I checked social media. Again. I really should have read a book or listened to a podcast. Or done something productive.

I clicked on Maya's profile, then on the hashtag for her band, only to see a photo of me as a go-go dancer. I was at the forefront of the photo, with Maya and another dancer in the background. My face felt hot, like I was blushing, as I read the caption. *Check out the Banshee Babes!* #Campathon #Lit #MusicFestivalBabes #BansheeBabes-PDX #BansheeBabes #BansheeBlues

I realized Bax had leaned over to look at my screen.

"Any chance you kept that dress?"

I shook my head, and Bax looked disappointed as he returned to his sketchbook. Guess we were back to normal. Although maybe Bax hadn't been annoyed when I'd asked about Maya, and had been focused on drawing.

On the stage, someone tested the microphone, followed by multiple instruments.

I clicked on the Changelings' account, scrolled through their photos of their performance, and then clicked on their band hashtag. I paused when I saw the same image from before, the one with Alexis and Ian arguing in the background.

"One, two, three, four." The next band started.

I paused.

The Changelings were onstage.

Without Maya, the band was all male now. Nate played guitar while singing lead. Dev, as expected, was on drums and even more handsome on stage behind the drum set. Something about being on stage makes people's relative hotness jump by a factor of eighty. I recognized the lead guitarist, a Black man with a deep voice who'd bought coffee, tipped well, and hadn't talked much. Although he had the sort of voice you want to hear drone on, even if he was just reading the phone book. I didn't know the blond bass player, so maybe he didn't drink coffee. Or perhaps he'd made his own tea or coffee in the kitchenette in the band's tour bus.

People streamed past us as the crowd next to the stage grew. We packed up our chairs, stowed them in Bax's bag, and joined the audience.

The Changelings barely waited for their opening song's final note to disappear from the air before jumping into their second song. They felt relentless, driving into each beat like they were living too hard to slow down.

The crowd was into it, and when they shifted gears into a slow song, the crowd swayed along.

I listened to the lyrics. "Mid-Morning Blues." Nate's voice

sounded like liquid gold as he crooned the lyrics, making references to classic lullabies twisted into a modern love song. The crowd sang along. I closed my eyes for a moment to listen, like not seeing anything would show me something earth shattering about the music. He repeated two lines three times.

> *So I'd sing you a lullaby*
> *'cept I only live the blues*

I opened my eyes and glanced at Bax. He leaned over so I could whisper in his ear. "The lyrics are sort of cheesy, right?"

"The crowd digs the song."

I tilted my head slightly and looked at him, and he grinned and wrapped his arm around me and pulled me toward him. We swayed for a moment, and I made myself forget Ian and the stress of the day and enjoyed the moment.

I was mostly successful.

Chapter 19

When the final notes from the last band of the night faded away, Bax held my hand as he led the way to Maya's tent. We wound our way through the crowd and then on paths through the trees.

"How do you know where Maya's set up?" I asked.

Bax laughed and squeezed my hand tighter for a second. "You're not jealous, are you? I'm not Maya's type."

"Just curious." But I heard the small note of hesitation in my voice. The part that knew Maya was vibrant and unique. And oh so magnetic.

"Her tent isn't too far from your brother's group."

A motley collection of people with guitars and ukuleles sat in a circle in a clearing where several paths converged. An enthusiastic tambourine player danced around, creating his own beat. A couple of battery-operated lanterns stood in the center, filling in for a campfire since real fires were banned everywhere except the official firepit in the beer garden.

Maya sat facing us. I recognized a few as musicians, and most of the crowd seemed to be festivalgoers. Someone was singing the Beatles' song "I've Just Seen a Face" as Bax and I found seats. People clapped when the song came to an end. After a moment, someone started a song that caused everyone to sing along.

A while later, someone pointed to Maya when it was time to choose a new song.

Maya strummed a few chords on her guitar and then launched into a song that sounded familiar. It took me a moment for a few connections to lock into my brain. This was the Changelings' big hit, "Mid-Morning Blues." It sounded soulful in Maya's contra-alto, instead of the over-the-top angst of the radio version.

Or maybe I just liked Maya a whole lot more than I liked Nate.

Someone sat down on the ground next to me. I glanced over.

Nate.

He watched Maya. I realized her lyrics were subtly different as she sang, "I'd sing you a lullaby, 'cept I only live the blues."

"Maya sounds haunting," I said. Nate startled slightly like I'd broken him out of a spell.

"She really brings out a different edge to the song," Nate said. "Hearing her reminds me of us writing this. I hear bits and pieces of her in the song, but I also hear me. But she's bringing out something I hadn't heard until now. Something special."

"If Maya cowrote the song, why is it copyrighted in only your name?"

Nate looked up at me. "What are you talking about?"

I told him about Faith checking Ian's files and how all of the Changelings' songs had been registered as Nate's creative property.

Nate shook his head. "That has to be wrong. When Maya, Joe, and I sat down and negotiated everything, we agreed Maya would get at least co-songwriting credit on the entire album. Ian suggested it as a way to help all of us move forward. It must have been a mistake."

"Or it was deliberate."

"If she's not getting what she deserves, I'll make this right," Nate said. "There has to be someone who can analyze the books and figure out what Maya is owed. This hasn't been announced yet, but we've signed licensing agreements for two of the songs. Maya deserves her share. And an on-screen credit, since 'Mid-Morning Blues' is being used in a movie."

"You might need a forensic accountant to analyze the books to see what Maya's owed," I said.

"And there has to be a way to fix the copyright if you're right. But I pray you're wrong."

Nate's lips were straight, and he had a mix of confusion and anger on his face. This was the most normal, the most human, he'd felt all weekend.

I realized I liked him more this way. And not just because he showed a deeply held sense of what's fair, along with respect for Maya.

I paused. Multiple people had mentioned that Ian was expecting a windfall. Could he have been embezzling Maya's share? But if he had, he must've been smart enough to not brag about it. And would it be enough money to qualify as a windfall? I didn't get the sense Nate was rolling in dough.

And more importantly, was it enough of a windfall to lead to his death?

Or, if Maya had found out Ian was embezzling from her, would that be enough to make her snap?

"You sounded great," I said to Maya. She offered me a swig from a flask, and I shook my head. She took a sip. Behind us, a man in the jam circle sang a bluegrass version of "My Heart Will Go On" along to the twang of a banjo.

"You'll have to join me sometime for a true camping trip. You can't beat beer and tunes around a campfire," Maya said.

"What's this about Sage and fire?" my brother's wry voice asked from behind me.

I laughed. "Maya, this is my brother, Jackson."

They shook hands. "Your rendition of 'Wayfaring Stranger' was amazing. You should record it," Jackson said. Piper joined us and we chatted about music until a human-sized mosquito wearing Buddy Holly–style glasses strode up.

Grace held out her phone. "I'm putting together a retrospective on my podcast about Ian Rabe. You're Maya Oliveira, right? I remember from interviewing Nate Green that Ian discovered you, too."

Maya snorted. "Discovered? Honey, I made his career."

"Says a musician without any hit songs."

Maya's eyes narrowed. "And what's this little blog you write for?"

Grace shifted onto her toes and thrust her phone under Maya's nose. "Where were you when Ian Rabe died?"

Ha, I knew her retrospective questions were a cover for her Nancy Drew–style ambitions.

Maya's gaze at Grace was intense, and she purposefully turned to Piper and forced a smile onto her face. "You said you just moved back to town? A group of us are going to a show at the Mississippi Studios over in north Portland next week if you want to join us. I'm planning to bug Sage until she agrees to come, too."

Grace made a snuffled groan, like she was annoyed. Piper gave her a side-eye glance before saying, "That could be fun."

"Everyone keeps avoiding the subject of Ian Rabe, and I want to know why," Grace said.

"Have you considered that walking up to people and clumsily interrogating them is definitely not the way to make friends and influence people?" I asked.

Jackson gave me his "quiet, I'm your lawyer" look, which Piper must have noticed because she giggled.

Grace glared at me. "You're going to regret mocking me. You and your little coffee business will pay. I promise you."

"I hope you didn't just threaten me and my business in front of witnesses, including a couple of lawyers. I doubt either of us wants to deal with a slander lawsuit."

Nate and Faith walked up. "Hey, it's the music blogger from earlier," Nate said.

"Podcaster." Grace sounded snippy, instead of the simpering tone she'd taken with Nate earlier.

"Oh! I see someone I need to introduce Sage to," Maya said. Her voice was too upbeat and breezy, and she practically dragged me away.

"Sorry," she said and let my arm go. "But I really needed to get out of that tableau."

"Tableau?" I asked.

"You know, a group of annoying people creating a scene of epically bad proportions. It's good we left, 'cause it could have turned Shakespearean."

"Hey, Maya."

"Hey, buddy." They fist-bumped.

Maya turned to me. "Sage, this is Davis. He's with the band Waffle Twaddle." She motioned to a guy with spiky hair who looked like he was in his late twenties and held stock in hair gel. "Sage makes the best coffee in the world."

"You flatter me. Keep on going," I said. Maya laughed. Someone called to her, and she turned away. Behind us, the jam session had moved into a funkified version of a song I almost recognized.

I looked at Davis. "You played at the children's stage today, right?"

"Yep, that was us. Did you enjoy the show?"

He looked so hopeful I couldn't bring myself to tell him I'd rushed to work at my coffee cart instead. "My boyfriend's son dug the show. How'd you get into performing for kids?"

"My band formed when we were all in the same master's program in early elementary education. Writing good music for kids is sort of our collective passion. Being around kids gives me a sense of what both kids like, and parents approve of. The two don't always go hand in hand."

"Do you teach music?"

"I teach fourth grade, but Cynthia, our keyboardist, is an elementary school music teacher. We practice our songs in front of her students because, man, once you figure out how to get honest feedback from kids, they're brutal."

I put an extra-heaping note of sympathy in my voice. "It must be a tough weekend for you, considering everything that happened."

"You mean Ian? I feel sorry for his family. We just signed with him a few weeks ago. I'm shocked he was able to get us into the festival, but he said he had an in with the organizers, and they were impressed by the band's educational focus. They had a band drop out, so we got in. We just finished our demo last week."

"How does one sign with a music manager, anyway?"

"Good question. I met Ian by chance. He volunteered in my school's afterschool program for a while—I should mention that we're one of the poorer schools in Portland and have a free program with an enrichment component. Ian ran a rock band class for us, pro bono. It was impressive. The kids performed the loudest version possible of 'We Will Rock You' at our end of the year festival."

I smiled. "Were the kids any good?"

"Let's just say they were highly enthusiastic. But Ian fostered their love of music, which is invaluable."

Davis laughed, but then his smile faded. "The program is going to miss Ian. He was great with the students. So patient. They loved him. I'm not looking forward to telling the kids that he won't be back."

"That's rough."

As we chatted, I realized this was a side of Ian I hadn't heard about. And the thought of the glad-hander I'd met surrounded by kids made me smile, but in a sad way. Ian must've been a guy with a bazillion shades of gray, but with also some excellent qualities. I wished I could've seen this side of him.

Stopping myself from yawning was getting harder and harder. After talking with Davis for a while, Bax had joined us, and then we'd joined Jackson, Piper, and his friends. My brother's crew had adopted Maya as one of their own and were making her play songs, which she did with a smile, and they were making overtures to Davis and his band. So I made my proverbial excuses to Bax and stood, ready to turn into a pumpkin.

"You sure you don't want me to walk you back?" Bax asked.

"Nah, enjoy the jam session. I'll be fine. Just because I want to get a few hours of shut-eye because of my early start doesn't mean you need to suffer with me."

Bax looked a tad uncertain as I walked away, like he thought he should escort me, but I knew he'd rejoin my brother and his crew.

I followed the fairy lights of the path and headed in the direction of the Ground Rules Subaru to pack my bag for the morning. I'd be way too bleary-eyed and in pain when it was time to wake up to pick out everything I needed to start the day.

After I passed my third jam group of musicians gathered in a circle, with several people holding guitars, the woods quieted down. Starlight filtered down through the trees. I passed a few tents. The occupants were either at the jam sessions, going for nighttime strolls around the grounds, or sleeping. The world felt almost silent, except for the occasional snippet of music that floated through the air.

The food carts had closed up a few hours ago. The door to the barn and its combo stage and bar were shuttered. The beer garden was empty. The firepit had been extinguished. The official festival programming was asleep, waiting for tomorrow to bring it to life once again.

My breath caught. A body huddled on the ground near the cars where I'd parked along with the rest of the vendors. Hopefully, someone was just drunk versus OD'ing. I took a deep breath and squared my shoulders, knowing I should check out the situation even though, after finding Ian, part of me wanted to run away. Something crunched under my foot when I stepped forward to lean next to the body. I used my phone as a flashlight and saw I'd stepped on a pair of chunky black-framed glasses, shattering the lenses.

"Grace?" My heart thumped in my ears. I felt like a girl climbing down into a basement in the middle of a slasher movie. But I couldn't run away.

I shone my phone's light on the person, taking in an arm protruding from a sleeveless collared shirt. My heart skipped a beat as I looked at her face.

It wasn't Grace.

Alexis.

My heart plummeted. I shook Alexis's shoulder, but she didn't react. Her silver necklace chain was broken on the ground beneath her.

A couple of guys walked by in the direction of the bathroom.

"Can you see if there's anyone in the medic tent?" I yelled at them.

They detoured to me.

"We're firefighters," one said, and they dropped down next to Alexis in fluid, synchronized motion. I sat back on my heels. My heart pounded in my ears, and I struggled to take in a deep breath, feeling like I was about to pass out. I sat back on the ground.

The firefighters looked at each other.

"This woman's dead," one of the firefighters said.

Chapter 20

"We meet again," Detective Adams said.

I didn't glance up from my spot sitting next to Ground Rules. One of the firefighters had called 911, and I'd texted Bax and Jackson. I waited with the firefighters until the first police car arrived, followed quickly by an ambulance. Then I'd retreated to the cart, where Jackson and Bax joined me. Bax had thought to bring our camp chairs, and he'd set them close enough to put an arm around my shoulders. Like I'd float away into oblivion if he weren't there to keep me grounded.

"Sage doesn't have anything to say," Jackson said. "Other than she found the body and flagged down two passersby for help."

"Who are you?" Detective Adams sounded snippy. I couldn't blame her; it was really late. I wished I were visiting dreamland.

"Jackson Hennessey. I'm Sage Caplin's attorney," my brother said. He stared at the detective with his patented poker face.

Bax tightened his arm around my shoulders.

"Your client just happened to stumble upon another body?" But Adams said "your client" like she actually meant something dirty. Like I was sketchy. My back tightened. Evidently I wasn't too tired to feel a few flickers of outrage, which felt warm against the quickly cooling night air.

But Jackson sounded calm, almost bored, when he responded. "From Sage's perspective, it was unfortunate timing. Obviously, for the murder victim, it was tragic. For the killer, unfortunate for the wheels of justice since they seem to have gotten away unnoticed."

Detective Adams stared at Jackson for a moment, like she was weighing his words and deciding which buttons to push. "Your client didn't disturb the crime scene in any way?"

I cleared my throat. "I did step on a pair of glasses."

Jackson turned and glared at me for talking while the detective eyed me. "Sunglasses?"

"Regular eyeglasses. Ones with thick black frames. They're still on the ground." I almost added that they had thick frames, like Buddy Holly. But adding too many details sounded like a bad idea, given the vibes flowing on the air around me, telling me to run away.

Jackson's look of annoyance reminded me he'd already told me to get his permission before answering any questions the police asked. His gaze my way rankled, but he had a point. Even if he usually dealt with kids, Jackson was an experienced attorney. And I could easily babble my way into trouble, especially if the detective suspected me.

"Were the glasses intact when you approached the body?"

I glanced at Jackson, who nodded at me, giving me permission to answer. "I didn't notice them until after I'd stepped on them. So I don't know."

"And you're still claiming you didn't see anything suspicious as you stumbled upon yet another possible murder victim?" If the detective's sarcasm was electricity, I could've powered the Ground Rules cart for a whole day.

"Of course she didn't. If Sage had seen Alexis being attacked, she would've called for help. We're not the enemy here, Detective." Jackson leaned back and folded his arms over his chest.

"You know, it's a bit suspicious for someone to happen to find a body and also happen to have an attorney on hand to deflect questions."

Jackson stood up straight, and his arms returned to his sides. "Or lucky, although I'm hesitant to talk about fortune when a young woman was struck down in the prime of life. And on this note, it's late, and my client has had a shock. We're leaving."

Jackson looked at me and jerked his chin upward, telling me it was time to skedaddle. So I stood. Bax followed suit and grabbed our chairs. We walked away.

I glanced back. The detective was staring at us. Like she thought she was letting a murderer walk away free.

Chapter 21

My chest felt heavy when I woke up as my alarm dinged under my pillow, like the weight of the weekend and the murders was pinning me to the ground.

Then I realized the weight was purring.

"How'd you get in here?" I asked the orange cat who'd been following me around all weekend. He—or she, since I hadn't gotten a good look at the cat's nether regions—purred louder. I silenced my phone.

"I have to go make the coffee," I whispered to the cat, and picked him up and moved him to the side. He promptly hopped up on Bax's stomach but shot me a look that said I'd broken his tiny heart. Then he lowered his head to a paw, happy enough with his new human bed.

I slid out of the tent into the still dark morning air. The grounds felt creepy. Like they'd morphed into woods where I might run into the Big Bad Wolf instead of the magical wonderland of music they'd felt like most of last night.

Going through my temporary morning routine and then opening the coffee cart Sunday morning felt weird. Would Alexis want me to continue on and brew coffee to keep the side up? Would the festival call it quits early like I thought they should? Or would they

let the afternoon shows go on to celebrate the life of one of their organizers? Would they try to hide the tragedy from festivalgoers? I
imagined I was a regular attendee, and I hadn't seen the police and
ambulance lights for myself. I'd guess people talking about dead bodies was a rumor.

Bianca from the Breakfast Bandits saw me and held up her hand
like she was warding me off. Like my mere presence would add evilness to her happy egg-and-cheese burritos.

Little did she know, my aura was currently more like jalapeños. I
almost smiled to myself but couldn't muster the energy.

I paused. Did she know about Alexis? Had she been one of the
rubberneckers last night? Or maybe she knew because she'd done it.
I told myself to focus on the cart. Wild speculation wouldn't help my
morning go any smoother.

Even the smell of brewing coffee failed to lighten my mood, but
I did my best to stay cheerful when the first bleary-eyed festivalgoers
came my way.

"A shot in the dark, please," one of my first customers ordered
and handed over a slightly dented stainless steel travel mug. "I wish I
could stay for the afternoon shows, but I need to drive home."

"Did you travel far to come to Campathon?" I gave his mug a
quick rinse.

"From San Francisco."

"You take your music seriously." Serious enough to drive about
ten hours one way, barring bathroom breaks and other needed stops.

"Campathon is special. When I worked in the business, it had the
reputation of treating the musicians well."

I set up the espresso machine since he'd ordered a coffee with a
shot of espresso mixed in. The machine hummed as I pulled the shot.

"You used to be in the music business?" I asked as I dumped his
espresso into his house coffee. I stirred it and then handed it over. He
picked up two of the vegan energy bars, and I added them to his
order.

"I'm a sound engineer. Now I work for the opera. Long story."
He paid with his credit card and then stirred a teaspoon of sugar into
his coffee.

Campathon was unique, and Alexis had to be a big part of that.
My heart thumped again. "I hope the deaths don't ruin the festival,"
I said without thinking. Thinking about the murders made me feel
tired, like I should go back to my tent, curl up in my sleeping bag,
and not move for a few days.

"Deaths?"

I told him about Ian and Alexis.

He bowed his head for a moment like he was engaging in a personal moment of silence. "I'm devastated to hear this, although it ex-
plains why the police had the parking lot roped off again. Alexis is a
good egg. I don't understand why anyone would want to harm her."

"Did you know Ian, too?"

"Slightly. I wasn't in the position to help out Ian's clients, and
I'm not female, so he didn't pay much attention to me." He held up
his coffee. "Thanks for this."

He walked off into the crisp morning air, heading in the direction of one of the festival's parking lots. Since I doubted he'd biked
from San Francisco.

Everything I heard about Ian made me think he regularly rubbed
people the wrong way, except for Davis and Ian's work with children. But Alexis? The musicians seemed to respect her. She'd seemed
patient, even when stressed, which was one of the highest virtues in
my estimation. And she'd had my back over the Grace situation, and
something told me she would've done the same for others if she
thought they were being wronged.

Could Ian have been killed over some inner musician fight that
Alexis had stumbled upon?

But why had there been a pair of glasses by Alexis? If the glasses
were Grace's, could she have attacked Alexis? Maybe she'd been
angry at being kicked out of the festival.

A trickle of customers kept me from wallowing too much. I scanned the cross-section of humanity that came through my line, wondering if I'd served the killer a drink this weekend. But no one had "I'm a murderer" scrawled on their forehead. Although part of my early morning crowd sported various marathon and organized run T-shirts, and glistened with sweat like they'd gotten in a few miles around the festival grounds.

A few people walked past lugging tents and gear, and I wondered how many people would stay all the way through the afternoon shows. A couple of the band RVs left, on their way to the next gig, with the festival just one in a long line of stops as they carved their way through the USA. I wondered how long it took for all the gigs, the towns, and the fans to become a blur. A mishmash of memories, like a Monet painting viewed up close. Maybe in a few years, when I thought of the different festivals and events Ground Rules had catered, they'd all run together in my mind. My team and I would argue about what happened at the events, mixing up years and jokes. But something told me this year's Campathon would be forever seared into my brain.

And I wondered if the festival could come back from two deaths in one weekend, and especially after losing Alexis, since it sounded like she pulled most of the organizational weight. Part of me doubted it, which made a secondary feeling of grief flood me. Whoever had killed Ian and Alexis had most likely destroyed Campathon as well.

Bax walked up. He drew his eyebrows together like something was bothering him. "Sage. I have to tell you something weird. When I woke up this morning, there was a cat . . . Ah! There it is again."

The orange cat rubbed against my boyfriend's leg, then looked at me, and went back for another pass, taking a moment to dig his chin into Bax's shin.

I laughed. "Trying to make me jealous, huh?" I looked up at my boyfriend. "The cat was in the tent with us when I woke up, too. He's been following me around all weekend. Or maybe she. You didn't get a good look at the cat's nether regions, did you? I defaulted to 'him' since orange tabbies are usually male 'cause it's a trait carried by the X chromosome. But this kitty could be a unicorn. Meaning, an orange girl tabby."

"Umm, no," Bax said. He blinked, like he was debating if he was truly awake. Or I needed to explain how a female orange tabby would need to inherit the orange gene on both X chromosomes, while male tabbies just needed to get it once.

And I clearly needed more sleep if my tiredness had destroyed my usual filter and turned me into a mess of random facts.

I poured whole milk into an espresso saucer and put it on the ground. The kitty purred and lapped it up. Bax left for the bathroom, still looking like he'd woken up in an alternate universe. Which mirrored how part of me had felt all weekend. Maybe I'd wake up, and all of this would be a dream.

And maybe this cat really was a unicorn in a furry orange body.

Logan stopped as he walked by. "You brought your cat to the festival?"

"Nah. It showed up and keeps hanging out." I watched the cat. Something told me he wasn't fully grown yet. Or he was destined to a life with out-of-proportion paws.

"It's probably hungry. People dump their pets out here, ignoring that it's usually a death sentence for a pet," Logan said.

"Who would do that to a poor cat?" I glanced down at the cat, which was way too sweet to abandon. There was no way I could leave the furball here. Maybe my dad would enjoy a kitty overlord? He had a whole house to himself, so he'd have plenty of room. And perhaps he'd like a companion once Jackson's dog went home.

Logan walked closer. Up close, his eyes were bloodshot. He looked stiff, like the sadness had made his body freeze up. He leaned awkwardly against the counter of the coffee cart. "I still can't believe Alexis is gone. I keep thinking she's going to walk up, and I'll realize the police calling me last night was a nightmare."

I shifted in place. Logan's grief felt heavy, like it could over-whelm the scent of freshly ground beans that permeated the cart.

"Would you like a coffee or something?" I offered since I couldn't do anything actually helpful.

"I'd adore a large house coffee. I didn't have a chance to make my morning brew." He handed over his official festival tumbler.

"Do you live on-site?" I asked as I poured his coffee, picturing the farmhouse on the edge of the property.

"Not full-time, but I stay in the house during the festival. My brother lives here full-time to manage the farm and helps with smaller events, but he usually splits town during Campathon."

"He doesn't like to stay and listen to the bands?" I grabbed one of the few remaining knit cup holders and put it around his tumbler before handing it over. I didn't want to add burned fingers to the trauma Logan was already dealing with.

"My brother likes the money the festival brings in and doesn't mind pitching in leading up to the festival, but he's not much for crowds. He's come a few times, and that was enough for him. He excels at the intimate events. A few people have thanked him for saving their weddings."

Logan ran a finger alongside the navy-and-yellow-striped cup holder like he was testing the wool, as he said, "I feel like I'm in shock. I was looking forward to meeting Alexis's addition to the Campathon family." He blinked hard like he was holding back tears.

So he knew Alexis had been pregnant. "Everyone who knew her must be devastated. I know I am, although I didn't know her well." And now I never would.

"Her parents are driving in tonight. I feel like I failed them."

A few people walked up. Logan handed over his VIP festival pass to scan. "You forgot to ask for this."

"I was happy for the coffee to be a gift," I said but still entered the code on his pass.

"If you decide to take the cat home with you, get it scanned for a microchip just in case," Logan said before walking away. More customers walked up, and I fell back into the morning coffee rhythm.

And I realized Logan's last-minute advice was right: if we took the cat home—and at this point, I didn't think I could leave him behind—we'd need to get him scanned to make sure he was an abandoned pet and not someone's beloved lost kitty.

If? I realized I'd already made the decision to take him home, even if I wasn't sure I could keep him at Jackson's house, since his dog finds cats scarier than thunder, the garbage truck, and nail trims combined. It's too bad our health codes wouldn't let the orange kitty be a shop or warehouse cat. Unlike my favorite local indie bookstore's resident cat, who even has her own staff picks. (She's partial to poetry by humans pretending to be cats.)

Bax came back, freshly showered. He looked around the cart, so I pointed out the cat, who'd move to its usual nap spot.

"Looks like you've been adopted," Bax said.

"I have to figure something out since I can't leave Kaldi here." The name came out naturally, and I knew, somewhere, pieces of fate had firmly clicked into place.

"Kaldi?"

"Seems like the perfect name for a coffee cat."

"Is that the name of one of Harley's blends in progress?"

As I made Bax a pour-over, I told him about how Harley was trying to make a blend she called the Greatest Of All Time, or GOAT, and about the Kaldi-the-goatherd story. "If Harley is ever satisfied, we'll call that blend Kaldi. And then she'll start working on a new GOAT blend."

"Did I ever tell you I used to have a cat?" Bax asked. "She passed away at sixteen. I miss hearing her chirpy voice."

As I looked at him, I knew we'd found Kaldi's new home.

My VIP walked up. "Cinnamon mocha, please," she said and passed over her mug. Bax waited, sipping his pour-over, as I made the drink, mixing housemade cinnamon syrup into the cup along with chocolate sauce and whole milk. I finished it with a dusting of cinnamon on top of the tree image I'd crafted in the foam.

"Perfect!" My VIP bounced as she walked away, even if this was her first (of, presumably, hourly) coffees of the day.

"Do you have plans for next weekend?" Bax asked after my VIP walked away. "Want to go camping for real? Just the two of us?"

I checked my calendar on my phone. "You won't have Niko?"

"Laurel's dad and stepmom are coming into town, so they're doing a mini family reunion. Laurel asked if she could swap weekends, and I agreed since they're great with Niko."

"I'm free."

As we decided to go backpacking instead of car camping, Bax said, "It'll be a good time to have some alone time since Laurel told you about her research trip."

"You'll be a full-time dad for a while," I said. I studied his face as a few nerves flickered inside me.

"I'm looking forward to it. Niko is growing up so fast," Bax said. He started to say something more, but a flurry of customers came by.

As I was dealing with the mini-rush, Maya walked up.

Bax grinned at Maya. "How do you feel?"

"Terrible. I must've gone to bed sober."

From the way they laughed, I guessed they were quoting something. Probably more Dashiell Hammett. I pulled a shot of espresso for her without asking.

"Really, Bax, you need to create a noir game so I can score it. I have so many ideas." She hummed a few notes.

"I'm working on the rough idea for a sort of fantasy noir idea. If it goes anywhere, I'll let you know," Bax said.

I put the shot of espresso down in front of Maya.

"Oh, you read my mind," Maya said. She held the tiny ceramic cup in her hands, like it was life-giving, before taking a sip.

"Coffee Angel," Bax mouthed in my direction, but quietly, keeping it just between us.

"You picked out a good one, Bax," Maya said. "In a way, she reminds me of Joe. They both have the same sort of sympathetic eyes that make you want to confess your darkest secrets. But Sage clearly has better taste."

"Hmm. I'm happy with my choice," Bax said and gave me the look he gives that says I'm special. At least to him. "And Joe's gorgeous. But what's this about taste?"

"You don't know about Joe and Nate?" Maya asked.

Wait. Nate and Joe? Nate felt entirely heterosexual to me. And I'd never heard Bax rate a guy before, let alone call a man gorgeous. Unless Maya meant Jo. Like in *Little Women*. What a difference an "e" makes. It's the sort of small, overlooked detail that can make a giant impact.

It also explained why Bax said he wasn't Maya's type.

"You mean they . . ." Bax asked.

"Supposedly, she quit the tour early because she's pregnant with Nate's demon spawn."

"Nate said he's having a baby girl soon," I said, realizing I'd made it sound like Nate was pregnant. They both looked at me. "Seriously, guys, as the main coffee vendor, I see pretty much everyone. Except for the banana-pants attendees who don't drink coffee."

"Freaks," Maya said. She shook her head. "I can't believe my ex is having a baby with Nate. It's just weird."

Maya's web with the Changelings felt even more tangled when I thought about how her ex-girlfriend had swapped one lead singer for another. Maya's animosity made sense. The grief of losing her band would've been bad enough without adding in a broken heart. Nate's sense of compassion toward Maya made me like him a smidgen more. But he'd also referred to Jo as one of his rotation, so maybe the relationship meant more to Maya than it ever had to Nate.

A new group of customers walked up. Maya left her ceramic espresso cup behind as she and Bax walked off together, talking. But I felt lighter than I had for days as they disappeared from view.

Jo.

★ ★ ★

Around lunchtime, as the first band of Sunday took the stage, a slow but steady trickle of people walked past the cart, carrying their tents and bags. It was like the crowd was fading before the final crescendo. But some of the people streamed back toward the stages, so hopefully, they were loading their cars and coming back. Like Bax had done after he'd loaded our gear into the Ground Rules Subaru.

Others were committedly holding on until the bitter end, soaking in all the music they could. Like the tunes were refilling their souls. Or maybe I was reading too much into it, and the remaining festivalgoers were simply getting their money's worth. And if the deaths went unsolved, and cast a shadow over me, the cost of the weekend would far exceed a weekend of strong coffee sales.

Detective Adams showed up, still rocking the Multnomah County Polo T-shirt with cargo pants. Plus heavy boots. The kind that are good for busting down doors and taking names.

"If you want to talk to me, I'll need to call my lawyer," I said.

She almost slammed a red travel mug down on the counter of my coffee cart. "Maybe I need coffee."

I took her mug and filled it from the French press, which I'd just brewed. "This is our house blend, Puddle Jumper. It's a medium roast with notes of dark berries and spiced dates. Hopefully, if you know anything about coffee beans, you'll understand when I say it's a mix of Bourbon and Caturra beans sourced from a fair trade co-op. There's a reason this is one of our best sellers."

"Is there a reason you're babbling about coffee beans?" The detective sounded grumpy. She definitely needed caffeine, stat. And maybe I should take comfort in her willingness to buy my blend. Or she needed coffee so badly she was willing to risk being poisoned by a killer barista.

"It's better than giving you the chance to ask questions." I put her coffee down on the cart's counter.

She grabbed the stainless steel carafe of half-and-half and added a liberal dose. "Coffee's okay, but I really just need the caffeine."

"We have sugar, too, if you need it."

"I wish. Sugar is one of the things I had to give up when I hit the wrong side of forty. Along with all of the fun carbs. I'm sick of brown rice and whole wheat pasta."

I wondered if the detective was trying to butter me up. Act friendly, slide into my good graces, and get me to slip up and admit I was secretly a serial killer. Although if she was willing to drink coffee I'd brewed, maybe she'd eliminated me from her list of suspects. Or was too desperate for caffeine to care.

The detective snapped her lid onto her travel mug, then looked up at me. "You've been talking to people all weekend. Who do you think killed Ian Rabe and Alexis Amari?"

I looked her in the eyes. "If I had any ideas, I'd tell you. But I honestly don't know. Maybe I'd have a theory if I knew them better."

She studied me for a second.

A lightbulb clicked in my brain, and I brightened. "You know, Logan's around somewhere. He's known for Alexis for years, and this is his festival."

"Logan?"

"Logan Pembroke? He runs the festival. His family owns this farm."

"Where'd you see him last? I've been trying to talk to him all weekend, but he keeps dodging me."

Her words made me pause. Logan had acted fond of Alexis and devastated over her death. Why wouldn't he talk to the police? Unless he wanted his attorney present, which was a sensible precaution, even if you don't have anything to hide.

And like Alexis, Logan knew what parts of the grounds were covered by security cameras and where to find the black holes. He probably knew the area better than Alexis had since his family owned it. He could've strategically planned the camera dead zones. Based on the twigs I'd seen in his hair, I suspected he'd been skulking around the grounds off-trail (or taking unofficial short cuts).

"Did the security cameras pick up anything around Alexis's death?"

The detective eyed me for a moment before shaking her head no.

I bit my lip. Was it chance or excellent planning that kept the killer from being caught on camera? Were there enough gaps in coverage that all sorts of activities had been going on beneath our collective noses?

"Back to my question: Where did you see Logan Pembroke go?"

"Umm, a couple of hours ago he went that way." I pointed toward the barn, which included the indoor stage and beer garden. "I've seen him around all weekend. Maybe one of the security guards could page him for you, or something? They have to have some way of getting ahold of him for emergencies."

"Did Logan seem normal? Or was he upset?"

"He seemed gutted over Alexis. He said he's known her since she was a kid."

My best customer of the weekend showed up with her VIP pass for her second hit of the day. Given her timing and ability to show up when I needed a distraction, I practically owed the customer a tip.

The detective dropped her business card on the counter in front of me, and I tucked it inside the cart before making an iced orange-spiced mocha.

As a thank-you to my VIP customer, I handed over a coupon for a free drink at the main Ground Rules cart.

"You've been our best customer all weekend. You deserve a complimentary drink at our other cart." I resisted the urge to add a Complementary Chocolate–style complement.

"Oh, I can't wait to try it! I love food carts and the Rail Yard is fantastic. Some of the bands that play there are legit."

We talked about how the menu at the main cart differed from the festival cart, including the plethora of additional ways we'd have to make coffee and the different seasonal drinks we'd offer.

"But as long as you'll have mochas, I'll be your fan for life," the VIP said before walking away.

If only it was always so easy to please people. One of the hardest lessons I'd learned is that you can do everything right, but someone else's actions can mess everything up. And when I thought of Ian's and Alexis's families and their grief, I couldn't complain about the detective looking at me a little too closely, even if I knew she was on the wrong track.

Chapter 22

All four of the Changelings walked up to the cart, including the elusive bass player I hadn't met.

Nate's hair stuck up like a broken, messy halo. "I need coffee, bad."

"A pour-over for me, please. Dealer's choice for coffee beans," Dev said, exuding a sense of calm like he was a still lake that no winds or storms could touch. I wondered if the drummer was always so zen. The guitarist ordered a pour-over as well, and the bassist hung back.

"Anything for you?" I asked. He shook his head. Maybe he didn't talk.

As I set the water to boil and made Nate's latte, the band chatted.

"You sure about the copyright issues with the songs on *Sanguine Sunrise*? That doesn't sound right. And Ian was way too professional for a mistake like that," Dev said.

"I'll see if we can get access to Ian's emails, and maybe his office files? There has to be a way to get this straightened out," Nate said.

"We don't have to worry about it now. I'm sure our whole financial situation will be a mess until we figure out if Ian had a succession plan. Given how organized Ian was, I'm sure he had something set up." Dev's words made me wonder if he talked Nate down regularly. Maybe that was one of his roles in the band. Keep the drumbeat steady. Keep the lead singer from melting down.

"Faith said it's all a mess," Nate said.

"Chill. She was an intern for just two months. She doesn't know anything."

I wanted to add, *a rather capable intern*, but didn't.

Dev kept talking. "She mainly created social media posts. It's not like she got into the actual business. I doubt she'd even know how to check a song's copyright."

"I'm not sure about that," Nate said.

Dev's head tilted ever so slightly. "Does anyone have Ian's old assistant's phone number? She might be able to help us out."

"She hates me," Nate said.

"But I always got along with her," Dev said. "Treat her with respect, and she's cool. You should try it sometime."

"You're always so full of wisdom. We all should've gone to sleep with the chickens like you did on Thursday night. Especially Ian. Then he'd still be with us." Nate's tone was bleaker than usual, and I felt the same current of honesty I'd heard when he talked about the agreement they'd come to over Maya's cowriting credits.

My hands paused, then continued pouring the water in a circular pattern. A sinking feeling in my stomach made me want to shake. Luckily my hands instinctively knew the familiar physical pattern I'd learned after pouring thousands of pour-overs. A row of dominos fell in my mind, knocking useless details that had complicated the weekend's story out of the way. And I knew.

I knew who'd killed Ian.

But was I right? Why would the killer target Alexis, though? Nerves made my whole body want to shake, but I focused on coffee, smelling the grounds as they bloomed, and slowly started to settle. I knew what to do.

After I'd scanned the band's passes and handed over their tumblers of coffee, I pulled my phone out of my pocket. I dialed the number on Detective Adams's business card. After a ring, she must've sent me directly to voice mail. Maybe she'd finally pinned Logan down.

"Detective, it's Sage Caplin. I think I have information on the deaths of Ian Rabe and Alexis Amari. It was . . ."

But my voice froze before I finished the message since the killer walked up.

"We need to talk."

I fumbled with my phone as I put it down in front of me on the counter. Faith looked at me like I was ridiculous.

"You okay, Faith?" I asked. I didn't call her a murderer, even though I suspected she was the killer. The pattern fit.

Faith glanced around. A couple of people were in line at the Breakfast Bandit cart. Her look back my way was speculative. Like she was reading me and then weighing me up like I was a mark she needed to sweet-talk.

The feeling in my stomach told me I was right. I'd taken a while, but I'd taken a case that felt like an impressionist painting and eventually pulled out the correct details to make a crystal-clear photo.

"So what do I need to do to keep you quiet?" Faith asked. "How much?"

"Excuse me?"

"I heard you talking with the band, and I saw your face. I shouldn't have lied about Dev being out late on Thursday. You know. I also know everyone has a price. I have a little money now, but when my grandfather dies, I can hook you up with a lot more."

Faith seemed relaxed and logical, just like she'd been when dealing with bands all weekend. I held down a frisson of anger that she thought I could be bought off. That I'd be willing to look the other way when Ian and Alexis deserved justice.

And even if I didn't have a conscience saying Faith deserved to face the music, logic said if I agreed to be paid off, she'd stick a knife in my back later.

"I stepped on a pair of glasses when I found Alexis," I said. I swiped my phone, feeling like it was a lifeline.

Faith's smile felt like air-conditioning. "Grace was having a conniption fit in the bathroom about no one answering her questions. She took off her glasses when she was crying, so I snagged them to plant by Alexis's body. Grace seemed like a good patsy."

"I just don't see why you'd need to hurt Alexis."

"It's my stupid half brother's fault. If he hadn't shown up, and my dad hadn't been all happy to finally have a son, Alexis wouldn't have needed to die."

"Your dad?" I asked.

Faith closed her eyes briefly. Something told me she was enjoying a chance to get this off of her chest. "My dad and grandfather, if you want to get all technical. My grandfather's estate includes a pretty good chunk of change going to his grandchildren, which is only me. Except my dad decided Ian deserved an equal share and hassled my grandfather until he agreed."

"Is that why you killed Alexis?" I asked.

Faith let out a combination snort and nod. "If my family found out about Ian's child, they practically would've disinherited me. I can hear them now: the poor fatherless baby will need our help, especially if it was a boy. Because I'm the afterthought. Even if I'm the one who busted her tail to get straight-As all through high school. Growing up, I was always in my cousin's shadow, even after he died in a car wreck. We don't live in a *Game of Thrones* world. It's not like they need a male bloodline to keep the family name going. Haven't they heard? The future is female. And I'm going to be my family's first female CEO."

I wondered if Faith was right about her family not valuing her because she was a girl. Or if she had the sort of chip on her shoulder that made her think what she received was never enough. Maybe her family had treated her cousin better because he was likable. Or they'd treated them the same, but Faith hadn't seen it that way.

"You lied about the copyrights of the songs, didn't you?" I asked.

Faith grinned, and instead of it feeling charming, I could see the malice deep inside. "I have no idea how, or if, or why, the songs were copyrighted. But the more people under suspicion for Ian's death, the better, especially if they act weird in front of the detective skulking around. I wished I'd known about Maya before the festival since she would have been the perfect fall guy. She's so all over the place emotionally. She should learn to toughen up."

I felt sick. "You didn't plan to kill your brother? Or Alexis?"

"My dad always says the great ones know when to be brave. So I saw a chance and took it. It's like you foretold in my coffee grounds."

Her words felt like she'd punched me in the solar plexus. Had I given her encouragement to kill Alexis? But my advice had been generic. The sort of ambiguous statements that worked well in newspaper horoscopes. The type of fortune the receiver makes into her own self-fulfilling prophecy.

"How'd you kill Ian, anyway?"

Faith tapped the side of her neck. "A chokehold. I stopped the blood to his brain through his carotid arteries. I need to remember to thank my dad for enrolling me in judo. It turned out Ian wasn't a fighter. Plus, I got a jump on him."

"So you just stalked him through the night?"

"He went for a walk; I followed. I wasn't sure I would go through with it, but then I decided it was the perfect moment to seize the day. I pretended I needed to talk to him and that I was crying. He fell for it."

Her words felt so cold. The lack of compassion for her half brother and Alexis made me feel sick inside. She acted like they were barriers to what she thought she deserved, versus people who were starring in a play called their own lives.

I glanced at her bare arms. No scratches or bruises and Faith must have followed my gaze.

"It was cold, so I wore a sweater. Thankfully Ian passed out pretty quickly," Faith said.

To stall for time, I asked one of the questions that had been bothering me. "Why was Ian carrying Alexis's coffee mug?"

Faith snorted. "He borrowed it so he could drink hot coffee without burning his hands. I didn't know Alexis well, but she strug-

gled to tell Ian no. He was charismatic, like our dad. She'd do anything for him. She was weak like that."

She eyed me. "We're coming back full circle: what'll it cost you
to keep your mouth shut?"

"You know, with your drive and commitment, you'd make a
good CEO," I said.

"Quit wasting time," Faith said.

The muscles in my back softened when Detective Adams walked
up. She asked, "What's this proof you claim to have?"

"How about a confession?" I held up my phone and pushed play.
Faith's voice said, "Grace was having a conniption fit in the bathroom . . ."

Faith lunged at me, but the detective was faster, although the
coffee cup in her hands went flying. As I stepped backward, retreat-
ing into the safety of my cart, the detective grabbed the twenty-year-
old murderer. The recording of her voice said, "She took off her
glasses when she was crying, so I snagged them to plant by Alexis's
body. Grace seemed like a good patsy."

Faith tried to wrestle away, and the detective slammed her into
the ground and cuffed her. A cloud of dirt floated around them as I
noticed a familiar face peeking out at me from behind a tree.

"Grace!" I called out and motioned her to come over. "I have a
scoop for your blog!"

Grace muttered "Podcast," as she scurried out, and she had an intent look on her face like she thought this story was her big break.
Today's glasses were dainty gold frames that made her look softer.
Grace took a photo as Detective Adams read Faith her rights. A
crowd of people gathered around, and multiple people started filming. Faith glanced at them like she was debating crying or trying to
throw herself on the sympathy of the crowd.

As the detective called for a police car to pick up Faith, Grace
held her phone toward the twenty-year-old former intern. "Will you
please tell the public why you murdered a promising and popular
band manager?"

"Oh, bite me," Faith said. Dirt was smudged on her cheek and across the front of her designer sundress. But the element that really brought Faith's outfit together was the coffee stain across her shoulder and flowing down onto her chest from the detective's cup.

The detective walked Faith to the parking lot, followed by a gaggle of filming festivalgoers like a twist on the Pied Piper legend.

My satisfaction from finding the killer was tempered with sorrow. Faith had killed her half brother, plus Alexis, for money. I knew what it was like to feel like you had a family legacy hovering around you. Even if mine was the sort I fought against, taking steps to make sure I didn't follow the easy road. And Faith had taken the low road as her journey to success. Even if it meant destroying everything in her path.

If she hadn't been caught, where would she have ended up in ten years? Twenty? Because there was no way the murders wouldn't have tainted her soul. And once she took the easy path, I suspected cutting corners in the future would've been easy steps even if she didn't commit the ultimate crime again.

As far as I knew, my mother had stuck to stealing people's money, and maybe their dreams, but left them physically intact at the end. If there was an evilness scale, murder was definitely heavier. Especially when it was purely for money. And Faith had an idea of the cost, as she knew the effect the deaths would have on her own family.

A trio of women came up after the police had marched Faith away. "What was that about?"

"Good question. She didn't look like a wanted criminal, did she?" I made my eyes wide and innocent, wondering if I was trying too hard to play dumb.

"I've never been front row for an arrest like that. It was different from TV," one of the women said.

"I wonder if she was on, like, the FBI's most-wanted list." The women looked at each other with open mouths. They discussed what Faith could have done and eventually ordered a couple of iced caramel lattes and an iced cinnamon mocha.

"Oh, this is, like, really good!" the mocha drinker said. I handed over a business card with the other cart's address at the Rail Yard.

"You should visit our other cart. We also sell beans around town, as well as through our website." The words felt automatic, like a shield between the reeling feeling still coursing through me and the business façade I'd snapped into place.

Jackson and Piper walked up. "We heard there was some excitement going down here," Jackson said. "I thought you'd be in the middle of it."

Which, of course, was the exact moment Detective Adams came back to the cart. She stood for a moment, looking at me, while my brother stared at her with his usual poker face that said he'd shifted into lawyer mode. Piper raised her eyebrows at me and mouthed, "What the fudge?"

"This is fun," I said to break the glacial ambiance threatening to turn all of the coffee I served into blocks of ice.

"That's one way to put it." Adams felt a bit different, more relaxed, even though she still looked tense. Something told me it was more of an "I still have a bunch of things to finish this case and send it to the DA" sort of energy. Versus a "is this coffee vendor secretly a serial killer?" sort of vibe.

"Is there something I can help you with? More coffee?" I turned to Jackson and Piper. "Oh, and the festival's murderer has been arrested. That's the drama you heard about. As you can tell, it wasn't me."

Detective Adams almost smiled. "We need to talk about the audio recording you made."

"Made in public in an area covered by security cameras with no expectation of privacy," I said, wondering about Oregon's laws about recording people without permission. "And she was trying to bribe me into staying quiet."

"What's this about a recording?" Jackson asked. I gave him a quick rundown, with Piper listening intently.

"Your client should be fine with the recording. But I will need a copy of it, and a statement." Detective Adams seemed exasperated. And tired.

"I'm sure we can arrange something," I said. Jackson's laser stare reminded me I was supposed to let him act as my lawyer during this moment in time. We scheduled a time for me to give a statement, and the detective hustled off.

The first real smile in what felt like days spread across my face as I looked at my brother and Piper, who were talking together quietly. But it slipped away when I thought of Ian and Alexis. But at least justice was being served.

"You sure lead an exciting life," Piper said.

"Trouble follows Sage around," Jackson replied.

"Isn't that the truth." I made them coffee, feeling the world had mostly resettled into its usual groove. Although everything felt like it should be swathed in a black ribbon of grief.

Chapter 23

The Changelings were the second-to-last band of the festival. The crowd waiting for them to take the stage was a tad smaller than the first two days, but the people still here, the ones hanging on to the very last note, felt passionate. And happy. Although maybe my sense of relief of having found the killer clouded my judgment.

I found Bax toward the back of the crowd, standing with Maya. I nestled up to him, and when he realized who it was, he pulled me to him.

"You okay?"

I nodded, bumping my head into his chest. "I have a story to tell you."

"I heard the police made an arrest," Maya said.

"Yeah." I turned to face Maya, and Bax kept his arm around me. I gave them a quick rundown of the morning highlights. "All I know is she's been arrested."

"I knew I should've sat outside your cart all morning," he said.

I didn't tell Bax that he's more like a golden retriever than an attack dog, but I appreciated his concern. I leaned against him.

"It's surreal to think we were tossing around Dashiell Hammett quotes a few days ago, ready for a weekend of fun, without knowing everything was going to take a horrible turn," Maya said. "There's a moment at the end of *The Thin Man* when Nora says the resolution of the case feels unsatisfactory. That's how I feel now. Nothing about this will ever make sense. Life won't ever feel the same."

"I'm sorry for your loss," I said.

Bax shifted and patted Maya on the shoulder, although he kept his other arm around me.

"It's not just my loss. I'm devastated for all our loss, including the music world. Alexis deserved more. So did Ian." Maya swiped her hand across her eyes, wiping away a few tears.

The Changelings took the stage and quickly jumped into a song, and I watched Maya as she watched the stage. I tried to read the emotions on her face. Hurt. Pride. Annoyance. Sorrow. Grief. She'd created this band, so in a way she was responsible for this moment in time. For the crowd around us hanging on every note of the Changelings' songs. In a way, for the grief hovering over everyone who knew Alexis and Ian, even if their sad fates weren't remotely her fault.

Toward the end of their set, Nate paused longer than normal and looked over the audience, like he was trying to see into the back corners.

"Is Maya Oliveira here? Because if she is, we need her on stage."

Bax called out, "She's here!"

And I'm glad Maya wasn't a killer because the look she gave Bax could've stopped a lesser man's heart.

Nate looked over the crowd, eventually zooming in on Maya's glare. I wondered if it felt hot, like a spark that flies off a fire. "You might not know this, but Maya cowrote most of the songs on our album. You might have heard her earlier this weekend, stunning the crowd as the lead singer of Banshee Blues. And I think you need to hear her perform a song with us. So come on up, Maya!"

The crowd parted as Maya walked through them. She looked like a panther that had stalked into the festival by accident as she hopped onto the stage, ignoring Nate's offered hand. But when she took her spot by the microphone, it looked like she belonged.

They performed "Mid-Morning Blues," with Maya singing lead and Nate leaning in to share the microphone as he harmonized on the chorus. They sounded fantastic.

I noticed Grace, the music blogger, holding her phone up to record the performance. Hopefully, this would be part of Ian and Alexis's joint legacy.

Hours later, I dropped Bax and Kaldi, the orange cat, at Bax's house. After a kiss and meow goodbye, I drove to the warehouse, where Kendall waited for me. We unpacked the Subaru and then gave the cart a thorough cleaning. I left the company car at work, pulled on my bicycle helmet, and rode my trusty bike through the late evening Portland streets. I detoured to the eventual site of the Button Building.

Eventually, our new coffee shop would look like a slice of pie in a circular building, with a sliver missing at the back. All of the micro-restaurants would open onto a central courtyard. The plans called for a firepit in the courtyard, with a ring of tables around it. Maybe I should get Maya to come by and bless it by singing "Ring of Fire" at the grand opening. Besides my coffee shop, there was room for six cafés, and most of us were food carts making the jump to brick and mortar.

I stood looking at the fenced-in lot and smiled when I noticed the FUTURE HOME OF GROUND RULES COFFEE BAR sign bolted alongside my uncle Jimmy's JONES & CO. GROUP DEVELOPMENT GROUP placard.

I couldn't wait to meet the future.

RECIPES

Peach & Lemon Iced Tea

To Ground Rules, peaches taste like summer. This naturally de-caffeinated drink basically combines iced tea, lemonade, and peaches into a summertime drink perfect for sipping in the shade.

Ingredients
4 cups of water
4 tea bags of rooibos
1 cup simple syrup
¾ cup fresh-squeezed lemon juice
1½ cups of peach juice or fresh pureed peaches

Preparation
Bring the water to a boil, then remove it from heat. Steep the tea bags in the water for five minutes, then discard the tea bags. Set aside to cool.

Mix the steeped tea, simple syrup, lemon juice, and peach juice in a pitcher. Store in your refrigerator and serve over ice.

Notes
You can buy premade peach juice or puree fresh peaches in a blender to make your own juice.

You can sub black or green tea in for the rooibos but be sure to check the recommended brewing time for the tea. If you use rooibos, this iced tea is naturally caffeine-free.

Mint Simple Syrup

Mint and cold brew coffee are perfect together!

Ingredients

1 cup of water
1 cup sugar
10 fresh mint leaves

Preparation

Bring the water to a boil in a saucepan; add the sugar and stir until it melts. Add the mint leaves and simmer for about one minute, then turn off the heat and let the sugar-water-mint mixture steep for 30 minutes. Strain the mixture through a sieve into a bottle, jar, or other closable (and airtight) container.

The mint simple syrup should last up to two weeks in the refrigerator.

Mint simple syrup is refreshing in cold brew and other iced coffee drinks.

Ginger Simple Syrup

Ginger syrup adds a delightful kick to coffee and tea drinks.

Ingredients
1 cup of water
1 cup sugar
Fresh ginger, chopped into small pieces

Preparation
Combine water, sugar, and ginger in a saucepan. Put on medium heat and stir until the sugar dissolves and the water comes to a boil. Reduce heat, cover, and simmer for about ten minutes.

Remove from heat and let it cool for at least an hour on the stovetop. Strain the sauce and store it in a container, like a mason jar with a reusable lid, in the fridge.

Note
Use this in fresh ginger lemonade, in hot or iced tea, in coffee, or in sparkling water for a DIY ginger ale. It also goes well in cocktails if you want a ginger kick.

Mint Cold Brew

First, you'll need to make cold brew concentrate. When making cold brew concentrate at home, Ground Rules tends to use mason jars, although you can buy fancy pitchers for cold brew. Or use a French press.

Making coffee is all about the proper ratio of coffee grounds to water. To make a cold brew concentrate, you'll need ¾ cup of coarse ground coffee to 4 cups of water.

You can double, triple, quadruple, etc. this recipe; just keep the ¾ cup of grounds to 4 cups of water ratio intact.

Ingredients
¾ cup coarse coffee grounds
4 cups of water

Preparation
Mix four cups of water and the ¾ cup of coffee grounds in an appropriately sized mason jar, and screw on the lid. Place in the refrigerator for 12 to 24 hours.

When the coffee has brewed to your liking, strain it into a clean pitcher or mason jar.

To make a mint cold brew
Put ½ cup of cold brew concentrate into a glass, along with ½ cup of water or milk (note: you'll want to keep your cold brew to milk or water ration at 1:1). Add a teaspoon of mint simple syrup (or to taste if you'd like a sweeter drink). Add ice, and you're ready to go!

Mint Coffee Soda

Ingredients
¾ cup cold brew concentrate
1 tablespoon of mint simple syrup
¾ cup of club soda
Ice

Preparation
Mix the cold brew concentrate and mint simple syrup in a wide-mouth, pint-sized mason jar (or glass of your choosing). Add ice to the top of the glass, then slowly pour in the club soda. Lightly mix, and your soda is ready.

Ginger Tea Soda

Ingredients

Tea of your choosing (black, green, white, rooibos)
Water
1 tablespoon ginger simple syrup
¾ cup club soda
Ice

Preparation

First, you'll make your tea concentrate. You'll want to dramatically up your ratio of tea leaves to water. If you are using a tea bag, instead of one tea bag to one mug of water, you'll add maybe just an inch of water in your usual cup.

Brew the tea for the usual amount of time (30 seconds to 1 minute for green, 3–4 minutes for black, 6 minutes for rooibos). Do not brew the tea for longer than normal—that will make it bitter. We want to make the tea stronger, not over-brewed.

Once your tea concentrate is done and you've strained it and/or removed the bag, you're ready for the fun part!

Mix the tea concentrate and ginger simple syrup in a wide-mouth, pint-sized mason jar (or glass of your choosing). Add ice to the top of the glass, then slowly pour in the club soda. Lightly mix, and voila! You have a tea soda.

Ginger Lemonade

Ingredients

Ginger simple syrup
1 fresh lemon, squeezed
Water
Ice

Preparation

Grab two glasses (Ground Rules recommends wide-mouth, pint-sized mason jars). Squeeze half of a lemon into each glass. Add a teaspoon of ginger syrup (or to taste). Mix. Fill about ¾ up with water, and mix again. Then fill the rest of the glass with ice.

Note

You can substitute club soda for the still water if you're in the mood for bubbles.

Strawberry-Sage Drinking Vinegar

Fruit shrubs date back to at least the Colonial era as a way to preserve fruit for the winter. This version uses strawberries and sage, but you can substitute pretty much any berry or fruit and any herb in this recipe. Just keep the fruit, sugar, and vinegar in a 1:1:1 ratio.

Fruit shrubs can be used in cocktails, but Ground Rules' favorite way to serve them is in club soda as a refreshing summer drink. This also mixes well with olive oil for a quick salad dressing.

Ground Rules recommends champagne vinegar because it has a delicate flavor. However, you can also use white wine vinegar or apple cider vinegar.

Ingredients

1 cup chopped fresh strawberries
1 cup granulated sugar
6 sage leaves
1 cup champagne vinegar

Preparation

Mix the sugar and fruit in a mason jar. Cover with a towel and let the bowl sit on the countertop overnight.

The next day, add the sage, stir, and put a lid on the mason jar. Store it in a refrigerator for 5–7 days.

After 5–7 days, put a fine-mesh colander over a bowl. Pour the fruit-herb mixture through the colander. Let the fruit solids sit in the colander for a few hours to fully drain.

Then remove the colander and discard the fruit solids. Whisk the champagne vinegar into the strawberry mixture, and pour into a clean mason jar(s) or bottle(s). Let the shrub rest in the refrigerator for at least seven days. It should last in the fridge for up to three months and will taste better as time goes by.

Mix a tablespoon (or to taste) of strawberry-sage drinking vinegar with club soda for a refreshing treat. You can also use the syrup in cocktails or with olive oil as a quick DIY salad dressing.

Chia-seed Pudding

If your goal in life is to eat out of mason jars, chia-seed pudding is a must-add to your breakfast repertoire. This makes an easy, home-made grab-and-go breakfast on busy days. Small jars work well as in-dividual-sized breakfast servings. You can also make this in a bowl with a cover and scoop out a serving each day.

Chia-seed pudding is versatile and surprisingly hearty with a good amount of fiber. You can even turn it into a dessert (consider adding cocoa and your sweetener of choice!).

If you'd like your pudding to be thicker, add more chia seeds the next time; conversely, add fewer if you'd like your pudding to be less thick. If you're making a week's worth of chia pudding at once, consider adding the fruit when you're ready to eat versus incorporating it into the pudding from the beginning.

You can use your favorite milk. Full-fat coconut milk creates a creamy texture; the pudding's consistency will vary slightly depending upon which milk you chose.

Ingredients for a single serving
1 tablespoon chia seeds
½ cup coconut milk (or your milk of choice)
Fruit (optional); Ground Rules preference: mango

Ingredients for a week's worth of pudding
3 cups milk
6 tablespoons chia seeds

Optional add-ins
Maple syrup or other sweetener
Chopped nuts
Cocoa
Vanilla extract
Peanut butter or other nut butter

Optional toppings
  Nuts
  Fruit
  Jam
  Granola
  Yogurt

Preparation
  Mix the chia seeds and milk in a bowl, and let the pudding sit for 5 minutes. Stir it again, taking care to break up any clumps of chia seeds, and add any optional add-ins. Once everything is combined, put the pudding in the fridge to set for at least 2 hours, ideally overnight, before serving.

Acknowledgments

Writing a novel during a pandemic and lockdowns was quite an experience. One thing that helped was Extracto Coffee Roaster's doorstop delivery program. Getting bags of freshly roasted coffee delivered to my porch kept me humming along all year. Thank you to Waylon, my Great Pyrenees, for making sure I took time every day to explore the neighborhood. He always showed me the best places to sniff, although I rarely took his advice. As far as advice I did implement, I owe a giant thanks to my agent, Joshua Bilmes, for his (as always) excellent editorial feedback and continuing belief in Sage and Ground Rules.

Thanks to Robin Herrera and Miriam Forster, my writing pals, critique partners, and good friends (even if one of you only drinks tea). Thank you to Esther, who answers my legal questions and didn't complain when I spelled her name wrong in the acknowledgments in *Fresh Brewed Murder*. Bill Cameron and Nevin Mays are also on my list of people who deserve all of the coffee in the world.

Thank you to John Scognamiglio, Larissa Ackerman, and all of the crew at Kensington Books.

Last of all, thanks to Jim, as always.